A DUKE FOR DIANA

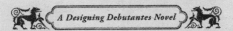
A Designing Debutantes Novel

SABRINA JEFFRIES

ZEBRA BOOKS
KENSINGTON PUBLISHING CORP.
www.kensingtonbooks.com

ZEBRA BOOKS are published by

Kensington Publishing Corp.
119 West 40th Street
New York, NY 10018

All Kensington titles, imprints, and distributed lines are available at special quantity discounts for bulk purchases for sales promotion, premiums, fund-raising, educational, or institutional use.

Special book excerpts or customized printings can also be created to fit specific needs. For details, write or phone the office of the Kensington Sales Manager: Attn.: Sales Department. Kensington Publishing Corp., 119 West 40th Street, New York, NY 10018. Phone: 1-800-221-2647.

Zebra and the Z logo Reg. U.S. Pat. & TM Off.

First Printing: June 2022
ISBN-13: 978-1-4201-5377-4
ISBN-13: 978-1-4201-5378-1 (eBook)

10 9 8 7 6 5 4 3 2 1

Printed in the United States of America

KENSINGTON BOOKS BY SABRINA JEFFRIES:

Duke Dynasty series

Project Duchess

The Bachelor

Who Wants to Marry a Duke

Undercover Duke

Designing Debutantes series

A Duke for Diana

*For my writer friends, Rexanne Becnel
and the late Claudia Dain—
thanks for teaching me everything I know about fashion
and how to make it work
for one's body type or coloring.
And thanks for the many years of fun times together.*

Prologue

London
Spring 1807

Hours into London's most poorly attended ball, not a single gentleman had asked Lady Diana Harper to dance. That didn't surprise her. Once one became a pariah in high society, one was sentenced to holding up the wall at all social engagements. Hence the term "wallflower." Except that she and her younger sister, Verity, were more like "wall-*weeds*," to be rooted out and stomped upon.

Still, they refused to give anyone the satisfaction of driving them home to hide. Who cared if Mama had scandalized everyone by running off with Major-General Tobias Ord? Who cared if Papa, the mighty Earl of Holtbury, was divorcing Mama for that selfsame act? It wasn't Diana or Verity's fault, and they refused to act as if it was. Instead, they went to every society affair they were invited to attend.

There weren't many.

Fortunately, their oldest sister, Mrs. Eliza Pierce, who had already wed by the time their mother made her mad dash for freedom, hadn't suffered quite as much. Whenever someone was cruel to Eliza, she could retreat to Mr. Pierce's strong arms. Diana and Verity could only put a good face on matters and dare the *ton* to torment them for what was *not their fault*!

Diana sighed. Perhaps if she said it often enough, she'd believe it. Perhaps then society might finally allow them to dance instead of forcing them to sit to the side watching their youth slip away.

Good Lord, but she was morose tonight, and the overpowering orchestra was giving her a headache that worsened matters. At this rate, she might as well go home where she could hear herself think.

Thank heavens the music ended with a flourish just then. Their good friend, Miss Isolde Crowder, approached them, her ash-brown curls bouncing. "I'm delighted you came. Mama wanted so badly for this to be a crush, but I knew it was unlikely."

Isolde and Diana were both twenty, their friendship forged when they'd embarked on their first Season together. This was their second, and, judging from how things were going, they might need a third. And a fourth and a fifth and—

Diana didn't want to think about that. Isolde hadn't "taken" during their first Season, not because of scandal but because she was a Cit. Marrying a Cit, even a wealthy one, wasn't au courant in society these days. Diana hadn't "taken" during her own first Season because of the rumors about her parents' flagrant infidelities.

Then Verity had only just been presented to the queen and had her début ball before the dance floor had been knocked out from under *her*, too, so to speak, by Mama's running off. At nineteen, Verity was now doomed to be an outcast in society. It simply wasn't fair.

Verity lifted one brow. "I'm surprised your mother even wanted us here, given our notoriety." The hint of bitterness in her voice reminded Diana that her sister had good reason to be bitter, given that she'd lost a serious suitor because of their parents' behavior.

"She didn't, but I told her *I* wouldn't attend if she didn't invite the three of you," Isolde said hotly.

"You're a good friend, and we appreciate that," Diana told Isolde. "I'm afraid everyone else thinks us as tainted by Mama's sin as if we'd jumped into the carriage with her."

"I hope it's not as bad as all that," Isolde remarked, ever the optimist.

Diana gave her an arch smile. "We both know Verity's and my Seasons have not borne the appropriate fruit so far."

Nearby, a lady chuckled, prompting Diana to look over. This was the second time tonight Diana had seen the woman eavesdropping on their conversations. Diana didn't recognize her, but no one else was standing close by, so the lady had to be laughing at their conversation.

Diana couldn't imagine why. "I believe a change of subject is in order." Putting her back deliberately to the lady, she swept her hand down to indicate Isolde's attire, a sheath of French gray silk with a silver net overlay and darling little bishop sleeves with ribbon bands. "Your gown turned out very well. It suits you."

Isolde beamed at her. "Thank you for designing it. I know that your help is why I've had so many more dances tonight. If I'd left matters to Mama, I'd be dressed in jonquil satin with large pink tambour-work blossoms over my . . . embonpoint."

"Good God," Verity said. "That sounds awful!"

The lady nearby laughed outright, reminding Diana that she and her sisters were under heavy scrutiny these days.

"Verity," Diana said in a low voice. "That's hardly appropriate language for a young lady."

"'Large pink tambour-work blossoms' over a woman's 'embonpoint' are hardly appropriate for a young lady either," Verity said grimly. "Thank heavens you intervened. Even I know Isolde would look abysmal in that shade of yellow. The color is perfect for my skin, but—" She flashed their friend an apologetic smile. "It would turn your lovely alabaster skin sallow."

"Surely the dressmaker would have discouraged your mother from that choice," Diana pointed out.

"I doubt it," Isolde said. "Mama patronizes Mrs. Ludgate's shop more than any other woman of the *ton*, so the dressmaker dares not gainsay Mama. *I* can barely gainsay her. She's stubborn to a fault." Isolde touched her necklace of jet beads. "And speaking of Mama, I couldn't ask her about this because I don't trust her taste."

"With good reason," Verity mumbled.

Isolde went on as if she hadn't heard Verity. "But I was hoping you could tell me if my jewelry matches my gown well enough."

"It matches beautifully," Diana assured her. "And your reticule is perfect—the simple gray silk and black ribbon ties contrast well with the sparkling net. As always, you have far better taste than you give yourself credit for."

"Thank you," Isolde said with a faint blush. "What a

relief." She turned to Verity. "I did try to implement your ideas about the décor, but Mama—" Her eyes went wide. "Oh, dear, she has spotted me. I'd best go mingle or I'll never hear the end of it."

Once Isolde was gone, Verity blew her droopy, golden-brown curls from her brow. "It's so hot in here." Verity snatched Diana's fan and started fluttering it over her unfreckled bosom.

Diana shook her head. "I warned you not to wear velvet in spring. This time of year, the weather is highly unpredictable."

"But I like velvet."

"I like parents who aren't engaged in a public war, but we don't always get to have what we like." Diana stared straight ahead, ignoring the matron who passed by while giving them the cut direct.

Her sister's brow darkened. "All the same, I'm determined to do as I please now that I'm rid of Lord Minton. He hated velvet, so I never wore it. I won't do that for a man ever again. Look what it got me! I'll wear what I like and to the devil with it."

"And you shouldn't curse either."

"I'll curse if I please. You should do a bit *more* cursing. Trust me, it is wonderfully freeing." Verity sneezed, then pointed Diana's fan at the massive arrangements of lilies, wisteria, and roses set at intervals of three yards apart. "Isolde's mother got to do and have what *she* pleased. Why can't I? Honestly, who would cobble those three flowers together? The scents are overpowering."

"Perhaps she was hoping to counteract the slightly off smell of the salmon cakes."

"You didn't eat any, did you?" Verity asked in alarm. "One sniff and I left them alone."

"I went nowhere near them. I confess I was disappointed in the biscuits, too. They were cloyingly sweet. Although the almond ones weren't bad. Isolde told me she'd chosen those personally because they were her favorite."

"Don't tell Isolde, but aside from her almond biscuits, I found most of the dishes lacking. The roast partridges were too dry, the crab patties too wet, and despite its pretty mold of a basket of fruit, the blancmange had a garlicky flavor. I shudder to think what ingredient was in it."

"Garlic, perhaps?" Diana quipped. "Trust me, Isolde tried to counsel her mother on everything involving this ball, but the woman wouldn't listen. Poor Isolde, to have such a mother."

"Not poor Isolde." Verity shook her head. "She lets it happen. She should stand up to the woman."

"The way we stand up to our father?"

"That's different. He's a man."

"True." A man they were utterly dependent on. Diana loved Papa, but sometimes he was so autocratic she wanted to scream. Still, she didn't dare. He could turn life in the house into constant misery if he was trying to make a point, namely that his way was best.

He was making that point now by pursuing a divorce. He'd tried shaming Mama into coming back, but she had known what half the *ton* did—that Papa hadn't been the marrying kind even after he'd wed her. Meanwhile, some said one of Mama's early amours had given Diana her brown eyes, dreadful red hair, and freckles. She was the only one with that coloring in her family.

Still, the rumor had to be false. She *hoped* it was false anyway. If it were true, Papa had never given a hint of it. His harsh words fell equally on all of them. And Mama had certainly never said a word about it. Sometimes Diana wondered, though. . . .

Verity stared out over the dance floor. "I'm just saying that Isolde should trust her own opinions more. The woman is smart and beautiful and has exquisite taste in clothing when she's not listening to her mother. If her mother wasn't always trying to steer her wrong—and Isolde wasn't always giving in—I daresay she'd be married by now."

Eliza joined them. "I agree. Dear Isolde would be a treasure for any man."

"You're not just saying that because she heeded your advice on the subject of hair, are you?" Verity asked.

"No, indeed." Eliza smiled. "I truly enjoyed helping her with her coiffure. And I *am* pleased she chose my idea for the ribbon arrangement over a turban. She's far too young to be wearing a turban to a ball." The music started again, even louder than before. Eliza gestured to them to join her outside on the balcony.

"Oh, that is so much better," Diana said as they moved to the far end of the balcony from the door. "I swear, my ears were bleeding."

Eliza nodded. "Anyone who hires a twenty-piece orchestra to play music for dancing when three players would do shouldn't be allowed to throw a ball." She sighed. "Isolde deserves better. Mrs. Crowder is a perfect example of the rule that just because you *can* have something doesn't mean you should."

"Mama is another example of that, I'm afraid," Verity said. "Why couldn't she simply wait until we were all married before running off with the major-general and forcing Papa's hand?"

"I'm sure she'd say she was in love," Diana said. "Although I suspect it was as much because he was a handsome widower and she feared somebody else would snatch him up before she could."

Someone cleared her throat. Startled, they turned to find that the eavesdropping lady had followed them outside. "I know it's not proper etiquette," she said in an accent that Diana couldn't quite place, "but I should like to introduce myself. I'm the Earl of Sinclair's new wife. I gather that you three are Lady Holtbury's daughters?"

Although wary of the woman's reason for asking, Diana made the introductions.

"I'm so pleased to meet you all," the countess said, flashing them a genuine smile. "I assure you, not everyone is against you. I personally think it a shame you should be tarred with the same brush as your mother. In any case, I couldn't help overhearing your assessment of this affair and I should like to know how you would have improved upon it." She winked at Eliza. "Other than hiring fewer musicians, that is."

When scarlet suffused Eliza's cheeks, Diana said hastily, "I'm sure we must sound terribly rude, criticizing an event we were charitably invited to attend—"

"Not a bit. I agree with everything you said. And more." Lady Sinclair shut the door to the ballroom. "Indeed, I would be most grateful if you would bear with me a moment and answer my questions. You see, I'm expected to throw a ball myself soon, and I'm American, so I've never done anything of the sort in London. I could use advice. For example, Lady Diana, what attire would you choose for me as hostess?"

Opting for caution with the woman, Diana said, "It appears you already have good taste in clothing, madam, because your muslin gown and plaid shawl are both fashionable and flattering to your figure."

"That's only because my lady's maid picked most of my attire for tonight. But last week she chose an Elizabethan ruff for me to wear with one of my day gowns. Even I know I don't have the neck for such a thing."

Diana relaxed. "No one has the neck for an Elizabethan ruff, not even Elizabeth the First herself." She glanced at Verity's willowy figure and long neck. "Well, perhaps Verity. But no one else I've ever seen."

"In any case," the countess said, "I can't trust my own judgment or that of my lady's maid. She's very new and very Scottish, and I'm still learning my way around the Scots. And the English, for that matter."

"If you're looking for someone to advise you on fashion," Diana said, "I would certainly be happy to do so. It's not as if I have a busy social calendar these days." And Mrs. Ludgate could use the patronage of a woman of standing like Lady Sinclair.

"I should enjoy that," the countess said. "But before we make our plans, I wish to ask your sister—Lady Verity, if you had control of the kitchen, what would you serve?"

Verity, having never lacked for self-confidence, answered boldly. "Mr. and Mrs. Crowder are wealthy enough to afford a variety of dishes, so *my* choices would be, among others, an assortment of sliced cold meats including roast venison and turkey, some lobster patties and minced lobster, Westphalia cakes, pickles of many sorts—"

"No roasted onions and anchovy toast, as Mrs. Crowder's cook is serving?" the countess asked.

"Certainly not." Verity leaned close to Lady Sinclair. "Who wants onions or anchovies on their breath while courting? Even if a lady knows to avoid them at a ball supper, gentlemen don't always think in those terms. They stuff whatever suits them into their mouths without a care for how it makes them smell."

The countess seemed to be fighting a smile. "True. What are Westphalia cakes?"

"Different recipes suggest different flavorings, but basically they're made from mashed potatoes mixed with eggs, butter, and milk, then formed into little cakes and fried. Sometimes they have bits of bacon or cheese in them."

"That sounds delicious," Lady Sinclair said. "And for dessert? We must have desserts—Lord Sinclair has quite a sweet tooth. What would you suggest?"

"You may not realize this," Verity said, "but for a fee, Gunter's will cater events such as yours, supplying ices, ice creams, and pastries. They're a very popular addition."

"And very costly, I'm sure," the countess said in an arch tone.

"I beg your pardon," Verity said with concern. "Is that an issue? I can suggest other sweets if you prefer."

Lady Sinclair laughed. "According to my new husband, it's not an issue in the least. But you know men. They'd prefer to spend less if they can manage it."

Or get the funds from someone else.

The part of the divorce trial going on right now was Papa's attempt to force Major-General Ord to pay him a substantial amount of money for alienation of affection. It was Papa's only way to get his revenge upon the man. But neither of the adulterous parties seemed to care what he did to retaliate. The major-general had a fortune, so Papa's demands weren't going to serve quite as well for revenge as he'd probably hoped.

"Well," the countess said, seeming to notice Diana's lapse into silence, "I do like a Gunter's ice, especially in summer. Very refreshing."

"Exactly." Verity smiled. "I could meet with the proprietors on your behalf, Lady Sinclair, if you think you might wish to use them for your future event."

"How odd that you should mention that. You see, while having the three of you ladies advise me would be helpful, I would much rather *hire* you to plan the whole thing." She gave them a sheepish smile. "Particularly as it's supposed to occur in two weeks."

Eliza gasped, Verity grinned, and Diana gaped at the countess.

Diana was first to speak. "You do know that . . . well . . . it would be rather frowned upon for us to take payment for . . . helping you."

Lady Sinclair blinked at them. "Oh! Of course. I forgot that such things aren't accepted in English society. But the truth is, I have no one to turn to. My servants are either new or only used to running a bachelor household, and my husband has no female relatives. Neither do I— not here, anyway."

Diana hastened to set her at ease. "I'm not saying we aren't perfectly thrilled to advise you, but we can't take payment for it. You understand."

"Speak for yourself." Verity handed Diana's fan back to her as if she were going to set out right that minute to help Lady Sinclair. "I am happy to take payment of any kind, as long as I'm given free rein in the kitchen for the ball supper."

"Verity!" Diana exclaimed. "Papa would . . . would never speak to us again."

"And that would be a loss?" Verity shrugged. "He won't notice anyway." Her voice hardened. "He's too busy trying to nail Major-General Ord to the wall."

Diana winced at her sister's cold—but accurate— perspective. "That's enough." She turned to the countess. "If you wouldn't mind, we would prefer to discuss this among ourselves more privately before we do anything. We live in Hanover Square. If you could visit tomorrow, we will let you know our decision about payment. But I think I speak for Verity and myself both when I say we would be happy to help you, paid or not. We don't exactly have men clamoring to dance with us or pay us calls or invite us to parties. And those that do have certain expectations . . ."

Verity arched a brow. "Let's just say they assume we're all like our mother—unacceptable as wives but suitable for a less respectable position. I'm sure you know what I mean."

"Sadly, I do." Lady Sinclair's blue eyes flashed. "Some of those men are looking for that sort of position with any pretty woman . . . if they can get it." She shot Eliza a pointed look. "But at least one of you has respectably married."

"That happened before the Incident, yes."

When the countess looked blank, Diana said hastily, "That's what we call Mama's elopement with a man other than our father. As a friend of mine said, Mama is 'married but courting.'"

"I see." Lady Sinclair faced Eliza. "Would you be willing to join them, too, Mrs. Pierce? I will definitely need your advice on music."

"I could use the money," Eliza said in a low voice, shocking Diana. When had Eliza and her husband begun having financial difficulties? "So yes, I would be delighted."

The countess grinned at them, as if their compliance was a foregone conclusion. "I'm afraid it is long past time I got back to my husband. I shall see all of you in the morning." And with that, she headed for the door.

Diana rounded on her sisters. "I can't believe you two wish to take money for this."

Verity narrowed her gaze. "Hasn't it occurred to you that we shall never be able to marry anyway now that the Incident has occurred? Our only choices are to live with Papa or become governesses—what fun that would be," she said acidly. "Or worse, we might end up working as companions to old matrons while they lecture us about morality and denigrate Mama."

"Surely Papa could and would support us for as long

as we need," Diana said, determined not to think of the other two choices.

"Even after he marries? You know that as soon as he gets his divorce, he will wed another—he still needs an heir. He'll find some buxom young creature to serve as his broodmare, and we'll slowly become the spinsters who watch over his new wife's children."

"You have *got* to stop reading those gothic novels, Verity," Diana said. "We do not live in a gloomy castle, and Papa is not the wicked villain who will treat us badly."

"No, he's worse," Eliza put in. "He's the father in the *Beauty and the Beast* fairy tale who accedes to the demand that his daughter take his place as the beast's 'guest.' Looking the other way and not defending your family is the insidious act of a villain. And where is Papa when we need him? Going to court to spread the family's dirty linen all over town. Who is suffering for it? The two of you. And me, in my own way. Lord knows Mama isn't. She's probably having the time of her life."

Something in her sister's despairing tone made Diana ache for her. To everyone else, Eliza looked the picture of the happily married wife. But Diana had noticed that Eliza's smile was forced of late, her blue eyes troubled, and her words tinged with bitterness. Was Eliza having difficulties because of Mama's bold act?

Diana would get to the bottom of it. Eliza deserved the best the world could offer. "By the way, I meant to tell you earlier that you look lovely tonight."

Eliza's lustrous hair was caught up in a delicate ban-deau just the right shade of nut-brown to accentuate her blondness. Her gown of silk primrose skimmed her hourglass form with loving care, and her shoes gave her some much-needed height. Diana had picked out Eliza's ensemble for her, of course—fashion was Diana's passion. But Eliza's gold jewelry seemed to come from her husband. Diana didn't recognize the intricate work and was rather surprised he'd purchased such a romantic piece.

"I feel like a cow in sheep's clothing," Eliza grumbled.

Her sisters closed in on her. Verity was the first to ask, "Are you expecting?"

"Expecting whom?" Then Eliza groaned as she realized what Verity meant. "Oh. No. Nothing like that. I just . . ." She sighed. "I suppose I might as well tell you; you'll find out soon enough. Apparently, my husband decided, without consulting me, that he should go off to war. To that end, he has bought himself an officer's commission, and he means to join his new regiment in Portugal as soon as possible. He does *not* wish for me to accompany him, even if it were allowed."

"That makes perfect sense." Diana grabbed her sister's hands. The very thought of sweet Eliza following the drum gave Diana heart failure. "It would be dangerous. He's only thinking of you."

"Is he? Three years married and he can't wait to leave me."

"To serve his country," Verity pointed out. "It's honorable, at least."

"Perhaps. But he didn't say that's why. It makes no sense. He never had an interest in serving as an officer before. Given his rank, he could have. The only reason I can think of is that he hates the scandal and gossip swirling about us. He says that's not why either, but—"

"You should listen to him." Verity hugged her. "Besides, it doesn't matter why. All that matters is we're here to support you however you wish."

"I appreciate that." Eliza looked as if she were on the brink of tears. "The house will be very lonely without him. I don't know how I will bear it."

"If we continue helping ladies with the social events they host," Diana said dryly, "we'll have to move in with you just so we can keep it out of Papa's view."

Eliza brightened. "What a brilliant idea! It will be so much easier to coordinate plans if we're all in the same abode."

"I spoke in jest, Eliza," Diana said.

"But we could do it, couldn't we?" Verity said. "It would be easy to convince Papa that Eliza needed us, on account of Mr. Pierce going off to war."

"Oh, yes," Eliza said, "and ever since I married, I've learned a great deal about running a household and keeping accounts. It can't be that much harder to manage a business. We could even charge high rates so that we're only doing it for those we prefer or know personally."

"Exactly!" Verity said. "Besides, the *ton* only respects something when they have to pay buckets of money for it. The higher our rates, the more they'll clamor to hire us. And if Eliza is going to live on an officer's salary, she can use the money."

Diana scowled at them both. "Verity, you realize that once you and I do this, *if* we do this, we can't go back.

There will be no more Seasons, no chance of finding a respectable husband."

Verity snorted. "As if we have any hope of that now. Besides, I've lost my desire to stand around at balls hoping for a few moments of conversation or perhaps a single dance with a man. I'd much rather feather my nest for my future as a grande dame in society, bestowing my advice on the ladies I deign to recognize." She cast Diana a sly look. "You must admit it would be a fitting revenge on all the society matrons turning up their noses at us. Lady Sinclair offered to pay us—why not take it?"

Because Diana feared she would come to regret it. Still, the siren song of a chance at independence, at living her life as she saw fit, was a powerful temptation. "I suppose if we wanted to keep from losing our standing, such as it is, we could always give our profits to charity."

"Exactly!" Eliza's face filled with excitement. "I wouldn't need much for myself, and the rest could go to charities we pick."

Sometimes Diana understood why their mother had tired of being under Papa's thumb and bolted; all of Mama's household duties had fallen to her and Verity. If they left, too, they could escape Papa's constant criticisms and incessant demands. This way, they would be in a different household, assuming that Samuel Pierce would even allow Eliza to move her sisters into their home.

And why shouldn't he? It would keep Eliza busy while he was away at war, and he could be sure she was looked after because her sisters were with her.

That was the main thing. Eliza needed them. How could they turn her down?

"Very well," Diana said. "We can at least try to make this work."

And on that night, Elegant Occasions was born.

Chapter One

Geoffrey Brookhouse, the newly minted Duke of Grenwood, lowered the window of the Grenwood carriage and thrust his head out so he could better view the heavily trafficked Putney Bridge. Each time he'd traveled into the City from the Grenwood hunting lodge in Richmond Park, he'd crossed the Thames by a different bridge so he could examine its engineering. Regrettably, this would be his last crossing for a while. Today they were moving into Grenwood House in London.

Determined to see every bit of this particular bridge, he slid over to the other side of the carriage and looked out. Just as he was marveling at how admirably the wooden structure had held up for over eighty years, his timid sister, Rosabel, cleared her throat. Again.

Reluctantly, he stopped pondering why the engineers had used twenty-six arches in a river that had regular barge traffic. "Yes?" he asked, keeping his gaze out the window. "Do you need something, Rosy?"

The pet name seemed to give her pause. That was when their mother, also seated across the carriage from him, chose to intervene. "She needs your full attention, Son."

Damn it all. "Fine." He sat back to gaze at Rosabel.

At nineteen, she was a woman in every respect. But at eleven years his junior, she was still a child to him, the little girl with curly black hair and green eyes who'd giggled as he'd hauled her around the house in a miniature carriage. It didn't help that she was wearing one of those white muslin dresses that never failed to remind him of christening gowns and innocence.

Although she'd been sheltered from birth, *he'd* been a bone of contention between his late father and late maternal grandfather—Josiah Stockdon, owner of the largest ironworks in England. Father and Grandfather had fought over his future until his grandfather had won.

Geoffrey didn't regret having chosen his grandfather's path—not one whit—but if he'd known then what he knew now . . .

No, it wouldn't have made a difference. All it would have done was make him fight harder to protect his little sister from the catastrophe looming if anyone ever learned . . .

"I don't want to go," Rosy said in a small voice.

"Go where?" he asked.

"To this Elegant Occasions place." Her fingers worried the white lace trim on her dress. "They'll talk about me behind my back as everyone else does, and—"

"They won't dare, and I won't let them in any case. Your brother is a duke now, remember?"

"You were a duke at that musicale last week and it did no good, did it?"

He sighed, remembering the whispers and condescending looks. To London society he wasn't really a duke. He certainly wasn't one of *them*. So he understood how she felt, what it was like not to belong in one's proper sphere, to be a river trout lost in an ocean of expectations and responsibilities that one wasn't equipped to meet. Just yesterday—

This was not about him, blast it. It was about Rosy. And their mother, too, whether she knew it. Given how intently Mother watched the conversation, perhaps she did. Was *she* feeling the same about giving Rosy a Season in London?

It didn't matter. He had to protect them, even if it meant kicking them out into the real world. Mother was still in mourning for Father, so her hiding could be excused for a while, but Rosabel had to find a husband now that her own mourning period was over. It was the only way Geoffrey could be sure she wouldn't end up worse off than she was presently. In England, a titled husband would be the best kind of protection money could buy.

"You're right," he said. "That musicale was . . . difficult. But none of us were prepared, having never been to anything that grand in Newcastle. That's precisely why we must hire people to help you . . . us." He forced a smile. "So you don't spend another social engagement hiding in a corner where no one can notice you. And you heard Mother's friend—Mrs. Pierce's company, Elegant Occasions, can ensure that."

He hadn't been in town long enough to do the research

he customarily did with anyone whose business he meant to frequent, but even if he could have taken the time, it would have made no difference. London was a place all its own, where he had no friends except some engineers, and none of them moved in high society. But since Mrs. Pierce had surprised him by agreeing to his request that he meet with her and her staff today, he'd seized the chance to survey the company in person. At the last minute, he'd decided to bring his mother and sister along, which he probably should have planned to do in the first place.

Being an older brother began to wear on him.

Rosy stared down at her hands. "I don't have to have a Season. I could stay at home the rest of my life with you and Mama. Or I could travel with you to anywhere you want to build tunnels and bridges and all that. I can keep house for you."

That was out of the question. Unfortunately, he dared not tell her why. Rosy wasn't the chatty sort, but if she slipped up and revealed the truth about Father to Mother or anyone else—

He shuddered at the thought. Realizing his mother had noticed his reaction, he reached out to clasp his sister's hands. "And when I go to Belgium and stay there months at a time? What about Mother? Would you leave her alone when I can't be with her?"

"Don't drag me into this," Mother said. "I've already tried—unsuccessfully—to win her over to the idea of having a Season."

He squeezed Rosy's hands. "In any case, you deserve a home of your own, poppet, with a husband and children you cherish. I firmly believe you will find someone who suits you if we can merely prepare you for a London Season. I daresay once you meet the staff of Elegant Occasions and feel comfortable with them, half the battle will be won."

She lifted an eyebrow. "Have you ever known me to feel comfortable with strangers?"

"No," he conceded, "but perhaps it's time you learned."

"So I can dance with a succession of gentlemen who are only interested in me for my fortune?"

"That's nonsense. You're a very pretty girl."

She tugged her hands free. "You have to say that. You're my brother. But I'm stout, and I can't help noticing that gentlemen don't like stout ladies."

"I do."

"You don't count. Again, you're my—"

"Brother. Right. I'm just pointing out that men like all sorts of ladies, including your sort."

Their mother patted Rosy's arm. "That nice Lord Winston Chalmers seemed to find you quite fetching at the musicale. Why else would he have called on you the next day?"

"Because he and I both love Beethoven. All we talked about was music and poetry. Oh, and art." She blushed. "He was very interested in my sketchbook."

"I'll wager he was," Geoffrey muttered.

Rosy shrank down in her seat. "What do you mean?"

He had to bite his tongue to keep from pointing out that art, music, and poetry were generally well-loved by ladies, so the scoundrel had made sure he knew all about them, as any good fortune hunter would.

At his continued silence, she paled. "Now the truth comes out. You think no man of rank would want me for his wife unless it was for my dowry." With desperation in her voice, she stared down at her gown. "Certainly I'm too dull and plump to hold the interest of a man like Lord Winston."

"Forgive me, angel, I didn't mean any such thing," Geoffrey protested. "And if I thought you boring or 'plump,' why would I be willing to spend on Elegant Occasions what will probably amount to a fortune, just so you would feel more at ease for your damned Season?"

"Language, Geoffrey," his mother murmured, as she did at least five times a day of late.

Rosy merely directed her gaze out the window.

Geoffrey gritted his teeth. If only he could direct *his* gaze there, too. No, there would be no point. They'd long ago crossed the bridge. He'd have to take a trip out to see it after they were settled into Grenwood House.

Forcing his attention back to the matter at hand, he said, "As for Lord Winston, you are far too good for the likes of him. I asked around about him. Don't let his honorific sway you—he's merely the fourth son of a marquess, so he has only an allowance, nothing more, and not a great one at that." When she blanched and Mother looked surprised, he added, "Neither of you knew that, did you?"

"It doesn't matter." Rosy sniffed. "You warned him off, so I won't be seeing him again anyway." She nervously tugged at her tight gown, refusing to look at him.

That worried him. "I can't keep him out of other people's balls and parties. I merely wanted to caution you about him and others of his ilk."

Rosy turned to Mother. "*You* understand, don't you, Mama? Papa gave up everything to marry you. Not that

Lord Winston would necessarily wish to marry me, and I wouldn't expect it, but if he did—"

"I didn't realize that Geoffrey had already investigated the man's reputation," Mother said, "but since he has, I agree with your brother. We should be careful around the fellow, around *all* the gentlemen, to be honest."

Mother released a heavy breath. "As for your father . . . you can't compare him to Lord Winston. Unlike you, I had no fortune. That was before my own papa became so rich. So there was nothing in it for your papa but me. Lord Winston, on the other hand . . . Why, you barely know the man. It can't hurt for you to meet a few more gentlemen before you make any decisions."

"That's all I'm saying," Geoffrey put in. "From everything I've heard, Lord Winston is best known for his skill at getting into women's beds."

"Geoffrey, good Lord!" their mother chided.

"Sorry," he said, though he wasn't. "Just being around the man is liable to tarnish your reputation, Rosy, and I'd hate to see that when you have a bright future ahead of you."

Rosy shot him a sad look. "Admit it—you despise men like him because of Papa. You always say people in high society act as if they're better than everyone else, the way Papa sometimes acted. But you're just as bad, talking with Grandpapa about the 'swells' in London as if you weren't born to be one, saying how they don't have any idea what the world is like. It's two sides of the same coin. You look down on them and they look down on you. Now that you're a duke . . . you can look down on everyone, and they don't *dare* look down on you."

That stung, partly because some of it was true. He and

his late grandfather had shared a fascination with civil engineering, which was why Geoffrey, and not his father, had ended up a partner in Stockdon and Son, even though his grandfather had left his father the company in his will. But who could have guessed that *Father*, a mere third son of a viscount, would have inherited the dukedom of Grenwood if not for his untimely death? That Geoffrey would himself end up inheriting the dukedom from his distant cousin?

Suddenly Geoffrey owned a ducal estate—Castle Grenwood in Yorkshire—and the hunting lodge in Richmond. There was also Grenwood House opposite Hyde Park that he'd been given to understand was for the Brookhouse bachelors. He hadn't had the chance to look it over, too busy with meetings about the Teddington Lock to do so, although he intended to use Grenwood House as the family's main residence while Mother and Rosy were enjoying the Season. The Richmond hunting lodge was too far from the city to be practical for Rosy's début.

His traveling coach shuddered to a halt, and he looked out to see that they'd apparently reached their destination. He checked his pocket watch to find it was 10 a.m., not too early for a business call in the City, he'd been told. A groom ran out to take the horses, and one of his own footmen put down the step.

He asked the footman to wait. He had to finish this discussion with Rosy before going inside. "I tell you what, poppet. If you'll agree to participate fully in your début this Season and put your best effort into it, then if you can't find a husband you like or you don't succeed at moving about in society, or even if you merely find yourself miserable at the end, I won't push it anymore. One

Season is all I ask. After that, you can do as you please. Just give it a go. For me. And Mother, of course."

Her gaze narrowed on him. "What if I decide at the end that I want to marry Lord Winston, assuming he would even offer for me?"

It infuriated him to think of such a thing, but how else could he get her to put her best foot forward for her début? He only hoped that after meeting several other eligible gentlemen, she wouldn't be as inclined to fix on Lord Winston for a husband. "That would be your choice," he said, trying not to choke on the words. "But he still isn't allowed to call on you until you've had a decent Season."

She cocked her head, as if trying to make out if he meant it. Then she nodded, looking for all the world like a princess regally bestowing a gift on him.

"Swear it, Rosabel Marie Brookhouse," Geoffrey said. "On Father's grave."

"Geoffrey!" their mother hissed. "She shouldn't be swearing, and certainly not on Arthur's grave. It's not genteel."

He snorted. As if his mother had any idea what *genteel* was, although he wouldn't say that to her for all the world. Thanks to Father, gentility was important to her.

But Rosy said primly, "My word is my bond."

Geoffrey fought the urge to laugh. "You don't even know what that means."

That took some of the starch out of her spine. "Fine. Then I swear—on our father's grave—that I will give my début a good chance. All right?"

He probably should take that for the olive branch she meant it to be. "That will do nicely, angel." He would simply have to hope that *some* respectable fellow offered for her before the end of the Season.

After jumping down from the coach, he helped them both out. But when he turned to face the building, he realized that the offices of Elegant Occasions were apparently in an impressive town house on a grand-looking street in Grosvenor Square. How peculiar. Then again, the company *was* run by a woman, so perhaps she preferred a more "genteel" setting.

He escorted his mother and sister up the steps. When they reached the top and he knocked, the door remained firmly closed. He knocked again. Nothing. Only after the third knock was the door opened by a butler who looked decidedly unsociable, especially after he surveyed them all and apparently found them wanting.

"I'm Grenwood," Geoffrey said, "here to consult with Mrs. Pierce of Elegant Occasions."

That didn't change the fellow's expression one whit. "Wait here."

When the butler started to close the door, Geoffrey thrust his foot forward to block it. "We are expected."

The butler looked as if he might contest that. Then he sighed. "Very well." Opening the door wide, he gestured to them to enter. "I shall still have to consult with my mistress. She and her sisters assumed you would arrive later, during the usual hours for paying calls."

Sisters? Had he come to the wrong house? But no, given the butler's surliness, the man would have sent him packing if Geoffrey had come to the wrong place. Instead, the butler pulled aside a footman and whispered something in the fellow's ear that had the footman scurrying up the stairs.

Geoffrey stared the butler down. "You realize this isn't a social call. These *are* the 'usual hours' for conducting *business*, are they not?"

"Of course, Your Grace." The servant chilled him with one look. "But the ladies were out quite late last night at an important affair for a very important client."

Before Geoffrey could ask what client's importance trumped a duke's, Mother said, "It's fine, Geoffrey. I believe Gunter's is nearby, and I've been wanting to try their ices and find out what all the fuss is about. We can return later in the day."

He could hear the embarrassment in Mother's voice and it fired up his temper. Continuing to hold the butler's frigid gaze, he told her, "We are not leaving. Or if we are, we're not coming back."

"That's fine by me," Rosy said under her breath.

Damn it all. Through clenched teeth, he told the butler, "Is there somewhere we can wait?"

"If you must. I am sure the ladies will be down forthwith." The high-and-mighty butler called for tea, then showed them into a nicely appointed drawing room more fashionable than anything Geoffrey had ever seen in Newcastle, filled with spindly furniture that would no more hold a man of his size than would a newspaper. Between that and the bright yellow taffeta curtains, he felt like a seagull lost over land. This was much too fancy for him.

Grandfather's house and offices had been furnished in goods of solid English oak, Leeds leather, and burnished brass fittings—a man's home and a man's place of business. Perhaps it had been different in his grandmother's day, but Geoffrey would never know, because his grandmother had died bearing Geoffrey's mother. Perhaps she'd have furnished it like this room, but somehow he doubted it. She'd been a farmer's daughter until she'd married an ironmaster.

In any case, Geoffrey found the whole place suspect. He roamed the Aubusson carpet, his annoyance exploding into anger the longer they waited. What kind of business did these ladies run anyway? He was a duke, for God's sake. Dukes were supposed to be given entry anywhere, or so he'd been told, yet Mrs. Pierce's butler treated him and his family as if they were imposing upon Elegant Occasions by attempting to give the company their business.

No *man* who ran a business would get away with such havey-cavey practices. Geoffrey had expected some sort of shop, not what was clearly someone's home. Then he remembered the butler's description of the ladies as sisters and conceded that the familial connection somewhat explained their working out of a town house.

A servant brought tea at last, but Geoffrey was still too irritated to have any. No doubt this shabby treatment of them had come about because Elegant Occasions had discovered he was one step away from being a commoner. Or worse yet, they'd learned he was *in trade*.

While Mother and Rosy had their tea, he paced over to the window, his temper further fueled by the sight of his carriage being held in front by a groom who seemed to be awaiting a signal from the butler before taking the carriage and horses around to the mews.

How dare they? Mrs. Pierce had agreed to this meeting, for God's sake. It wasn't *his* fault that she'd meant him to come later in the day.

He'd nearly decided to leave when his mother whispered, "Geoffrey." He turned toward the doorway and lost all power of speech. Because there, framed by a ray of sunlight, stood the most beautiful creature he'd ever encountered.

Yes, her rich, auburn hair looked as if it had been hastily done up in its simple coiffure, and her frown at spotting him and his family marred the perfection of her wide, pearly brow. But still, all he could do was stare. Like an apprentice engineer confronted for the first time with a skew bridge, Geoffrey wanted to figure out how all her parts fit together to create such a magnificent whole.

Other than being statuesque, the lady had "parts" that weren't particularly unique: warm, brown eyes, a fetching face with a delicate sprinkle of freckles across her nose, and the requisite curves for a woman, or as much of them as he could see. The very fact that he wanted to see more of them was unsettling. So was the way she ignited a pulsing heat in his temples that coursed straight down to his loins.

That had never happened to him, or at least not immediately upon meeting someone. But under the circumstances, it would be unwise, to say the very least, to acknowledge it or contemplate acting on it or anything of that nature.

She strolled into the room and held out her hand. "You must be Grenwood."

"And you must be the proprietor of Elegant Occasions." He took her hand and shook it for a fraction too long. He'd taken off his gloves and she wasn't wearing any, so the skin-to-skin contact had his pulse racing. Which was absurd, of course. "Mrs. Pierce, is it?" he asked.

With a lift of one elegant brow, she tugged her hand free of his. "Wrong proprietor. I'm Lady Diana Harper."

He tensed up. "You're a lady of rank?" By God, he really should have spent more time learning about Elegant Occasions.

Judging from how she stiffened, she agreed with him. "I'm not sure why you're here if you didn't know that."

Though her name sounded familiar for some reason, he couldn't place where he'd heard it.

His mother stepped in. "Forgive us. We're a bit out of sorts. I'm Mrs. Arthur Brookhouse. My son asked for this meeting after my good friend recommended you. I believe she's related to someone who used your services previously? Anyway, she only knew the name 'Mrs. Pierce' when telling us how to find you in Mayfair. I assume that Mrs. Pierce works for you?"

"Not exactly. Eliza Pierce is my widowed sister, and this is her home. My other sister is Lady Verity Harper. We three run the business together, but my sisters are still dressing, I'm afraid. You took us all by surprise. We expected you later."

"So we were told," Geoffrey clipped out. "I assumed that because businesses usually start early in the day, you would all be available."

Her frozen expression showed he'd put her on her guard. That gave him a certain churlish satisfaction.

"Our company is unique," Lady Diana said in a brittle tone. "Most of what we do requires us to be at social engagements well into the wee hours of the morning. So I hope you can understand why we do not operate during the hours of a typical business concern while the Season is going on."

"Of course," Mother said, shooting him a warning look. "How could you? And we are very pleased you could see us today."

Lady Diana smiled at Mother. Apparently, he was the only person she didn't smile at, for she turned an even brighter smile on Rosy. Every ounce of her seemed to soften, as if she could tell his sister was uncomfortable. "You must be the duchess," she said kindly.

Before he could correct the woman, Rosy blinked, then gave a nervous laugh. "Perish the thought! Geoffrey—the duke—is my brother. He's hoping you can help me with my début."

Lady Diana looked mortified. "Please forgive me, but my sister didn't say exactly whom we were to help."

"It's an honest mistake," Geoffrey said. "No harm done."

She gazed at him as if trying to figure him out. "So that's why you and your mother came here with your sister?"

He nodded. "I should explain. We . . . that is, Rosy . . . Rosabel—"

"My daughter is shy, Lady Diana," Mother said, looking at him in bemusement. "She's not used to high society—indeed, none of us are. My late husband was the third son of Viscount Brookhouse, but we were never . . . part of that world. So we went on in Newcastle in our own merry way until my husband died. Shortly afterward, some duke—a very distant cousin of his—died, too, and Geoffrey inherited the dukedom out of the blue. So now we're in this situation." She looked at Geoffrey. "Yes?"

"That about sums it up," he said, relieved to have his

mother do the explaining. Lady Diana was unnerving him with her beauty and her perfect manners and her hard-won smiles.

Lady Diana stared at him. "Oh, you're *that* duke."

He tensed. "What do you mean?"

"There was talk of an heir to the Duke of Grenwood last year, but I'd completely forgotten about it, mostly because rumors about who the heir was were rather wild. Some said he was an American, which was why no one had ever met him, and others claimed that the Brook-house family disinherited him for being a blackguard, leaving him only the title of duke, because they couldn't take *that* away from him. The most outrageous one was that he'd been under everyone's noses all this time, working as an engineer in Newcastle."

"That last one is true," Rosy said cheerfully. When they all stared at her, she added, "And a bit of the middle one, too. Well, Geoffrey isn't a blackguard, and it was really Papa who was disinherited, but that happened before I was even born." She must have realized they were still staring at her, for she said, "What?"

Lady Diana chuckled. "So, definitely not an American, then? I'm just making sure."

Rosy blinked, then shook her head, pulling into herself the way she always did when strangers focused on her.

Lady Diana shifted her gaze to Mother. "And she's shy, you say?"

"Not always, apparently," Geoffrey said dryly. "Or at least not with you."

"That will certainly make matters easier," Lady Diana said. "Assuming you agree to engage our services." Before he could answer, she added, "Ah, here are my sisters at last."

As she performed the introductions, he noticed that, in his own opinion, neither of the two was as attractive as Lady Diana. Granted, Mrs. Pierce had blond hair, blue eyes, and a curvy figure, a combination he sometimes found appealing, but she was too short—given his height, he would tower over her. As for Lady Verity, her hair was a slightly darker shade than Mrs. Pierce's, and she had green eyes, but while every bit as tall as Lady Diana, she was too thin.

He liked some meat on a woman's bones, especially in bed. He didn't want to feel he might crush a chit every time he lay atop her. And despite Lady Diana's elegance— something he'd always associated with fragility—she did seem well capable of bearing his weight.

He groaned. Already he was thinking like a duke, auditioning prospective wives to bear his heir and winnowing them down to the one he found most compelling. But none of these women were remotely acceptable, even if he did plan to marry, which he didn't. Or not anytime soon anyway. He might be a duke, but they were far above him in manners, breeding, and all the other things that mattered to their sort. They wouldn't give him a second glance, even if *they* planned to marry, which it appeared they didn't or they wouldn't have started this business in the first place.

A pity, then, that he found Lady Diana so fetching. Indeed, if the trio of sisters hadn't come so highly recommended, he would turn around and leave right now. But he could tell from the excited chatter of Rosy and Mother that they liked the ladies, which counted for something with him.

After several minutes of discussion, Lady Diana

whispered to her sisters. Then Mrs. Pierce asked his mother if she'd like a tour of the town house, and Mother readily assented. As those two walked off, Lady Verity asked Rosy if she'd like to go sample some of the pastries left from the previous night's event. Never one to refuse pastry, Rosy gave a quick nod and those two headed off, too.

He and Lady Diana were now left alone, obviously by design. So when she gestured to the settee, apparently expecting him to sit on it, he did so, albeit reluctantly. The damned thing felt as flimsy as it looked.

Lady Diana perched on the chair opposite him as gracefully as a swan. "Shall I call for more tea, Your Grace?"

"No need. This shouldn't take long."

With a frown, Lady Diana picked up a portable writing desk like one he might use in the field. When she took up a pencil and licked the tip of it, a fleeting and very wicked image entered his head. He stamped it out at once.

"I hope you don't mind if we have a private chat, just the two of us," she said. "I'd rather discuss what we offer without three people asking questions. It goes more quickly this way. So, can you tell me what sort of help you desire from us for your sister's début?"

He propped one ankle on his knee. "I don't know enough about débuts to tell you even that much."

Lady Diana nodded, as if that wasn't unusual. "At a minimum, I would think you'd wish us to prepare her for her presentation to the queen."

"Certainly. That is, I'm aware she must be presented, but I'm not sure what that might entail." Feeling impish, he asked, "Is there a début orchestra? Does Rosy wave to the queen from across a room? Must Rosy give a series of curtsies? Or is that the queen's duty?"

She eyed him askance. "You aren't taking this seriously, are you?"

He sobered. "I am. But I'm so entirely out of my depth that I don't know what to ask for."

"Would you prefer that your mother participate in this discussion?"

"She won't be the person paying you." The chit actually winced at his mention of payment. "Besides, I fear Mother is no more knowledgeable about débuts than I am. She was born into a long line of ironmasters and was raised in a household of men. None of them knew a damned thing about débuts and women's fashion."

His curse made her frown. "I see. So you've come to us to make sure your sister has a successful début."

"Yes. But before we start discussing that, I need to tell you a few things about Rosy."

A ghost of a smile crossed her pretty lips. "You already claimed she's shy."

"She is, despite her surprisingly forthright remarks about the silly gossip high society feeds on."

"*Only* high society?" she said archly. "You do realize that gossip exists in every village, town, and city in England and probably the world. Are you claiming that the ironmasters of Newcastle never gossip?"

He could hardly claim that, given the gossip that had been going around town ever since his father's death. The worst was that he'd killed Father to get his hands on the dukedom, which was ludicrous. For one thing, the dukedom came *after* Father's death, and he'd had no idea he might inherit such a thing. For another, Geoffrey would give the dukedom back if that were possible. But if the powers-that-be insisted on naming him duke, he figured he might as well have whatever went with the blasted title, which wasn't as much as people probably thought.

"I'm not saying they never gossip," he said. "But they are too busy putting food on their families' tables to do much of that. It isn't worked into the very fabric of their world as it is in London."

"I see. So these are highly principled ironmasters." She wrote something in her notebook.

He leaned forward. "What are you writing in there?"

"Whatever I must to help me make sense of your family's peculiar situation, so I can do what I can for your sister. Also, I made a note to remind me and my sisters to call her Lady Rosabel."

"Why? I'm the one who inherited the damned title."

That prompted more scribbling in her notebook. He could only imagine what it said, probably something like, *Make His Grace stop cursing.* Which only made him want to curse all the more.

When she lifted her gaze to him again, her lips were drawn into a tight, prissy line. "The rules of address for titles have their idiosyncrasies, and one is that when a man inherits a title, his siblings inherit whatever form of address they would have had if their father had lived to take the title himself. That's assuming you have gone through the process to obtain a warrant. If you have not, then we should set about doing that at once."

"I have not. And if you think it will help Rosy's

chances, then by all means do so. Does that make Mother a dowager duchess, then?"

"The rules don't extend to your mother, because she married into the family. Just your sister. So your mother is still Mrs. Brookhouse, but your sister is now Lady Rosabel Brookhouse."

"That makes no sense."

"The rules aren't designed for the sort of unusual circumstances your family finds itself in. In such a case, they are bound to seem nonsensical."

"Nonsensical sums it up, to be sure." He checked his watch and noted that they'd been there three-quarters of an hour already. He rose to pace again.

"I'll make this quick, because you seem impatient to get it over with."

"How could you tell?" he said sarcastically. "I could have designed a bridge in the time I've spent here."

"A whole bridge?" She matched him sarcasm for sarcasm. "Either you are a very accomplished engineer or you waited for me far longer than I realized. I couldn't have designed a single gown in that time."

The tart words surprised him. She certainly had more backbone than any society woman he'd ever met. "I . . . may have exaggerated a bit."

"Imagine that—a man exaggerating. I've never seen that before." She pointed her pencil at him. "Look here, if you're sincere about wanting our help, we have to be sure what you need, which you don't seem able to tell me."

She licked the tip of her pencil, and he stifled a groan. While she wrote something in her notebook, he gazed at her lovely mouth, wondering what it would be like to kiss those full, seductive lips.

When she spoke again, it took him a moment to register what she was saying. "So perhaps I should tell you everything we do to ensure that a young lady has the best possible début. Then you can pick and choose which things you'd like us to do for her."

"Very well."

"Perhaps you'd prefer to sit while I go over everything?"

"I'd prefer to stand. I get restless when I sit. Especially on that flimsy piece of furniture." He gestured to the settee.

"You roaming around is making *me* restless," she bit out. "And don't let that Sheraton settee's looks deceive you. It is built sturdily enough to outlast even a robust fellow like you."

"If you say so," he grumbled and took his seat again. "Can we get on with this?"

"Of course." She picked up another notebook and began perusing it. "Generally, if we are helping a young lady through her entire début . . ."

Thus began Geoffrey's descent into hell.

Chapter Two

Diana tried to be patient as she explained again why an intimate dinner entertainment at the duke's town house should follow Lady Rosabel's presentation to the queen. But the man made her wary, and for the life of her, she couldn't figure out why.

In the past four years, she had worked with the daughters and wives of earls and baronets, admirals and generals. She'd even dealt with the occasional captain of industry. Some of the men had lacked manners; others had looked down their noses at her because of the scandal. But she'd always been able to paste a smile on her face and continue on.

And the few who'd been so unwise as to make disgusting proposals to her or her sisters? Those had found themselves charged quite a large fee for the privilege of having Elegant Occasions deign to endure them. Yet not even they had maddened her the way the duke was doing at present. It made no sense.

Well, it made *some* sense. Apparently, the man couldn't pay attention to anything but her pencil, because every time she licked the tip of it, he got a funny expression on his face and focused only on that. As he was doing now.

She put down her pencil. "Don't you agree, Your Grace?"

He stared blankly at her. "To what?" Then his gaze narrowed on her. "Oh, right, the intimate dinner entertainment. I bow to your superior knowledge of the field."

Amazing. She'd feared he might walk out because of her rather costly plans for Lady Rosabel. Before he'd even arrived, Eliza had made sure Diana and Verity understood the importance of taking on this particular client. Eliza had assumed a new duke would pay well to have his sister fully armed for the Season. From what Eliza had learned, his sister's previous years had been spent in the industrial wasteland of the north, so her triumph in society would be *their* triumph, a genuine caterpillar-to-butterfly transformation.

Eliza had said it would be best to accept him, regardless of whether they took to him and his sister. They'd never had anyone as lofty as a duke come along who required their services. And they always needed money to get them through the roughly eight months of the year when there was no Season, if only to better help their charities through winter.

Just as Verity had predicted, Papa had married again, probably hoping the widowed mother of three little boys would give him an heir. When she and Verity had first moved to Eliza's, they'd said they were doing so to keep their sister company, and he'd accepted it. But once he'd found out about the business they were building, he'd said they would only get their allowances if they lived under his roof. It was a typical attempt on his part to force them back home, where he could bully them to his heart's content.

Little did he know his daughters. She and Verity dug in their heels and left home for good. Elegant Occasions had saved them, allowed them to venture out from under Papa's thumb. After Eliza's husband died, Elegant Occasions had also become Eliza's sole support. Her husband had left her only a pittance in his will, falsely assuming he'd end up as a heroic soldier covered in glory instead of blood.

"You still haven't addressed my biggest concern," Grenwood said impatiently. "What good does all of this do if Rosy just sits in a corner to avoid people? That's what she did at the musicale, and neither our mother nor I could coax her into the crowd. She's just too shy."

Diana stiffened. Yet another mention of his sister's shyness. It was time to put an end to that perception. "She's not shy—she's self-conscious about her looks and, frankly, overwhelmed. As any young lady would be in her circumstances."

He started to speak, and she held up her hand. To her surprise, he shut up, though a tad sullenly. Most men would have barreled on.

Be honest, Diana. Plenty of men wouldn't go to this *much trouble for their sisters.*

"Many, *many* women are self-conscious about their looks," she went on. "The only way to change that is to find trappings—flattering clothing, better jewelry, more enticing coiffures—that present the ladies' fine qualities so truthfully that they can't help but see them for themselves. Your sister is quite pretty, you know, which will make it easy. By the time we finish redoing her wardrobe and training her maid to properly dress her hair, she'll feel like a princess. And the fact that we are taking over such a task for her will go a long way toward solving her other problem—that she feels overwhelmed."

"I'd say that the fact I'm paying for it should help her feel less overwhelmed."

His vulgar remark about money made her stifle a sigh. The man knew nothing about how a duke should behave. "Does she have pin money of her own?"

He muttered an oath. "No. I should probably give her an allowance. It didn't occur to me until now."

Obviously. With great difficulty she bit back the word. "So, you know what pin money is, then?"

His gaze turned frosty. "I'm not such a barbarian as all that. I graduated from Newcastle-upon-Tyne Academy and am also a member of the Literary and Philosophical Society of Newcastle-upon-Tyne."

That shocked her. He didn't seem the literary type. "You learned what pin money is from a literary society?"

He tightened his jaw. "I've heard it spoken of, yes, enough to know that women like my sister and mother should have some. But I hardly think there's a need for new gowns and such. They have plenty of gowns already. Why can't they just use those?"

How would she get it through his thick head that a successful début required new everything? "I know women whose families have gone into debt paying for their débuts."

Looking alarmed, he started to speak.

She cut him off. "And not women who were our clients either. We try to save expenses where possible."

"I daresay what I mean by 'save expenses,'" he drawled, "differs markedly from what you and your sisters mean."

"You'd be surprised," she muttered. "In any case, the new gowns are essential to her début. Judging from today's attire, Lady Rosabel seems to have outgrown her present ones. That explains why they appear ill-fitting and outdated, which means whenever she gazes at herself in the mirror, she sees a *person* who's ill-fitting and outdated. If she can't see past that, you can hardly expect other people to do so, neither lords nor civil engineers nor footmen. Not even the women she might want as friends, and every woman in society needs influential friends."

That was how they'd succeeded in this business venture. Lady Sinclair had praised them to her husband's sister, who'd told her best friend, and before long, they'd had plenty of work to keep them busy during the Season. "Have you never heard that clothes make the man?" she asked. "Well, they also make the woman."

"If you say so," he said, not for the first time in the past hour. She began to think it meant, *You're wrong.*

Bullheaded dolt. Oh, dear, she mustn't use such language even in her head or she might call him that to his face. "I take it you disagree."

He stood up to pace. Again. She ought to do the same, following him around the room like a teacher with an unruly student.

Unfortunately, he wasn't remotely her student. He was too large, too overbearing, too . . . omnipresent. Like her strict, demanding father, Grenwood put her on her guard with every word. But Papa didn't have the added dimension of the duke's size. She could handle Papa . . . sometimes, but she wasn't sure about the duke. Although she was tall for a woman, she would guess Grenwood was over six feet, with a broad chest and muscular arms, judging from how he filled out his clothes. That made him feel more dangerous to her.

And more attractive.

Goodness, what was she thinking? He was *not* attractive. It was just that he lacked the softness she associated with gentlemen of his rank. He was all sharp edges, from his chiseled jaw and high cheekbones to his pointed Hessian boots. Coming from a family of ironmasters, he was a gentleman in name only. She got the feeling that if all his clothes were stripped off, she'd find not an ounce of fat on him. That made sense, given how he'd apparently spent the past few years, but it didn't make her feel any easier around him.

Not that she would be seeing him without clothes. Heaven forbid!

On the other hand, as a woman who sketched everything, she could appreciate the male form in all its glory. And he looked to have quite the impressive one, although it was hard to be sure. Lady Rosabel wasn't the only Brookhouse who needed better attire.

He halted to glare at her, his eyes a peculiar shade of Prussian blue, no doubt accentuated by his cobalt-blue wool coat. And he did have the most beautiful head of wavy, raven hair just begging to be riffled by some enterprising lady.

Like her. She winced. Not on her life.

"Let me see if I have this right," he said. "My sister will need a new wardrobe. Various people—she and her maid, for example—will need to be trained in the vagaries of high society. After her presentation, I'll be hosting a dinner for important people who can introduce her to eligible gentlemen. Sometime later, I will host a ball to which many of said gentlemen will be invited. As if that isn't enough, I should contrive to get Rosy a voucher, whatever that is, to Almack's, whatever that is."

Diana hid how impressed she was that His Arrogant Grace had paid that much attention. He had certainly learned the high-handed manner of a duke to perfection. "You have it right, indeed. And without even taking notes."

"I don't need to take notes. My brain is in good working order. Besides, when I'm in the woods surveying a route for a canal, it helps to be able to make mental notes." He scowled at her. "And my mental notes tell me this will all require a great deal of money."

"You're a duke," she said archly. "It shouldn't be a problem."

"Money is always a problem, dear lady. I've suddenly inherited a woefully mismanaged estate and other properties that require refurbishing. Who knows what any of *that* will cost?"

"A gentleman should never talk about money so blatantly, you know. It makes him seem boorish."

To her surprise, he chuckled. "Aren't dukes always boorish?"

"No. They're condescending. It's not the same thing."

"Right." With a glint of mischief in his eyes, he waved his hand to indicate repetition. "Keep going. You're demonstrating condescension quite well."

She didn't know whether to laugh or to chide him. She settled for shaking her head. "Now I see why your sister is 'shy.' She's intimidated by you."

"What? Never." A troubled frown crossed his brow as he seemed to consider the possibility. Then his brow cleared. "Not Rosy. It's just as you said—she's . . . self-conscious. She thinks no one would ever look twice at her, no matter how much I tell her otherwise."

That softened Diana toward him a bit. "As her brother, you're biased."

"That's what *she* said. And I told her there were plenty of men who would find her attractive."

"Did you mean it, or were you just trying to make her feel better?"

"Of course I meant it! My sister is an angel—she's too good for most men in society. Still, I'd like to see her wed to a respectable fellow of her choosing. That's where you and your business come in."

"Quite right," she said. "And we're happy to oblige."

"For a large fee."

She lifted an eyebrow. "It depends on what you mean by 'large.' At the very least we expect you to cover the costs of her new wardrobe and the various entertainments." While a bit of their fee would go to supporting her and her sisters, the rest would go to the Foundling Hospital and the Filmore Farm for Fallen Females, their two charities of choice at present.

He sat down again, thank heavens, and crossed his arms. Did she prefer him sitting because it made him seem less overbearing? Or did she simply find it wiser to stare at his face than at those powerful thighs and calves, molded quite effectively by his tight buckskin breeches and well-worn riding boots? When he paced, she felt a savage and unexpected desire to sketch him unclothed.

Heavens! She'd never had such thoughts before. It was a trifle unsettling.

Plenty of men had flirted with her, or teased or kissed her. Before the Incident, she'd been rather popular with gentlemen despite her cursed red hair and freckles. But their advances had always left her cold.

Until now, she'd assumed Mama had taken all the family penchant for passion, leaving her a dry husk. Why this particular gentleman challenged that assumption was beyond her. He warmed her to an unconscionable degree.

She'd always thought if she ever met a man who roused her that way, she might consider seducing him, if only to determine whether she'd like the physical part of being a wife. Because if she didn't, there wasn't any reason to try marriage, assuming she could ever find a man who would brave the wagging tongues to marry her.

She'd even gone so far as to find out how a woman might protect against having children. She certainly didn't want to find herself with child and forced to either give up her babe or live a secluded life abroad. Or, worse yet, become a woman like Filmore's "fallen females." That was not in her plan for the future. Fortunately, that very charity had some inhabitants more than happy to share what they knew about enjoying their "fallen" status without suffering long-term consequences. She'd told them she needed the information for a pamphlet she was writing. They hadn't questioned that.

Thank heavens. And thank heavens, too, that Eliza had been kind enough to explain how sharing a man's bed worked, solely because she didn't want her sisters to be as ignorant as she had been on her wedding night.

"Are you sure Rosy can succeed in society if I hand her

début over to you and your sisters?" he asked. "Can you really increase her confidence and get men to notice her?"

She tamped down her inappropriate reaction to the duke. "Certainly. There's nothing wrong with your sister that a new look and some training won't improve. The intimate dinner entertainment is key, a sort of practice social event, so to speak. That will keep her from feeling overwhelmed while also helping her make friends."

"And you'll be there. All of you, I mean. Your business concern."

"We'll be there beforehand, making sure Lady Rosabel's attire and coiffure are perfect, and reinforcing her confidence where needed. We'll already have set up a scheme of decoration that is subtle but memorable, with food that persuades your guests to stay late and get to know your sister. But we wouldn't actually be guests." Especially not given the scandal attached to their names, which she was oddly reluctant to warn him about. "Still, once the dinner begins, she can speak to us whenever she likes, because we'll be behind the scenes in your town house, orchestrating the entire affair."

"Ah," he said. "She'll find that reassuring."

"Trust me, over time she'll gain enough confidence to be comfortable in society. Her new wardrobe alone will ensure that. I will personally oversee the dressmaker to make certain all your sister's gowns are designed exclusively for her. Once that's taken care of and she's had her presentation and her dinner, we'll set up a series of events that, over the first two weeks, will increase in size and importance of guests. That way we can build her confidence gradually."

"Not too gradually. She'll need time afterward to acquire suitors."

"Honestly, I don't think it will take long. By the time we graduate to throwing a début ball for Lady Rosabel, she will be the toast of the *ton*. My sisters and I will do everything in our power to ensure that."

He looked her over, as if sizing up an opponent in a boxing ring. "Now we come to the point. How much will all this cost?"

She wasn't accustomed to having to offer an estimate. The people she dealt with were used to throwing their money at anything. But she wasn't about to tell His Boorish Grace that.

Quickly, she jotted down some figures and what they were for. She included the Elegant Occasions fee and added up all the numbers. Then she leaned forward to hand him the paper.

He must not have taken the time to read over what every figure signified, for his gaze went immediately to the bottom and he said, "Bloody hell! That's highway robbery!" He tossed the sheet down on the tea table between them. "I won't pay it."

A voice came from the doorway. "You most certainly will, Geoffrey Arthur Brookhouse!" His mother marched over and picked up the sheet. She glanced at it and gulped. Then she walked around the tea table to hand it to Diana. "He can afford it." She glanced at her son. "For Rosy, he can."

Fully expecting him to give his mother what for, she was surprised when he instead rubbed his temples and groaned. "It seems I am overruled, sentenced to being plagued by busybodies for the next few weeks." Then he fixed Diana with a determined look. "I will pay for everything you listed . . . on one condition."

"What is that?" Diana asked warily.

"You guarantee that all your work will lead to Rosy having several suitors."

That baffled her. "I'm not sure I understand."

"Do you stand by your services?"

"Of course, but—"

"No shilly-shallying, Lady Diana. You either stand by them or you don't." He stared her down. "I'll make it easy for you. I will pay the *expenses* of the début regardless. That's only fair. I always demand that in my own contracts, and so should you. But whether I pay your *fee* will depend on whether your efforts result in suitors for Rosy."

"Are you demanding any particular number of suitors?" she asked sarcastically as his mother watched the two of them with seeming interest.

He leaned back and crossed his arms. "I should, shouldn't I? I won't even demand that you produce callers after her presentation and the 'dinner entertainment.' But after her début ball, I wish to see five callers a day for the first week."

She wasn't sure she could meet his expectation, but she was annoyed enough by his smugness just then to want to try. Five callers a day indeed. Hmph.

"If she gains that," he went on, "I will not only pay your fee, I'll double it."

Double it! "And if she *doesn't* gain five callers a day? What then?"

"We can negotiate a reduced fee, depending on the number of callers she actually has. But I warn you—if there are no callers, I will pay no fee."

"Geoffrey!" his mother hissed. "This is for Rosy."

"Precisely," he told her. "And if I am to pay some trumped-up fee, then I mean to get my money's worth for Rosy. Otherwise, what's the point? The enticement of a doubled fee will make them work all the harder for her."

"Our *reputation* will make us work all the harder," Diana said and cast him her chilliest look. "Come to think of it, I have a condition of my own."

"Oh?" he said with a raised brow.

"*You*, sir, must agree to accept our services for yourself." She had the delicious satisfaction of catching him off guard. She'd never seen a man go from self-satisfied to insulted so fast. "We won't even charge you, as long as you cover expenses. 'That's only fair.'"

He jumped to his feet. "Expenses!" he roared. "What could you possibly need in expenses for *me*?"

She rose. "Bills from a tailor, a cobbler, a glover . . . I'm sure the list will be endless, if I am to judge from *this*." She swept down her hand to indicate his attire. "Your inappropriate clothing for paying calls."

"I was *not* paying calls in the social sense," he said irately. "This was a business call."

"That's no excuse for wearing riding boots and buckskin breeches. Were you raised in a barn?"

"He was not," his mother said as she sank onto the settee. "But he might as well have been. He never listens to me."

"Now see here." He glowered at Diana. "There's nothing wrong with my clothes. I simply hadn't expected ladies of rank to be running the dam— . . . the business, all right? And anyway, beyond my poor choice of attire today, I see no reason for me to use your services for myself."

"No?" She ticked off his transgressions on her fingers. "You arrived at an hour never used for paying calls. You cursed without apology, and in front of ladies no less. You hovered over them in a most ungentlemanly manner. You sat with your ankle across your knee, for pity's sake, splaying your legs in a vulgar pose."

"Plenty of men sit that way," he said defensively, though a flush crept up his face.

"Perhaps in the country taverns you obviously frequent," Diana said, "but not in polite society, I assure you."

A burst of laughter came from the doorway. Diana looked over to see that Lady Rosabel and Verity had returned.

But Lady Rosabel was the one laughing. "I've never seen a woman stand up to the almighty Geoffrey before." She entered the room and clapped her hands. "Impressive work, Lady Diana!"

"Watch it, poppet," he said. "I'm the one paying for this dressing down, you know."

"And another thing," Diana said, beginning to enjoy herself. "You discuss financial matters in the crudest way possible! Even when I tell you it's uncouth."

There was a decided glint in his eyes now. "You said it was boorish. Not the same thing."

"Close enough," she snapped. "So, Your Grace, will you agree to *my* condition?"

He searched her face, as if looking for a crack or weakness to exploit. Then he surveyed the four other women in the room and let out a long, ragged breath. He'd obviously realized he was outgunned and outmaneuvered at present. "If I must."

His mother rose. "You must, my darling." She winked at Diana. "Or else we won't be able to hire them, will we, Lady Diana?"

"Absolutely not. Our efforts would be all for naught if your son undid them with every word out of his mouth."

"No need to club me over the head with it," he grumbled. "I've already agreed to your condition."

"Excellent." She turned to Lady Rosabel. "I shall call on *you* and your mother at your family's town house first thing tomorrow. We can assess your wardrobe before going off to the dressmaker's, where you're to be fitted for new gowns and whatever else your wardrobe lacks."

Lady Rosabel looked nervously at her brother. "I don't know. That sounds dreadfully expensive."

"Remember what I told your brother about not discussing money?" Diana said gently.

"Right," Lady Rosabel said, blushing a little. "I shall remember that next time."

"Besides," her brother put in, his voice kind, "I've already agreed to the gowns. And you should have them. You deserve to have them. I can afford them."

That he spoke so lovingly to his little sister put a lump in her throat. Until she remembered that the tight-fisted fellow had argued against new gowns when his sister wasn't around.

"Geoffrey, you're not to speak of money, remember?" Lady Rosabel chided him.

"It's all right." He shot Diana a sly look. "I've already been deemed 'uncouth' and 'boorish.' One more cursed epithet won't hurt me. What's it to be this time, my lady? Rude? Crass? Utterly lacking in social graces?"

"Careful, Your Grace," she warned, struggling not to smile. "Don't make me reconsider taking you on as a client. Especially when you just cursed in the presence of ladies again."

He cocked his head. "Because I said 'cursed'? But you said 'curse' to chide me for cursing."

"I used the verb, which is perfectly acceptable. You used the adjective, which is not."

"Good God, woman!" he said with a roll of his eyes. "This is why I never wanted to go into polite society. You're all quite mad. Good day. I'll find my own way out." He glanced at his mother. "I'll call for the carriage and wait for you and Rosy there." With that, he marched to the door.

But Diana was having far too much fun to stop. "If it makes you feel any better," she called after him with great glee, "your use of the past participle for 'curse' was appropriate and not uncouth at all!"

He came back to glare at her through the doorway. "It does not make me feel better. It doesn't make me feel anything at all. Feelings don't come into it. To hell with you. And yes, I know 'hell' and 'Good God' are not suitable for society. I just don't care!" Then, whirling on his heel, he left.

All of them froze as his hurrying steps sounded the entire way down the stairs. Only after they heard him leave through the front door did they burst into laughter.

"He's such a *man*," Eliza said a bit wistfully because she sorely missed her late husband.

Diana, thinking of Grenwood's stalwart form, said,

"That he is." Then she realized they were eyeing her quizzically and blushed. "Because he must always have his own way, I mean." And because he was nothing at all like the last duke she'd met, an old, bald fellow with scrawny calves and a roving eye.

Remembering the look in Grenwood's eyes as she licked the tip of her pencil, she caught her breath. Perhaps all men had roving eyes. Then again, he might just have wondered *why* she was licking it. Yes, that must be it. After all, he'd made it perfectly clear he didn't like her.

"That boy has had a mind of his own since the day he was born," Mrs. Brookhouse said, her pride in the duke leaking through her words nonetheless. "He never let anyone but his grandfather tell him what to do, and even then, if my father was wrong about the engineering of something, Geoffrey would inform him of that, even at ten years old." She swept her gaze about the room. "But Rosy and I should go. We're probably keeping you ladies from your work. Besides, Geoffrey will wonder what's taking so long."

"I'm sure he will," Diana said. And probably blaming *her* for it. Or wishing he'd never taken up with them. What had his sister called him? Almighty Geoffrey. Diana dared not call him by his given name, but the Almighty Grenwood sounded exactly right for him.

His mother and sister said their farewells and headed down the stairs chattering. Then, as she and her sisters always did after taking on someone new, the three of them headed to their private parlor that overlooked the square to exchange notes on their impressions of their new client. Or clients, given the bargain Diana had struck with Grenwood.

Verity went right to the window to look out over the street below, and Diana followed her. They watched the Brookhouse ladies make their way down the steps toward their carriage, still chattering amiably.

"Lady Rosabel seems promising, a diamond in the rough," Verity said as she watched them. "As long as she can be trained to behave in society, you can easily turn her into a diamond of the first water. She has the looks for it, or she *would* when not wearing an awful gown, with her hair unfashionably dressed. You have plenty to work with, Diana, and you're always so good at transforming ladies into their best selves."

"Thank you," Diana said, then narrowed her gaze on Grenwood, who'd jumped out to help his mother and sister climb in. "It's *him* I'm worried about."

"The duke is certainly not like other gentlemen, is he?" Verity said.

Diana could feel her sister's eyes on her. "No. Because he's *not* a gentleman, I fear. And I'm still not sure if that's bad or good. Lord knows we won't be able to control him. I only hope the great lout doesn't pick up some suitor and toss him off a balcony for not showing Lady Rosabel suitable respect."

"That I would like to see," Verity said with a chuckle, "though I have no doubt he could do it. He's quite an impressive specimen of masculine good looks, isn't he? He could take on even the accomplished Gentleman Jackson."

"I'm sure Papa would beg to differ. You know how he loves Gentleman Jackson." A disquieting thought occurred to her. "You're not setting your cap for him or anything, are you?"

"Gentleman Jackson?" Verity asked.

"Of course not. Grenwood." The very idea alarmed Diana, for reasons she didn't want to examine too closely.

Verity laughed. "No, but you clearly are."

"Don't be ridiculous," Diana complained. "He'd be as bad a husband as Papa, if not worse."

"Whatever you say." Verity turned away from the window. "Is it true Grenwood promised to double our fee if you could get his sister five new callers a day in the week after her début ball?"

"It's true," Eliza said from her favorite spot on their comfy parlor sofa. "That's when Diana dressed him down and said he'd have to meet *her* conditions."

"Oh yes, that's where I came in." Verity took a seat beside Eliza. "So, what did *you* think of him, Eliza?"

"I think any man willing to double our fee is perfect," Eliza said. "I can see why Diana has set her cap for him."

Diana turned on them in a temper. "I have *not* set my cap or anything else for the duke."

"Ooh, I wonder what 'anything else' means," Verity said, her eyes dancing. "It sounds most unladylike."

"And you sound unprofessional," Diana retorted. "This is a business concern, and you two need to remember that."

"Aye, aye, Captain," Verity said with a salute. "Careful, Eliza, or she'll crack the whip. Wait, do you think *that's* what 'anything else' means? I somehow doubt Grenwood would enjoy such a thing."

Diana sighed. "You two have spent far too much time reading gothic novels."

"Trust me," Eliza said, her eyes gleaming, "there is no whip cracking in gothic novels. We learned about *that* from our support of the Filmore Farm for Fallen Females. And have I ever said how much I hate the term 'fallen females'?"

"Repeatedly," Diana and Verity said in unison.

Eliza ignored them. "I mean, no one calls the men who use their services 'fallen,' do they?"

Verity snorted. "That's because we live in a man's world." Even after four years, Verity was still bitter about losing her suitor due to the Incident.

"Speaking of a man's world, Eliza," Diana asked, "is Grenwood really a civil engineer?"

"How should I know? I'd heard nothing of him until he sent a note on the Duke of Grenwood's stationery saying he wished to consult with us about the début of his sister."

"You never told me it was for his sister."

"Didn't I?" Eliza said. "I could have sworn I did."

Heat crept up Diana's cheeks. "I thought she was his *wife*. It was quite the embarrassing moment when they corrected me."

"I would have paid good money to have seen *that*," Verity said. "You, embarrassed in a social situation—will wonders never cease? That happens so seldom as to be rare indeed."

Diana glared at her. Her sisters laughed. Honestly, Diana didn't know why they always treated her as if butter wouldn't melt in her mouth. She had plenty of difficult moments in society. She just didn't dwell on them.

Time to change the subject. "Verity, you never said whether you saw your 'phantom fellow' at the ball last night."

"Oh, right." She glanced at their other sister. "As I recall, I only told Eliza, but yes, I did see the phantom fellow at Lady Castlereagh's ball. And once again, the footman I encountered refused to tell me his name. Well, really, he claimed he didn't know who I was talking about. Which is absurd. Someone has to have seen the fellow, *know* the fellow."

For the past few occasions they'd been involved in, Verity had insisted that she kept seeing the same man lurking in the hallways. She was sure he was up to some nefarious purpose, but he was dressed well and had the look of a gentleman. So how nefarious a purpose could it be?

"I still say he works for the Foreign Office, rooting out French spies in society," Eliza said.

"He could be a circus performer for all I care," Verity said. "I just want to know his name."

"And why does he only show up around you?" Eliza asked. "You'd think *someone* else would have noticed him."

Verity and Eliza speculated for a while, leaving Diana to sit in precious silence. Her sisters were clearly not ready to begin a serious discussion of their new clients. Nor could she blame them. They'd never had a pair quite like this one, making it hard to guide the Brookhouse siblings when not even the mother knew what was proper.

But Diana at least intended to find out what exactly a

civil engineer did, and how a viscount's grandson had come to be one.

Tomorrow should be an interesting day.

Geoffrey scowled out the window while his sister and mother talked of the next day's plans. He would contrive to be gone when Elegant Occasions arrived at the town house tomorrow. Lady Disdain's assessment of his fitness as a gentleman still smarted, and he wouldn't give her another chance at condescending to him. The woman had a mouth that would sear a man's skin.

Not to mention inflame other parts of him. He hated to admit it, but her lips had the most enticing shape. And her sweet little tongue . . . Every time she'd licked the tip of her pencil, he'd wondered what it would be like having her lick the tip of a certain part of him.

God help him. Arguing with her roused him in ways he'd never thought a fine lady could, even as she'd been insulting him! There could be no more of that, however much it stirred him. Too dangerous.

Besides, she hadn't been entirely wrong about his need for more fashionable clothing. He'd been putting off having new attire made until he was in London, but that could no longer be postponed. The Season was upon them, and his need for new trousers had become dire, especially if he had to escort Rosy anywhere.

He did have one suit of clothing that would do. But it was for dining with the Society of Civil Engineers tomorrow evening.

"You're very quiet," Mother said. "Are you all right, Son?"

"I'm fine. Or I will be once this début is behind us."

"You could always change your mind about Elegant Occasions," Rosy said lightly. "We could go home to Newcastle and I could look after you for the rest of our lives."

He searched her face. "Do you still want to?"

Her expression was comical. She seemed truly conflicted. Then she sighed. "No. They're very nice women. I think they can help me become a real lady, like . . . like Lady Diana."

"God forbid," he muttered under his breath.

"What?"

"Nothing." He looked her over. "I hope they help you come into your own as Lady Rosabel. That would please me most." When she smiled shyly at that, he added in a teasing tone, "By the time this is over, I expect you'll have thirty-five suitors."

"Thirty-five! I'll be perfectly satisfied with three."

He laughed. "Lady Diana would not be satisfied with that, I assure you." He noticed that the uppish female hadn't turned down his offer to double their fee. She might not approve of *talking* about money, but she was certainly happy to spend it, especially when it was someone else's.

Not that he intended to watch her do it. He'd be a bull in a china shop if he accompanied them to a dressmaker's. Best to let the ladies do that on their own.

Instead, he would head off to a tailor before they even arrived. Lady Disdain would never lecture *him* about clothing again if he could help it. The next time she saw him, he'd be well-dressed if it killed him.

And it just might, given tailors' usual reactions to his size. They always called in their apprentices to gawk at him. He was *not* looking forward to that, to be sure. Tall, muscular fellows were uncommon in society as far as he could tell.

That was something Lady Disdain had in her favor. She didn't seem to mind his size. Although how could he be sure when her sort didn't share their true feelings about anything?

He caught Mother staring at him. "What is it?"

"You were rather rude to them, you know."

"Was I?" Of course he was. Sometimes his temper got the better of him. "I found them to be somewhat full of themselves."

"I found them to be quite nice," Rosy said, "especially considering what has put them in their present position."

That got his attention. "What position is that? Sisters running what is probably a lucrative concern?"

"Daughters of an adulteress and her vindictive husband," his mother said. "Their mother ran off with her lover, ignoring the effect that would have on her daughters. Then their father, also selfish, divorced her for it in a very public trial that had the family—the sisters—being gossiped about for months. Even though those ladies had done nothing to deserve it."

That sobered him. *Now* he remembered why the Harper name had sounded so familiar. He'd heard it mentioned in the gossip rag Rosy loved to read to them at breakfast.

"So that's why three pretty women of rank are still unmarried," he mused aloud. "I did wonder. Especially when Lady Diana showed me their fee. Couldn't imagine how the three of them managed to gain such hefty fees despite being unable to marry themselves."

"Mrs. Pierce is a widow, so she at least married once," Rosy pointed out. "Her husband died in the war."

"Good God, how did you learn all this?" he asked. "I knew nothing of it."

Rosy shrugged. "Lady Verity told me. She assumed we knew why they'd decided to strike out on their own."

"A very bold step in a society that doesn't allow unmarried women to do anything but live off their family's wealth, become governesses, or subject themselves to possible humiliation as lady's companions." Mother stared at him disapprovingly. "You can hardly fault them for hiding behind their pride."

"Well, you needn't worry about me insulting them tomorrow," he said. "I plan to make myself scarce. You wouldn't want me around anyway."

"We certainly wouldn't," Rosy said. "You have no taste at all when it comes to fashion."

Et tu, Brute? Geoffrey thought, though he didn't bother to say it. He had a fondness for Shakespeare that his mother and sister didn't share. It had actually been the one thing he and Father enjoyed together.

The thought of Father reminded him why he was here in London in the first place—to make sure Rosy and his mother wouldn't have to endure the sort of vile gossip the Harper sisters had. To see them settled in a good situation in case the worst happened and Father's secret was revealed.

Yes, he would definitely stay out of this début nonsense to the greatest extent possible. Because if he got involved in it, he might soon find himself mired in a different kind of rumor and speculation. One in which he became besotted with a certain voluptuous vixen.

And *that* he could not tolerate.

Chapter Three

The next morning, Diana sat at the dining room table and spread her usual piece of toast liberally with butter, then poured herself a cup of tea. Verity was still filling her plate and Eliza was probably still asleep, as usual.

When Verity approached to sit down, she gaped at Diana. "That's all you're eating? We have a long day ahead of us, so it would be wise to prepare."

"You appear to be preparing for Napoleon's army," Diana said, with a nod to Verity's plate, piled high with tartlets, Westphalia cakes, various combinations of fruit on skewers, marzipan figures, ham slices carved in the shape of pigs, and turkey slices carved in the shape of turkeys.

Her sister poured herself some coffee and added cream. "I am, in a way. These are the items I mean to suggest for Rosy's ball."

"Lady Rosabel," Diana corrected her.

"Right. And I will call her that when she's around."

"You will call her that everywhere, so you don't slip up and call her the wrong thing in front of anyone important."

"My dear sister," Verity said with a sniff, "I can see that after yesterday's contretemps with the duke, you are flexing your dictatorial muscles. But aside from the fact that I'm only a year younger than you, I am also an important part of this business concern and you are not in charge, whatever you may think. If anyone should be in charge, it's Eliza. It's her house and she's the oldest. But we agreed a long time ago that we all have a stake in decisions."

"You're right." Diana stirred some honey into her tea. "Forgive me if I'm being . . . bossy. I'm just a bit out of sorts this morning. I didn't sleep well last night. I had disturbing dreams."

"I would wonder if you'd dreamed about the duke, but I doubt you would call dreams like *that* disturbing."

"No, indeed." Diana *had* dreamed about the duke, but not in the way Verity probably imagined. She'd dreamed of him nude. She had *never* dreamed of a man nude before. And that wasn't even the disturbing part! That had come when he'd put his hands on her, kissed her, and touched her all over . . . and she'd liked it. She'd awakened to find herself rubbing her breast with one hand and between her legs with the other. How shocking!

Lord help her. Was this how it had happened for Mother? Was Diana destined to be a wanton, too?

"In any case," Verity said, "you needn't be so stuffy about what we call *Lady Rosabel*. She doesn't care about all that. She does, however, care about the food at her ball. Which is why I'm eating this peculiar breakfast. I wanted to see how the items hold up if done by Eliza's half-decent cook and eaten in the hours of the morning after one has risen."

Diana laughed. "You're already planning the ball supper dishes? This is a new height of care indeed."

"Actually, the idea occurred to me during the last ball supper we took charge of. The cost of hiring that expensive chef would have bankrupted us if the client had not agreed to pay that expense. Eliza's cook isn't bad, so why not use her?"

"Let me guess," Diana said archly. "Lady Rosabel cautioned you not to spend too much of her brother's money."

"Well, yes. I couldn't figure out, however, if he's just a pinchpenny or if they are actually cleaned out."

"I suspect neither. Grenwood merely dislikes high society, so he resents wasting extravagant amounts on his sister's début."

"But he's a duke." Verity bit into what looked like a marzipan swan.

"I said the same thing to him. It didn't faze him. Apparently, he inherited a number of debts along with the properties."

"That doesn't surprise me. From what I heard about the previous duke, he wasn't careful with money."

"Exactly." Diana got up to fetch a second slice of toast.

"Do you want one of these cheddar tartlets?" Verity asked. "They turned out rather well."

"I'm not eating that for breakfast," Diana said. "When I eat something rich first thing, I feel ill later. And I need to be prepared for anything at Grenwood's town house. For one thing, we don't know what condition the place is in."

"True. We've never been there, have we? Isn't it one of those fancy places near Hyde Park, surrounded by trees? Still, it might be too small to host our dinner entertainment.

Mrs. Brookhouse did say it had once been used as a place for the Brookhouse bachelors."

"So it might not have a ballroom," Diana said. "In fact, we don't even know if Lady Rosabel can dance."

"She can," Eliza said sleepily as she entered the room. "I asked. She said her brother had paid for her to have lessons while she was in mourning. Although we probably should make sure she can dance *well*. Who knows what passes for a dancing master in Newcastle? By the way, I didn't realize you truly meant we should be ready at this ungodly hour of the morning until my maid told me you two were expecting me downstairs any minute."

"It's ten a.m., Eliza," Diana pointed out. "I realize that's early on days after we've worked most of the night, but not when we've all been in bed by nine."

"Careful," Verity told Eliza. "Diana has been on the rampage ever since she got up."

Eliza went to get her usual breakfast—porridge and pears. "She can be forgiven that. We are all on edge these days, with Papa going back to his old ways." She made a tsking noise. "Those poor little lads. The new Lady Holtbury must be breeding. Otherwise, Papa wouldn't be so blatant about his indiscretions."

"We don't know anything for sure," Diana said. "For now, it's just gossip."

"Perhaps," Verity said. "But he was seen in the company of Harriette Wilson."

"Half of London has been seen in her company," Diana said. "That means nothing."

"If you say so," Eliza said.

Diana suppressed the irritated remark that came to her lips. She did *not* like having the duke's "if you say so" thrown at her again, even by her beloved sister. "Glad we've settled that. We need to turn our attention to our plans for the day."

As they lingered over breakfast, they discussed what to tackle first. Obviously, they should focus on Lady Rosabel and her clothing. Diana pointed out that Mrs. Brookhouse would need little improvement because she was still in mourning and couldn't change much of her current attire anyway. The woman had also impressed all three of them with her ladylike behavior, so, assuming they saw nothing glaring during their time at Grenwood House today, there would be little need to advise her on her manners.

"But what are we to do about the duke?" Verity asked. "He can't go about cursing as he does. And his clothing . . ."

They all sighed together.

"The problem is," Diana said, "he doesn't take direction well."

"As we all noticed yesterday," Eliza said. "But you must admit he's one fine-looking fellow. That goes a long way with the ladies in society, who might be predisposed to overlook his language for the pleasure of gazing at him."

"It won't be a pleasure if he continues to dress badly," Diana pointed out.

"He definitely needs a better tailor," Verity agreed.

A short while later, when they headed off to Grenwood House with their marching orders, Diana couldn't settle her pulse. The thought of seeing the duke again, of *sparring* with the duke again, had her overheated. She tried envisioning the gowns she might design for Lady

Rosabel, but all she could think of was what outrageous remarks Grenwood might make today.

Then they came to the drive in front of Grenwood House, which was located down a side road across from the Hyde Park Barracks.

"It is quite a bit larger than I would have expected a bachelor's house to be," Verity said. They turned down the drive to discover it had acres of pleasure gardens and a house befitting a duke. Like some of the wealthiest lords, his abode in town was similar to abodes out of town for lesser lords.

Already her mind was leaping ahead to how they could use the pleasure gardens to good effect for Rosy's intimate dinner entertainment. She pointed out to her sisters where they might place a small band of musicians to allow for some dancing outside. They could even dine outside, assuming the weather was fine. Why not? Wouldn't that be splendid?

She couldn't wait to see what the duke thought of her idea. So she was vastly disappointed when they discovered he had left early and would not return for some time.

It wasn't as if she'd expected him to join them on a trip to a dressmaker, but she hadn't *not* expected it either. He was refreshingly unpredictable, which wasn't true of any other man she'd ever met. Besides, she'd been looking forward to suggesting clothes to complement his . . . robust build. But perhaps he would return before they left late in the afternoon.

She had no more time to think about the Almighty Grenwood, because she and her sisters were instantly shown into the drawing room, where Lady Rosabel and

Mrs. Brookhouse were waiting. The two ladies were eager to start the tasks at hand. "Lady Rosabel—" Diana began.

"Oh, do please call me Rosy. Everyone does."

Verity started to laugh, but stifled it when Diana glared at her. Diana had half a mind to inform Lady Rosabel that she shouldn't be so free with her Christian name, but the young woman looked so eager to fit in that Diana couldn't say a word of it. "If you wish . . . Rosy. And please do call me Diana."

"And me, Verity." Her sister shot Diana a smug look. "Oh, wait, I already gave you leave to do that yesterday. Silly me."

Rosy beamed at her and Verity.

Just then a footman entered. "Lady Rosabel, you have a visitor."

"Oh!" Rosy said. "I forgot to have the door knocker removed for today. Who is it?"

"Lord Winston Chalmers."

That took Diana completely by surprise. Aside from the way Rosy lit up at the news that he was paying her a call, Winston was also her and her sisters' second cousin.

Diana was about to reveal that to the Brookhouse ladies when Mrs. Brookhouse said to the footman, "Didn't His Grace tell the staff that Lord Winston is always to be informed we aren't at home?"

The footman blanched. "I didn't know, ma'am. Nobody told me. And Lord Winston seems very eager to see Lady Rosabel."

"Can I see him for just a few moments, Mama? Ten minutes? You can chaperone."

"I'm sorry, dear, but remember what you promised

Geoffrey," Mrs. Brookhouse told Rosy. "No visits from Lord Winston until after your début. And I am not going behind his back to allow it."

Rosy nodded glumly. "No one ever goes behind Almighty Geoffrey's back."

Now Diana was dying of curiosity to know exactly how Winston and Rosy had managed to meet.

"Besides," her mother said, "you wish to look your best when you see him again, don't you?"

Rosy's brow furrowed. "What if he doesn't come back?"

"He will, I'm sure. This is his second visit, so he's obviously interested. And if he's not, you don't need him, do you? Now, why don't you go with Lady Diana and have her take a look at your closet while I introduce Lady Verity to our cook?"

"All right," Rosy said, watching as Mrs. Brookhouse and Verity walked off, with Verity clutching sheafs of recipes.

Soliciting the help of a footman, Eliza hurried away to survey the Grenwood ballroom before she was needed to help assess Rosy's closet . . . and her lady's maid. They'd long ago put Eliza in charge of coiffures because she was so good with hair. She always evaluated the lady's maids of their clients in that respect.

Meanwhile, Diana and Rosy headed down the hall toward the stairs leading up to the young woman's bed-chamber. Diana slanted a glance at her. "So, you know Lord Winston, do you?"

Rosy nodded. "I met him at the musicale. He saw me sitting in the corner, asked our hostess to introduce us, and then asked me to dance. But I couldn't do it, not in front of all those people. So Lord Winston sat with me instead, and we talked about books and music and everything. He was *wonderful*." A dreamy expression crossed her face.

Diana suppressed a snort. Winston often inspired that look in ladies. He had a way with women, to be sure. A novice at courting like Rosy wouldn't have stood a chance.

"I've never met a man so intelligent," Rosy went on, "other than Geoffrey and Papa, of course. Besides that, Lord Winston paid me a visit the very next day. Do you know him? He's very handsome."

He certainly was. That was the problem with a man like Winston. He never had to fish for women. Women leaped into his boat. Which begged the question—why was her cousin throwing his fishing line into the pond for Rosy? "Your brother disapproves of him?"

"Geoffrey *says* he asked around town and discovered that Lord Winston is a fortune hunter and a seducer of women." Rosy hurried to the stairs. "But the truth is, Geoffrey just doesn't like anyone with a title. It's on account of Papa, you know. Papa fell in love with Mama despite her being an ironmaster's daughter, and even though he married her, he . . . Anyway, you don't want to hear all that."

Oh, yes, Diana wanted to hear every word. But she shouldn't want it. She already had an unwise fascination with His Grace.

But in this particular case, she shared his concern for his sister. "Well, I will only caution you that Lord Winston does have a reputation as a rakehell. But I've never heard a word about his being a fortune hunter."

That seemed to make Rosy very happy. Diana and her sisters would have to work hard to get Rosy other suitors now that they knew of her infatuation with Winston. Perhaps Diana shouldn't have told Rosy that last part without first consulting with the duke.

She strode stiffly up the stairs behind Rosy. What was she thinking? The poor young woman deserved to find her own way in society and not be bullied by her brother. Indeed, that was something else Diana wanted to know about Rosy and Grenwood.

When they reached the top of the stairs, Diana paused to get Rosy's attention before they entered her room and found themselves surrounded by other people. "Does your brother dictate to you all the time?"

"No! Well, not really." Rosy wrapped her arms about her waist. "Only about things he deems important."

"Like your début."

"Not the début so much as his insistence that I find a husband."

"I have no brothers, but my understanding from people who do is that all brothers want their sisters to marry. Some because they want their sisters to be happy, and they think marriage is the only state in which a woman can be happy. Others because they don't want to have to support their sisters for the rest of their lives." Diana forced a smile. "Which one is the duke?"

"Neither really. He didn't start talking about the importance of me marrying until after Papa died. Before then, he'd never mentioned it or even tried to find men to court me."

"How old were you then?"

"Eighteen."

"Your father's death probably made your brother realize

you'd reached the age for a début. And then inheriting a dukedom made him even more aware of it."

"Perhaps."

Clearly, Rosy was skeptical, but Diana was nearly certain she was right. "So, is the duke forcing you into this début?"

"Sort of. I'm truly terrified at the prospect of being presented to the queen and possibly making a mistake that haunts me forever. But after meeting you and the other ladies . . ." She gifted Diana with a shy smile. "I know I have friends to help me get through it. And honestly, before I met Lord Winston, I would have said marriage didn't suit me at all, but now I realize marriage can be quite nice with the right man."

Good heavens, the young woman was already envisioning herself *married* to Winston. That was troubling, to say the least.

Rosy sighed. "Besides, I don't want Geoffrey and Mama worrying about me. It's just . . . he makes me so self-conscious sometimes. I mean, he's very talented at what he does, and the things he's in charge of engineering are so . . . big and important that I feel insignificant next to him. In case you hadn't noticed, Geoffrey can be very intimidating."

"Oh, I noticed, believe me," Diana said.

Rosy walked down the hall. "Did you know he designed a stretch of the canal between Leeds and Liverpool? Because of him, people in Leeds can get their coal to market in the west of England, and even to places beyond if they use the Liverpool port. It saves them countless thousands of pounds and lowers the cost of coal for all of us."

That was more words than Diana had seen her speak all at once since they'd met. And about engineering, no less. Some part of Rosy was clearly an ironmaster's granddaughter.

The young woman stopped outside a door. "So I can see why Geoffrey finds this whole début business wearing, with all its rules that make no sense to him. They make no sense to me either, but I don't have his prospects. Either I marry or I become a spinster. And to be honest, I don't care which it is. I promised him I'd do things his way until the end of the Season, but after that I will do as I please. I mean, I would like to marry, but not without love. If I can't marry for love, I'd just as soon keep house for Geoffrey the rest of my life."

Finding herself sympathetic to Rosy's situation, Diana offered the young lady some advice. "Love is highly overpraised, my dear. As I'm sure you've heard by now, my mother ran away—left my father—to marry the man she'd fallen in love with, only to discover that none of her friends would talk to her anymore. She thought she'd be the next Lady Holland, thumbing her nose at London society while being celebrated for her salons."

She shook her head. "Unfortunately, Mama doesn't have Lady Holland's circle of friends and doesn't understand how to cultivate artists and writers and other interesting sorts. Instead, cut off from the society she used to dominate, she's lonely and miserable. And my father has—"

Diana halted before she revealed too much about her and her sisters' situation. "In any case, don't marry for love. That makes you dependent on someone else for happiness. Marry for the pleasure of running your own household or for riches, or even for companionship and the joys of having children. But not love. Love is fickle and sometimes even unkind." She thought of Verity's suitor and shook her head. "There are far better reasons to marry."

"I shall keep that in mind," Rosy said but didn't sound convinced. And when Rosy opened the door to her room, Diana knew her advice had fallen on deaf ears.

Very well. Diana had done her best. Now she would do what Almighty Grenwood was paying her to do—turn his sister into a swan.

As soon as they entered, Diana knew she'd have her work cut out for her. Rosy's bedchamber was frilly and fussy, more like the sort of room a girl would have, not a woman. Then again, Rosy hadn't been here long enough to have chosen the trappings, so perhaps the young lady didn't even like it. Diana would at least give her the benefit of the doubt.

Then Diana threw the closet doors wide open. She wasn't terribly surprised to find a sea of white gowns in muslin, velvet, and sarsenet. After all, white was the color of choice for gowns these days. Here and there were flashes of showy colors like Mazarine blue and bottle green, mostly in spencers or pelisses, but white predominated.

It wasn't just that, however. The overly frilly designs weren't in fashion, and the gowns proved to be too small when Diana insisted that Rosy try them on. Diana started a discard pile at once, then began working her way through the dresses.

"First of all," Diana said as she tossed a gown into the discard pile, "clothes that are too small for you only make you look larger."

"I *am* larger," Rosy said glumly. "I'm stout."

Diana stiffened, remembering the many times Mama had made her slouch to hide her height and Papa had said she should stop eating butter on her toast and rolls because "no gentleman likes a plump wife."

"Did your mother or brother tell you that?" Diana asked, annoyed on Rosy's behalf.

"Certainly not. They say I'm beautiful. But I have a mirror, you know. I can see what I look like."

"Nonsense. Looking in the mirror when you're alone is quite different from how others see you in public. For one thing, you're the only one to see yourself bare, and you're also seeing yourself from only one perspective. But everyone else, save your husband one day and your lady's maid, sees you clothed and in the round. So you can shape how you are viewed just by how you dress and wear your hair. Besides, you are not stout. I daresay you and I are of the same size around."

"Perhaps, but you're tall, and that helps."

Diana had to concede the truth of that, although she'd also long ago decided that if she had to give up butter for her toast, she would simply have to be "plump." Rosy, however, was not plump by any stretch of the imagination—she just wore unflattering fashions.

Fortunately, Eliza had arrived a few moments after Diana and Rosy and was consulting with Rosy's maid, Mrs. Joyce, on coiffures. "Eliza!" Diana called out to her sister. "Would you mind coming here for a moment, please? And you, too, Mrs. Joyce."

The two women joined Diana and Rosy. Diana hunted through the discarded clothes until she found one of similar cut to Eliza's. Then she told her sister, "If you would try this on for me and Rosy, I should like to demonstrate something to her. There's a screen over there you can use while changing. Oh, and don't forget the sash. Mrs. Joyce may help you."

"The gown won't fit me," Eliza warned.

Rosy grimaced. "Of course it won't. You don't have my figure, so it will probably be far too big for you."

Eliza laughed at that.

Diana turned to her young charge. "Now, Rosy, before Eliza changes, observe what she's wearing at present. What do you see?"

"She looks very elegant. The pink is pretty. She could use more ornamentation over her bodice or perhaps a lace fichu?"

Diana bit back a smile. "Go on then, Eliza." As her sister and Mrs. Joyce went behind the screen, Diana said to Rosy, "This is as good a time as any to teach you about color. While you look radiant in white, my dear, so do many other young ladies. In a sea of white, you want to be the pretty pink shell or the vibrant blue fish. The gentlemen must first notice you if you want them to court you."

Rosy nodded.

"So," Diana went on, "to stand out from the other ladies, I recommend you insert color here and there in your ensemble—a border of embroidery at your hem and sleeve cuffs, a colorful silk shawl, a fichu-cravat perhaps, or even gloves, shoes, and hair ornaments that match each other. If you prefer, you might even wear a colored gown, perhaps one in a pale lavender or cool yellow. In spring, light pink is good as well, especially for a young lady of your coloring."

Diana pulled out a gown from Rosy's closet. "This one isn't too bad. It's the right shape for you and looks as if it would fit." She put it back in the closet. "Ooh, this month's *La Belle Assemblée* has a perfect gown for spring, and no one has seen it yet."

"Since we know the editor," Eliza said from behind the screen, "she shows us all the fashion plates before they go into the magazine. Thanks to her, we can order gowns for our clients that are new to everyone else. That puts them at the forefront of fashion instead of the hindside. It's a good place to be if you're striving to impress everyone."

"The design of this particular gown gives you a bit of both worlds when it comes to having a flattering look," Diana said. "You can have both a white underdress and a Pomona green overdress that would look delicious with your vibrant emerald eyes."

"And that's good?" Rosy asked. "Looking 'delicious,' I mean?"

"Of course. You want the men to eat you up, don't you?"

"Not literally," Rosy said, looking horrified.

Diana suppressed a laugh. "We aren't advocating cannibalism, my dear." She suddenly flashed on the expression of sheer hunger on Grenwood's face when he'd first met her. Remembering how she'd shivered beneath the power of that all-encompassing stare, she shook her head. Really, she was behaving quite daft today. And over Almighty Grenwood, too. How absurd. "But men do have a way of . . . how do I explain it . . . *devouring* you with their eyes."

"They've never done that to *me*," Rosy said.

With a pat of her hand, Diana said, "They will, I assure you."

At that moment, Eliza emerged from behind the screen. "Just as I said—it's too small." She twirled slowly to allow Diana and Rosy to see it in full.

Diana touched Rosy's arm. "Look at Eliza now. What do you see?"

"She . . ." Rosy winced. "Forgive me, Mrs. Pierce, but you look as stout in that as I do."

"Exactly," Diana said, pleased that Rosy had made the connection. "The two of you are actually about the same girth and height. But Eliza's own clothes are designed to minimize her flaws and maximize her virtues, so she looks as if she's closer to the ideal female form that society prefers. Whereas in your gown, she . . . Well, that sash around the natural waist is too thin, so it looks as if Eliza is spilling over it, which makes her look plump. The bodice is too tight, which also exaggerates her already full bosom. And the length—"

"Oh, yes, I see what you mean!" Rosy said. "With her white stockings showing, she appears shorter than she actually is." The young lady paled. "Is that how *I* look in it?"

"Do you want the truth?"

"Always," Rosy said.

"Then I'm afraid you do. It's easier to tell these things on another person, especially when that person has the same shape as you. Also, whenever you look in the mirror, remember that you're seeing only the one view." Diana gestured to Eliza to stop twirling. "What about the trim? What do you notice about that?"

"The ruffles make her look childish, I'll admit." Rosy sighed. "The thing is, I like ruffles."

"You can have ruffles, but let's restrict them to your hems for now. Too many ruffles make the gown look fussy instead of elegant, like Eliza's own gown, which has less adornment."

Rosy stared at Diana wide-eyed. "So I can have dresses created that make me look elegant?"

"Not only will you look elegant, but you'll look as beautiful to yourself as you do to your mother and brother. As beautiful as you truly are. There's nothing wrong with being our shape. You just need gowns that display it best."

Excitement lit Rosy's face. "That would be nice for a change."

A short while later, Diana and Rosy, along with her mother, who wanted some gowns made for herself, too, were off to Mrs. Ludgate's, leaving Verity and Eliza behind to figure out ideas for decorations, music, and food.

So far, everything was going very well. Perhaps Diana should consider herself lucky that the duke hadn't appeared. Why didn't she?

Diana, Rosy, and Mrs. Brookhouse spent a very satisfying afternoon at the dressmaker's. Diana had brought a few of Rosy's more acceptable gowns to be altered so she would have dresses to wear until the others were made. Diana had also chosen to have made the gown she'd told Rosy about, but in different colors.

Every necessary part of Rosy and her mother had been measured, and then Diana had helped them pick fabrics. Mrs. Brookhouse had been limited to half-mourning colors—white, gray, and lavender. Rosy, on the other hand, had more choices, so she and Diana picked some colors for Rosy's gowns that would complement her coloring.

By the time they left Mrs. Ludgate's establishment, Mrs. Brookhouse and Rosy each had a fashion doll in their arms, with gowns and accessories to try on them so the ladies could better tell how the fabrics lay and how the colors appeared in various lights. That way they could determine what alterations they might like made to the designs.

But by then, Diana was exhausted. She never knew why these bouts with the dressmaker and clients wore her out, but they did. There was so much negotiating between what could be done rather than what wild imaginations thought were reasonable. So instead of riding back with the Brookhouse ladies, she cried off, saying they would have plenty more to do once they met with her two sisters, who awaited them at Grenwood House.

But they refused to leave her to walk alone, instead saying they'd carry her to Eliza's house, an offer she gratefully accepted. Once home, she asked that tea be brought out to her in the garden, and she took her sketch-book, charcoals, and pencils with her so she could draw designs while she drank her tea.

Eliza's garden wasn't large by any means, but it was large enough for Diana's purposes. She vastly enjoyed watching the blackbirds and wrens, and would sometimes leave seeds for them so she could sketch them. She'd spent a good hour doing so before she realized a storm was brewing. Swiftly, she took a new page to capture the blackness building like bruises on the sky and the distant lightning like electric fingers piercing the clouds to arc toward the ground.

Her pencil fairly flew in her attempt to get it all on paper before the rain assailed her little corner of London and forced her to view the dramatic crescendo from inside. So when a footman came to announce, "His Grace the Duke of Grenwood," it took her a second to react.

Then she swiftly cut out her sketches of the storm and tucked them at the back of the book, leaving her gown designs on top. Her nonfashion sketches showed just a little too much of herself for her comfort. Besides, given the Almighty Grenwood's dislike of what he considered trivial, she couldn't bear hearing him mock her for them.

He entered the garden just as she closed the sketchbook. She rose. "Your Grace, I wasn't expecting to see you tod—"

"How dare you encourage Rosy's interest in Lord Winston?" he snapped. "The man is indeed a fortune hunter, whatever *you* may have heard! I can assure you, my information about him was credible. And even if it wasn't, you have no right to involve yourself in our family affairs, damn you!"

The unexpected attack roused her temper. "That *is* what you're paying me and my sisters to do, isn't it?" she shot back. "Involve ourselves in your sister's début?"

He glowered at her. "That does not include going behind my back to approve her suitors."

"I wasn't going behind your back. You weren't there. Rosy asked me what I thought of the man, and I told her the truth—that I'd never heard he was a fortune hunter. But I also said he has a reputation as a rakehell, and I cautioned her against encouraging him as a suitor."

That seemed to take him completely off guard. "You told her that?"

"Yes. If you press her on it, she may even admit it." *Or she may not, given how much you intimidate her.* Best not to say that aloud. He was still their client, after all.

Which was also why she dared not tell Grenwood that Winston was her cousin. She doubted Grenwood would stay a client of Elegant Occasions if she did. And she rather liked Rosy. She didn't want their association to end merely because the duke had some problem with lords of the realm. She'd also have to dash off a quick note to Winston telling him not to reveal their connection. Oh, and warn her sisters not to speak of it, too.

Grenwood began to pace the garden, no small feat given the little space available and the length of his strides. "Damn it to hell."

"You really should stop cursing." Relieved that he seemed to believe her, she resumed her seat on the garden bench.

He uttered a harsh laugh. "*That's* what you're focused upon at this moment?"

"That . . . and the fact that Rosy obviously omitted some things when she related to you my conversation with her."

Not to mention the fact that he was dressed rather spectacularly. He couldn't possibly have had clothes tailored for him in one day, so he must have owned these already. Even the highest stickler in society couldn't have found fault with his present attire—from his black tail-coat, figured white waistcoat, and perfectly tied cravat to his fawn breeches, white stockings, and highly polished black shoes. He even had a fancy gold watch fob.

He looked splendid. No, *delicious*. But she simply wasn't going to think about that right now. There was always tonight, in her dreams.

Good Lord, she was in so much trouble. For the first time in her life, she'd found someone she desired and he was entirely unacceptable. A duke in name only, a true rebel against the rules she still clung to.

That made him quite dangerous.

Chapter Four

"You're blushing," he said in a low voice.

The observation seemed to startle Lady Diana, which was probably why she shot back, "No, I'm not." Even though she was.

By God, he'd made her blush, and he didn't even know why or how. *Careful now, Geoffrey. This way lies madness.*

Still, he wished he could do it again. Seeing it stirred something wild in his blood.

"Anyway," she said hurriedly, "Rosy probably didn't tell you exactly what I said about Lord Winston because she didn't want to add to your disapproval of him. Besides, it hardly matters if your sister is smitten with him for the moment. It makes perfect sense—he was the first eligible gentleman who paid marked attention to her. But by the time our work is done, Rosy will have many more acceptable suitors, and Lord Winston will fade from her memory."

Did she really think it would be that easy? Geoffrey walked up to where she was sitting. "You seem rather sure of yourself and your abilities for someone who's only known Rosy a day."

"Two days." She cast him a cool look. "Which was plenty of time to figure out that she can easily become the toast of London if she lets us help her." To his shock, she reached out to tug on his watch fob. "I'm not so sure about her brother, however, because he continues to loom over ladies."

He barely suppressed an urge to laugh. She really was a piece of work, never letting a body forget the rules while breaking them herself. He might not know much about her world, but he was fairly certain tugging a man's watch fob wouldn't meet anyone's standards for high society behavior.

Now prepared for anything, he took a seat on the other end of the garden bench, so he wasn't *looming* over her. With her sketchbook the only buffer between them, he had to resist the urge to look inside. Especially when she kept glancing nervously at it.

"You might know how to build a bridge or a canal, Your Grace, but my sisters and I know how to build a début. If you don't trust us to do that, why did you even start this in the first place?"

She had a point. If he'd been dithering like this over a project, he would have been ousted at once. "You're right. Forgive me for assuming that you, and not my sister, were in the wrong."

She blinked. "Will wonders never cease—the great duke has stooped to offer an apology."

"I won't do it again if you intend to gloat every time I do."

A laugh bubbled out of her. "There's something different about you today. Aside from the apologizing, of course."

She gave him a teasing smile that fired his blood. "Is it the hair? No, not that, because it looks much the same as yesterday. Could it be your walking stick? No, you don't have one." She tapped her chin. "I know. It's your scent. You're wearing Hungary water, aren't you?"

He eyed her askance. "You know dam—*perfectly* well I'm not wearing any Hungary water, whatever that is." And just to prove she wasn't the only one who could be sarcastic, he added, "I'm wearing the same common scent I wear every day. You may be familiar with it. I believe they call it soap."

"That must be it, then." She smirked at him. "That and the fact that you're dressed rather finely for dinner at home. You should be careful. With the storm coming, you may end up regretting your fancy attire. Especially when the rain muddies up your nice white stockings."

"I have a carriage," he drawled. "That's how we dukes keep out of the rain."

"You must be going somewhere special indeed if you put the carriage into use."

"If you must know, I'm attending the Society of Civil Engineers monthly dinner as the Society's guest. Despite what you think, I do know how to dress for something important."

"So you do, indeed." She turned serious. "But that's the problem. You don't consider Rosy's future to be as important as your bridges and canals. You'll dress finely for the latter and not for the former."

He chuckled. "Clearly you don't know me at all. I don't dress finely for the latter either. High society in Newcastle-upon-Tyne is fairly limited, and until recently, after I inherited the dukedom, I wasn't part of it. I'm not sure anyone in town even knew my father was the son of a viscount. Or if they did, they didn't think much of it."

"So why are you dressing so well today? For this event?"

To show you you're wrong about me.

Right. He would never give her the satisfaction of hearing him admit it. Besides, it wasn't just that. "I'm advising on the engineering of the Teddington Lock. That's why I was invited to speak at the Society's dinner. I dressed well out of respect for the men who attend it, all of whom are well-known in their field."

"I see." She cocked her head. "Tell me something. What exactly *is* a civil engineer?"

"An engineer who's polite to his workers," he quipped.

With a thin smile, she said, "I'm serious, you know."

She folded her hands in her lap, and he noticed that not only was she not wearing gloves, but her fingers were stained black. From ink? Charcoal?

He was about to ask when she said, "Admit it, you think me some shallow female who does nothing important in the world, don't you? Simply because I don't design locks and dig canals, or whatever a civil engineer does."

Belatedly, he realized he'd insulted her. He hadn't meant to. He rarely got the chance to use that joke, and hadn't thought beyond that. "A civil engineer uses his knowledge of the natural world to harness the power of nature for the benefit of mankind. For example, the founder of the Society whose dinner I'm attending was a man named Smeaton. He improved water wheels, designed lighthouses, and engineered viaducts, bridges, canals, and, yes, locks. Thanks to him, we can better train nature to do our bidding instead of being at its mercy."

Her soft, gratified smile pleased him more than any beautifully crafted tunnel. It made him realize he should answer her other question, too, before they went any further.

"As for my thinking you a shallow female," he said, "that's not true. You deal in a world of subtleties I can't grasp."

"Or prefer not to."

He conceded the point with a nod. "Your business is navigating *human* rivers. I must confess that Rosy's self-confidence seems to have already improved—I just wasn't paying attention to that after she said what she did about Lord Winston. You clearly have a better way of reaching my sister than I do. I honestly don't know what to do to help her."

"You mean, beyond what you're already doing?"

"Yes. I want to see her married well, but I don't know what that would mean for her. Should I let her choose the man she wants and risk her repeating my parents' mistake?"

"Eliza said that according to her and your mother, your parents were happily married."

A happily married couple didn't keep secrets from each other. "Mother and Rosy . . . have only a part of the picture, I'm afraid." When interest flickered in her eyes, he cursed himself for saying even that much. "Which is why I'm afraid to trust Rosy to make the right decision. Marriage is—or should be—for life, after all. I've set aside funds for a substantial dowry for my sister, but beyond that, how do I keep her from ending up with the likes of Lord Winston?"

"You don't. You mustn't. All you can do is advise her and give her opportunities to meet other gentlemen, which you're already planning on doing. In the end, she's the one who has to live with whatever man she chooses."

"That's sensible advice coming from a 'shallow female who does nothing important in the world.'" When she lifted her eyes heavenward, he laughed. "I mean it, though. You have a way with young ladies. It probably comes from having practiced on two sisters. Rosy has only me to practice on, and I don't look nearly as fetching as you in a gown." The minute he realized he'd come right out and called her "fetching," he groaned. "What I meant was—"

"I know what you meant," she said, her gaze enigmatic. "But sadly, my sisters don't let me practice on them any more than you let Rosy practice on you. And honestly, Eliza—who's the oldest—is no trouble at all. She keeps the books for us and takes care of the music for various events, and she's generally very good at both."

She sighed. "Verity, on the other hand . . . Please don't misunderstand me. She does her part, too—she's excellent at dealing with cooks of all sorts in preparing the menus for our various balls, parties, what have you. And she's also excellent at arranging decorations that are stunning without being expensive. But like most artists, she thinks only of her creations, which means she's often up in the middle of the night painting backdrops or fashioning decorative items out of papier-mâché. At least *your* sister keeps regular hours."

"True." Geoffrey gave in to temptation and opened her sketchbook.

"By all means, be my guest," she said archly.

He ignored her, intent on taking in the excellently rendered drawings of a woman's gowns, along with each feminine thing to accompany it. "Your own designs, I take it?"

She nodded.

"Clearly Lady Verity isn't the only artist in the family." He paged through a few more. "These are very well done."

"For a shallow female," she said.

"I should hope we can dispense with that term for good now. It doesn't suit you." He paused in his perusal of her sketches. "Why do you choose to run a business instead of spending your time with your charcoals and pencils and watercolors? Aren't gently bred ladies such as yourself not supposed to work for pay?"

"That's true. But here and there you find a few who break the rules, writing novels or designing Wedgwood china patterns or what have you, for money. Like me and my sisters. We didn't fancy becoming governesses or paid companions, and living under Papa's roof became intolerable, so this is what we chose. I'm quite content with my choice."

"But surely you could have found a husband to appreciate your talents and enjoy watching you exercise them."

Lady Diana leveled a decidedly frosty stare on him. "Of course. Why didn't *I* think of that?" She shook her head. "By now you must be aware of what happened between my parents during the time of my come out."

Should he admit it? He couldn't see why not. "Mother

and Rosy told me a bit." But he wasn't about to reveal that he remembered the gossip about it in the papers. No point in rubbing salt in the wound. "They said the divorce spawned a great deal of scandal."

"'Spawned' is an excellent word for it," she said grimly. "Every gossip rag wrote about it for months, we were shunned at every social occasion—*if* we were even invited—and no one called on us, afraid of being ostracized by association."

Outrage seized him by the throat. "And this is the society you want me and my family to be part of?"

"No," she said firmly. "This is the society you said you aspired to for your sister. If you simply want a good husband for her, I'm sure you could find a very respectable one among your engineer friends, assuming she found any of them attractive."

He cast her a rueful smile. "I doubt she would—most of them are my mother's age." Then he sobered. He could hardly tell her he wanted Rosy's husband to be a titled fellow. Because then he'd have to tell her why. "In any case, this is what *she* wants. Or rather, it's what she wants now."

"I understand."

Did she? Perhaps he should get her off the subject of Rosy's future husband. "But we weren't talking about Rosy. We were talking about you. And I still can't imagine that a woman of your fine qualities would be ostracized for long. There must really be something wrong with titled gentlemen if they can't look past a bit of scandal to see your marriageability."

A bitter laugh escaped her. "You must be joking. Once

you learned we were ladies of rank, you didn't even want to hire us. And what do you know of my 'fine qualities' anyway? You haven't yet seen what I can accomplish on your sister's behalf."

"I've seen enough to know you're talented as an artist. Engineers notice these things. Drawing is part of what we do." He gestured to her folded hands. "And I've also seen enough to know you're the epitome of elegance. By rights, you ought to have gentlemen of your sort battering down your door."

"My sort?" She sounded irritated. "In case you hadn't noticed, *you* are considered my sort now."

"Only on the surface. We both know that beneath the title I'm not your sort in the least."

"No one is my sort," she blurted out. "That's why I haven't married."

Ah, now they were getting to the heart of it. He wanted to know the reason, and he also didn't, because it meant he cared about the answer. "How could that possibly be?"

She blushed. "I shouldn't have said that."

"But you did." He traced the outline of a finely gowned woman on the page. It kept him from looking into Diana's face and frightening her off before she could answer. "I will not judge. Just tell me."

She looked away, her gaze steady, thoughtful. "The truth is, I fear I'm not the marrying sort. I'd much rather sit and sketch or work with fabric or even read a book than tie myself to a man."

"Why would you have to choose? You could be tied to a man and still do all those things."

"Perhaps with the right man. But that's not the only

reason. I . . . fear I'm too . . . cold for marriage, if that makes any sense. I can't imagine caring so much for a man that I would give up everything to have him. Like whatever prompted Mama to run away with the major-general. And if that impulse isn't there, what's the point? Elegant Occasions provides me and my sisters with more than enough to meet our financial needs, and my sisters provide me with companionship."

She reached for her sketchbook, obviously intending to end their tête-à-tête, so he bent forward to close it. Between the two of them, it was knocked to the ground, where some loose sketches spilled out.

"Sorry about that," he muttered and began to pick up the scattered pages. That was when he noticed what was on them.

He froze, captivated by the images in charcoal of windy moors and an ancient forest bounded by a river. "Is this Exmoor, by any chance?"

"Yes." She looked surprised. "You've been there?"

With a nod, he gathered up the sketches and put them on his lap before paging through them. "I stayed in the Simonsbath House Inn while considering a project. I did a good bit of roaming thereabouts."

"I was born near Simonsbath," she said softly. "That's where Papa's estate, Exmoor Court, lies."

"Ah. That explains why these drawings are so evocative. You must have spent a great deal of time sketching them. You're quite the artist."

"Thank you. To paraphrase your definition of civil engineering, I like to use my 'knowledge of the natural world' to portray 'the power of nature' for the pleasure of mankind."

"I can see that."

Then he came to a sketch that clearly wasn't of Exmoor. Instead, it appeared to capture the storm gathering directly overhead. Had she been sketching this very image as he was being announced? Somehow she'd captured the swaying of the trees and the black clouds looming in the distance. He fancied he could even hear the sky rumbling, though no thunder had actually rolled their way yet.

Or at least no thunder beyond the drumbeat of his blood through his veins. He lifted his gaze to hers. "The woman who sketched these with such fervor isn't 'cold' in the least."

She wore a vulnerable expression he hadn't seen on her before, and the gathering clouds with their threat of rain pushed him to do what he'd been wanting to ever since meeting her yesterday. Reaching over to cup her chin in one hand, he bent his head to press his lips to hers.

It was a wild, unwise impulse. Yet when she didn't protest or push him away, he allowed himself to exult in that victory, taking her lips more boldly.

Her mouth was as tempting as he'd guessed it would be—a soft, sweet wonder of a mouth—and she smelled of strawberries, his favorite fruit. She placed her hand on his cheek, so he placed his behind her neck where tendrils of red hair spilled over his fingers. Then he was lost, wrapped in the pleasures of touching her delicate skin and silky locks, of the taste of honeyed tea on her lips and the warm breaths that mingled between them. It was the most delicious pleasure, and at the same time not nearly enough.

So he pulled her nearer and sank his tongue into her mouth.

Chapter Five

If any other man had kissed Diana like this, she would have slapped him. But none had ever dared to try, and that alone was a potent temptation to allow the duke's kiss. Grenwood's tongue delved into her mouth in slow, steady strokes that burst through her inhibitions like a buck crashing through Exmoor Forest. Her heart beat in a frenzy, and her blood pounded not only in her ears but in the places she'd touched herself last night.

So this is passion. Diana could never have guessed it to be so . . . all-encompassing, taking over her body like . . . like . . .

Her mind went blank. She had no words for this.

He paused, and she thought he might stop. She didn't want him to stop, so she caught his head in her hands to stay him. With a groan, he renewed the kiss, and she lapped it up like cream. His hair was so soft and thick. She took a moment to riffle it, as she'd so been wishing to do. Then she let her hands slide down to rest on his broad shoulders, which were clearly not padded.

My oh my, wasn't he a muscle-bound Adonis?

He stopped kissing her mouth, only to kiss a path

over her cheek to her ear. "We should stop," he whispered unconvincingly.

"Yes," she said, equally so.

Now he was kissing down her jaw to her throat, and the fires it lit inflamed her, especially when he wrapped his hands around her waist to pull her close. It felt natural to have his large hands there, natural to have him brushing kisses along her neck to where her pulse beat fiercely, so fiercely. . . .

The rain came, fat drops that splattered them all over. She jerked back. "Oh, no, you'll get your fine clothes wet!"

"I think it's too late to avoid that."

But he swiftly rose and tucked her sketchbook inside his coat, then grabbed her hand to draw her inside. Once they were in the morning room, he glanced around, probably to make sure no one was there. Right now, the room was dark except for the fire in the hearth, which crackled and spit as if to compete with the storm. The dark clouds blotted out the light that would normally come through the windows.

Her common sense had started to assert itself now that the potent drug of his kisses was wearing off. She should say something to prevent further overtures. Except that she didn't want to prevent further overtures. Which made everything even worse.

Drawing her sketchbook out from beneath his coat, he offered it to her. Her hand accidentally brushed his, and he jerked back as if burned. She didn't know whether to be insulted that he now clearly regretted touching her earlier or pleased she got such a strong reaction from him.

He ran his fingers through his inky hair, creating even

more disorder in the waves that wind and rain had already ravished. Only with an effort did she resist the impulse to reach up and smooth the errant locks.

"Lady Diana, I did not mean—"

"Call me Diana," she said softly. "Your sister already does."

Instead of setting him at ease, that made him stiffen. "I wouldn't presume . . . that is, I don't want you to think that I—"

"It's all right." She wasn't sure what he planned to say, but she doubted it was good.

With a deep breath, he looked her in the eye. "I don't generally take advantage of someone in my employ," he clipped out. "I might lack proper manners, but I'm an honorable gentleman, not a scoundrel."

"I don't think you a scoundrel." She eyed him warily. "And you didn't take advantage of anyone. I was a willing participant. Besides, our association feels more like that between equals than employer and employee."

"I suppose that's true." He still sounded uneasy, though. "All the same, I apologize and assure you it won't happen again."

What a pity.

No, she dared not say that. She wanted to ask why "it won't happen again," but when she thought of other men who'd stolen kisses and then turned into octopuses when they caught her alone, she figured it was prudent not to ask. Better just to settle it now, and keep their association professional. "Of course. It wouldn't be appropriate."

"Exactly."

She couldn't resist a small smile. "Although it does seem odd that *you're* the one concerned about propriety."

He seemed to fix his gaze on her mouth for a moment. Then he went rigid. "I must go or I'll be late for my dinner. No need to show me out."

When he turned and nearly ran from the room, she felt both bereft and confused. Had their kiss been *that* bad for him? It certainly hadn't been bad for *her*. It had set all her assumptions about married life on its ear.

A voice sounded from the armchair with its back to her. "So what awful thing did our burly duke do anyway?"

Diana jumped. "Eliza! You scared the devil out of me. Were you there the whole time?"

Eliza rose and came toward her. "Didn't you just see me enter the room?" When Diana frowned, she laughed and added, "Of course I was there the whole time. But I wasn't about to interrupt that rather interesting scene." She came close enough for Diana to make out a magazine in her hand. "I dozed off while reading this article His Grace wrote about skew bridges. It was deucedly dull. Although from what I read, he really likes bridges."

"And canals and tunnels and all sorts of public works, apparently. I had no idea there were so many men engineering those things. Did you know he's speaking at the Society of Civil Engineers tonight? He had to explain to me what a civil engineer is." When Eliza opened her mouth as if to speak, Diana said, "And no, it's not an engineer who is civil to people."

Eliza's chuckle halted Diana's steady babbling, thank heavens. Diana never babbled. But then, she'd also never kissed a duke in the rain or thrust her fingers through his hair or felt such wild impulses that they made her blush even now.

"So what awful thing *did* he do?" Eliza's voice had

hardened. "I came in here as soon as I heard he'd demanded to see you and was in a temper. I started to go outside to give you moral support, but when I peeked out, it looked as if you had everything well in hand. So I settled down with the journal to wait and I dozed off . . . until your voices woke me just now."

"Were you *spying* on me?" Diana asked, mortified at the possibility that Eliza had seen their entire exchange.

"It's called 'chaperoning,' my dear. I know I rarely practice it, but then, you rarely give me reason to. So, for the last time, what awful thing—"

"He did nothing awful to me."

Eliza's gaze narrowed on her. "Then why was he apologizing?"

"Because he thought he had." She pretended to be straightening the cuffs of her gown. How was it that Eliza could make her feel like a five-year-old again, apologizing for some infraction even though she wasn't sorry? "But I explained to him that he hadn't."

"Hmm. Would you tell me if he had?"

Diana eyed her aghast. "Of course I would! But he didn't. So there's no reason for all your concern."

She might still have told Eliza about the kiss if Grenwood hadn't made it perfectly clear he considered it a mere thing of the moment, something he'd instantly regretted. While that stung, Diana should probably take the same tack. Much as she wanted to savor it, she must let *his* behavior be her guide.

After all, Grenwood was sure to return to his boorish self tomorrow, after the gentlemen at the Society of Civil Engineers sang praises to his skills tonight. If, as a result, nothing came of her association with him but cordiality, she would hate having revealed the details of their tête-à-tête in the garden to her sisters.

And if he *did* start behaving differently toward her? If he approached her again, tried to kiss her again?

She tamped down the sudden thrill that gripped her. That was a bridge she'd have to cross when she came to it. *If* she came to it. Because that was by no means certain.

If not for the rain and his "fine clothes," Geoffrey would have walked to his dinner. He needed to clear his head, to remind himself of all the reasons he shouldn't entangle himself with Lady Disdain . . . no, *Diana*. He groaned.

Lady Disdain had sure as hell disappeared while he'd kissed Diana senseless. The woman was proving to be more than he'd bargained for. That mouth of hers, oh God, so warm and wet. And her soft skin and her pretty eyes . . .

What was he going to do about her? He wanted her in his arms, in his bed. That was out of the question, of course, but it didn't change the fact that he did. And why couldn't he stop thinking about that incredible kiss?

He couldn't believe he'd actually kissed the woman. He couldn't believe she'd actually let him. No doubt she would give him a piece of her mind once she got over her shock, but by then he'd be calm enough to remind her of his apology, and to point out that the matter was done. Then he'd pray that his impressive title and willingness to pay their exorbitant prices would convince her not to throw him out on his arse.

Just then, his carriage drew up in front of the tavern

where the Society met. He'd never been so glad to see a building in his life. Now he could finally put the intoxicating Diana out of his mind. For good, with any luck.

But three hours later, after a fine dinner and a bit of good ale, he was back in his carriage and thinking of Lady Deadly once more. No, Lady Disdain. No, *Diana.* The woman he was clearly going to have to avoid from now on, because even a long dinner with the most fascinating men he knew couldn't blot her from his brain.

Worse yet, once he reached Grenwood House, he discovered his mother and sister had been waiting for him the entire time he'd been gone.

"Geoffrey!" Mother cried from the doorway of the drawing room before the footman could even take his greatcoat. "How long do dinners with engineers take anyway?"

He handed off his coat to the footman. "As long as needed to discuss advances in engineering for the past month. Or five. It was all business, I assure you."

She came up to kiss his cheek, then drew back to eye him skeptically. "You've been drinking."

"Only an ale or two, no more than what I drink every night at dinner. Don't worry, Mother. I'm not turning into Father yet."

"I should hope not. Drinking is what killed him."

Drinking and laudanum. But Mother didn't know about Father's use of laudanum, and he wanted to keep it that way.

She squeezed Geoffrey's hand. "But regardless of his . . . lapses, I hope you know he was very proud of you. When he was in his cups, he boasted about your inventiveness to all who would listen."

The remarks sliced through him. "That's doing it up a bit brown, don't you think?"

"Just because he rarely did it around you doesn't mean he didn't do it at all, Son."

Her assertion boggled his mind. He'd never once had the sense that Father even knew what Geoffrey did when he marched off to work at Stockdon and Sons or left for a months-long period to oversee the digging of a canal or tunnel.

But he tamped down his shock as he walked toward the drawing room with her. Right now, he needed to spend time conversing with the living, not the dead, if only to reassure Mother and Rosy that all was well. Ever since Father's death, Rosy had been prone to worry about him.

Oddly enough, it wasn't relief he saw on her face when he and Mother entered. It was wariness. That certainly gave him pause.

"What happened?" Rosy sounded hurt. "Where have you been all this time? Did you . . . did you dismiss Elegant Occasions?"

That caught him by surprise. "Did you *want* me to?"

"No!" She wrapped her arms about her waist. "But you were gone so long, and . . . and when you left you said you were going there, and I was afraid—"

He pasted a smile to his face as he approached her. "Surely you know your brother better than that, poppet. I growl and grouse, but once my temper cools, I turn sensible again."

Her face cleared. "So you *didn't* go there?"

"I did. But Lady Diana and I parted on good terms."

He chucked her under the chin. "She revealed what *else* she told you, the part you didn't mention."

Rosy swallowed. "I–I don't know what you mean." Turning her back to him, she hurried over to stoke up the already blazing fire.

He followed her and took the poker from her, setting it down in its holder. "She told me that Lord Winston does indeed have a reputation as a rakehell."

She faced him with a defiant expression. "A man can change, can't he?"

"Everyone can change, angel. But that doesn't mean they do."

Crossing her arms over her chest, she said, "You're already changing. Yesterday, you would have refused to continue working with Diana if you'd known what she told me. Today you were more tolerant."

Today he'd kissed the woman, too, which somewhat colored his perceptions. Not that he was going to tell his sister that. She'd be ringing wedding bells over his head in an instant. "Lady Diana was honest with me—unlike my little sister—so I'm willing to take a chance on her and her business. Might as well see what happens."

"Oh, I'm so glad!" She beamed at him, which made everything better. "I thought for sure you would dismiss them, and they've been so wonderful to me that I couldn't have borne it."

Then she and Mother proceeded to tell him about every single thing they'd done with Elegant Occasions that day. He was forced to watch them parade their fashion dolls in front of him and explain what gowns they had ordered. By God, what had he landed himself in?

At one point, he stealthily looked at his pocket watch.

Apparently, he wasn't stealthy enough, because Mother asked, with a raised brow, "Are we boring you, Son?"

"Certainly not," he said blandly. "Watching you four show off your gowns is fascinating."

"We four?" Rosy asked.

"You, Mother, and your two dolls."

When she giggled, he relaxed. He could always be sure she was fine if he heard her laugh. But when she and his mother demanded to know what he'd ordered at the tailor, he'd had enough of fitting and fabric talk for one evening.

"You'll see soon enough." He rose. "Now forgive me, you two, but I'm off to bed." And if he was lucky he would fall asleep without thinking of the fetching female who kept intruding on his thoughts.

Clearly, for the next few days he'd have to find somewhere else to be.

Chapter Six

*D*uring the three weeks of plotting and preparing for Rosy's first event as Lady Rosabel—Diana refused to count the disastrous musicale the poor girl had attended—Diana had expected to see the duke occasionally. To her chagrin, no matter how much time she and her sisters spent at Grenwood House, she didn't see him once, even in passing.

He talked to her sisters, though. They were helping him prepare for what was also to be *his* presentation as a duke. He'd somehow managed to get an agreement from the Earl of Foxstead to sponsor him. Apparently, Lord Foxstead was an investor in one of Grenwood's projects. But Grenwood said not a word to her, about that or anything else.

It was hard to ignore the truth. He was avoiding her. As that became more apparent, she felt a sickening lurch in her belly very much like the one at that first ball after the news broke that Mama had run away. Everyone had avoided her as if she hadn't bathed or dressed correctly, and now he was doing the same.

Grenwood had kissed her and found her wanting. What other explanation was there?

Now she and Rosy and Mrs. Ludgate were in the young woman's bedchamber in the early morning. Mrs. Ludgate was tucking here, snipping a thread there, and generally making a lovely gown into an outstanding one.

Meanwhile, Diana had been putting the finishing touches on Rosy's ensemble. Today was the big event— Rosy's presentation and her intimate dinner entertainment afterward. But due to the strangeness of court dress these days, all their focus was on Rosy's dinner gown, made of bronze-green silk gathered artfully just under the breasts. The dark hue of green with shadings of blue accentuated Rosy's beautiful emerald eyes, and the silk was embroidered around the bottom. White beads ornamented the neckline as well as the sweet little sleeves.

"It's finished," Mrs. Ludgate pronounced and stood back.

"What do you think, Diana?" Rosy spun slowly to show it off.

"I think it's splendid, don't you?" Diana said. "Mrs. Ludgate, you have outdone yourself. Rosy looks even more gorgeous in that gown than usual."

As Mrs. Ludgate murmured a thank-you, Rosy blushed. "I'm sure I don't look gorgeous, but do I look at least pretty in this? I've been too anxious about tonight to gaze in the mirror."

"Well, you absolutely must do so now." Diana turned Rosy to face the mirror and waited for her reaction.

Rosy gaped at her own reflection. "Is that really *me*? I . . . I look like a princess."

"You do, indeed. A princess setting out to gain many, many admirers. Especially once Eliza finishes with your hair this evening." She called across the room to where her sister was sewing something. "Eliza, that turban fillet *will* be completed by the time for the dinner, won't it?"

"It will," Eliza said, never taking her eyes off the long tube of fabric she was ornamenting with rows of beads. "If people stop interrupting me, that is."

"You'll have no time to work on it once you leave for the Queen's Drawing Room," Diana said.

"I'm aware of that," Eliza bit out.

They were all growing testy the closer it got to time for Rosy to meet the queen, and they were finding it harder to hide their testiness.

Verity appeared in the doorway. "Is Rosy presentable to a gentleman?"

"Depends on the gentleman," Diana said. "Her hair is down."

"Oh, I daresay her brother has seen that a time or two," Verity said with a laugh.

Then she pulled the duke into the room, and Diana lost all capacity for speech. He was wearing another blue coat—this one of indigo, not a particularly fashionable color, but one that suited him. With his cream-colored silk waistcoat, linen cravat, and well-tailored pantaloons, which were shoved into highly polished top boots, he looked particularly delicious.

Not to mention uncomfortable to find himself in a room full of women. And her. He avoided her gaze, which set her straight about how he felt.

She'd hoped that their kiss meant she had a future

possibility of marriage, not necessarily to him but at least to someone. But she'd obviously been putting too much importance on what to him must have been a moment's whim. And if she couldn't even entice the socially unsophisticated duke into behaving recklessly again, she would never get some other enterprising fellow to look past the scandal and actually *court* her.

It was probably a good thing she hadn't expected to marry. She swallowed the tears gathering in her throat. She absolutely mustn't make a cake of herself, and over a client no less. She knew better. And she was definitely too proud to let him think she was chasing him or some such nonsense.

"Lady Verity," he began, with a swift glance at Diana. "I don't mean to intrude—"

"Geoffrey!" Rosy cried. "You must come see how I look."

He approached, his eyes fixed on his sister. His reaction when he saw Rosy was all Diana could have asked for. "My God, Rosabel," he said in an awed voice. "You look like an angel. A real one, from heaven."

"I know! Isn't it wonderful?" She twirled for him. "Lady Diana designed it, and Mrs. Ludgate created it. Mrs. Ludgate, come meet my brother."

The dressmaker appeared shocked by the very idea that a duke's sister would introduce *her* to him, but she quickly hid her response and allowed Rosy to do so. To his credit, Grenwood was more cordial to the dressmaker than he'd been to Diana the first time they'd met. No one would ever have guessed that Mrs. Ludgate was far beneath him in consequence, and Diana was grateful for that. She adored the dressmaker's work.

Then Grenwood came over to ask Diana in an undertone, "What about jewelry?"

Surprised he was speaking to her after three weeks of silence, she said, "We are making do on that score. I assume you did not inherit any of the Brookhouse jewels because neither your mother nor your sister could find any in the house. And you weren't around to enlighten us on the subject. So we have some pretty bead necklaces for her to wear. And my sisters and I intend to loan—"

"Will emeralds do?" he asked, taking Diana completely off guard.

"Why? Do you have some in your pocket?" When he smiled at her joke, though not at *her*, she added, "Yes, emeralds would be perfect with that gown for dinner. But they're rather costly, you know. And to be quite frank, I'm more concerned about the diamonds and pearls women are expected to wear at the Queen's Drawing Room."

"Is that where the presentation takes place?"

"No. Well, yes, it takes place there, but the occasion at St. James's Palace involving the queen giving young ladies her blessing—or newly minted dukes like you—is also called the Queen's Drawing Room."

"That makes no sense," he said, his eyes still riveted to his sister. Apparently, he'd do anything to avoid looking at Diana.

"What makes no sense is the all-white gown Rosy will have to wear for it—it looks like a gigantic dollop of whipped cream with a fashionable bodice stuck on top like an afterthought. Add a train and several tall feathers in one's tiara and the ostentatious picture is complete."

"I see," he said, making it clear he did not see at all.

"Oh, I almost forgot what we were discussing in the first place. The jewelry. The young ladies being presented are expected to put as many diamonds and pearls as possible on their persons. Full diamond parures are preferable, of course—"

"Of course," he said sarcastically.

"We have no full parures of anything, but I loaned Rosy the diamond tiara from my own presentation," she said, "complete with feathery excess rising out of it—though we had to replace some of the ostrich feathers because they were too worn and droopy after seven years and three women's débuts. They were handed down from Eliza to me to Verity." *Stop babbling, Diana!*

She drew in a deep breath. "We've gathered an assortment of our own diamond and pearl earrings, but we don't have much in the way of necklaces and brooches, so we'll make do with paste . . . anything that glitters, really, because I believe that's the point. Oh, and Eliza intends to loan Rosy some of the jewels her late husband gave her."

"Good God, you should have mentioned this to me sooner."

"You haven't been around, remember?" she said in an icy tone. "And your mother and sister were reluctant to bother you concerning jewelry because you weren't even sure Rosy should have new gowns when you spoke to me three weeks ago."

His face flushed. "You have a point. And I probably should have said something before, but when the will was read some months ago, the attorney I inherited from the previous duke showed me the Brookhouse jewels he'd been keeping in a safe. I've been meaning to bring them here anyway, so when I'm at the solicitor's office signing papers this morning I'll fetch back the casket of jewels. I know for certain it has a parure of emeralds Rosy can wear for the dinner, and I suspect it has some other things you can use."

"That would be wonderful," Diana said. "Thank you."

"Don't thank me just yet." He smiled faintly, and this time his gaze met hers. "You'll have to choose the proper ones for the various gowns."

"What a trial," she said dryly. "I'll be forced to play dress-up with what are probably spectacular jewels." She pretended to be having the vapors, complete with pressing the back of her hand to her forehead. "But I shall persevere."

He laughed. "I'm glad I can amuse you." He nodded to Rosy. "And I'm very glad you're taking care of her attire. She told me she has to wear a hoop skirt, of all things. I haven't seen a woman in one of those since I was a lad, and I'd definitely have no idea where to purchase one."

"The hoop skirts are why the gowns look like dollops of whipped cream."

"I like whipped cream," he said lightly, though his gaze on her had turned rather intense.

"Ah, but you can't eat these gowns."

"That's a pity." He fixed on her mouth. "I've had no breakfast, and I'm feeling rather . . . peckish."

How was it he managed to make his every remark feel like a caress? And why was he flirting with her again as if nothing between them had changed?

Just as she thought that, he seemed to catch himself, for he returned his gaze to his sister, who was now talking to Verity. "You've transformed her, you know. I daresay once her hair is up, I won't even recognize her."

"You'd better. You're accompanying her today. Not to mention, you're having your own presentation. Or have you forgotten?"

"I remember."

"The clothing for men is very specific."

"I'm well aware. Rosy has reminded me of it repeatedly. White bag wig. Breeches. Old-fashioned coat. Buckled shoes."

"Are you sure you won't get caught up at the attorney's office and forget to return home in enough time to change?"

He crooked up one brow as he met her gaze. "Why? Are you planning to dress me?"

She could feel heat rising in her cheeks. Once again he was flirting. She might as well flirt back. "I will if I have to."

Something passed between them that electrified the very air. She couldn't breathe. Her heart was pounding. She would swear he felt it, too.

He bent close to whisper, "Feel free to dress me anytime you like, Diana." Then he straightened and seemed to realize they had an audience—one that wasn't paying any attention to them, but still . . . "You may not have noticed," he went on, "but I own a watch, which keeps perfect time. I'll be here at the necessary hour, I assure you."

She forced herself to take a breath. Then another and another. After that, she was able to compose herself. "Do you have a chapeau bras?"

"What's that?"

Feeling a sudden panic, she said, "Perhaps we can get you one from—"

He chuckled. "I know what a chapeau bras is. Good God, you must really think me a green lad. My new tailor sent me right off to the only hatter he approved of. The same for a cobbler and a glover. But as it happens, I already owned a chapeau bras. I wore it to the Society's dinner. You just didn't see it because your footman took it from me when I arrived at your sister's house."

She relaxed a fraction. "Then you know about carrying a sword."

"I plan to dub several gentlemen knights of the realm."

"Do be serious. You have to wear a sword. It's required."

He eyed her skeptically, then called Eliza over. "Must I wear a sword to the Queen's Drawing Room?"

"Yes. Not a big one, mind you, but a genuine sword. A ceremonial one will do."

"You may be surprised to hear this, but I haven't been in any situation where a ceremonial sword was appropriate." He shook his head. "Why, pray tell, do I need one? In case I need to defend Rosy's honor in the garden?"

"The queen dictates these rules," Diana said. "But I'm not sure of the reasoning behind the swords." She cast him a mischievous smile. "Be sure to ask her while you're there. I wouldn't dare to do so myself, but you're a duke—you can get away with anything."

"I have no desire to converse with the queen beyond an introduction. If *you* disapprove of my cursing, God only knows how Her Lofty Majesty would react." As Diana fought a laugh he headed for the door. "But I'll solve this sword problem right now."

Oh, no, that didn't sound good. She hurried after him, wondering what he could possibly mean. But it was too late. He'd already found his valet.

His valet? What in heaven did he expect his valet to do?

"Tell me, Webb," Grenwood said, "did your previous master have a sword he used for court things?"

Webb stared at him wide-eyed. "C–court things, Your Grace?"

Diana sighed. "He means a sword to use when appearing at court. Like for Lady Rosabel's presentation this afternoon. And his own."

"Ohhh," Webb said. "Yes, Your Grace, I believe your predecessor did have such an item. I shall have it found at once."

"In time for him to use it this afternoon?" Diana asked.

"Yes, my lady," Webb said. "I will make sure of it."

The valet rushed off, gathering footmen to look for the sword as he went.

Grenwood stared at her smugly. "There. Problem solved."

"*If* they find it in time. Which is by no means certain."

"Diana, calm yourself," he said in a low voice, "I can see you're worried about this afternoon and tonight."

Startled that he could tell, she blurted out the truth. "Of course I'm worried. These two events could destroy Rosy's confidence if they go badly. She'll blame herself. And we've worked so hard to give her confidence." She shouldn't have said that. One of their cardinal rules was never to confess their own fears and weaknesses to a client.

"Admit it," he said, "that's not the only thing you're worried about. You're concerned I won't follow the rules. I promise I won't shame you. I will use my best manners."

"That hardly reassures me."

"Fortunately, you will be able to keep me in line."

"I beg your pardon?"

"Aren't you accompanying me and Rosy for the presentation? She said you were."

"I can't. I'm unmarried."

"So is she."

She folded her hands over her waist. "I'm not being presented to the queen. After a woman is presented, she goes to no drawing rooms at St. James's Palace until she marries. But you needn't worry. Eliza, the only one of us three who can sponsor Rosy, will make sure everything goes well. Your mother would normally be the one to do it, but she cannot because it must be someone who has already been presented to the queen, and your mother says she never even came to London after your parents met in Newcastle."

"That seems damn—*very* complicated. If you're not sponsoring Rosy, why did she say you were going with us?"

Diana had been waiting to tell him, hoping to find the right moment. Now, right or wrong, the moment was here. "Rosy got me to agree to at least riding in the first carriage with her and waiting until you both come out of the palace. I think she's hoping for some last-minute wisdom to give her courage. Either that or she considers me a sort of magical talisman to give her good luck."

"*Or* she has begun to rely on your counsel of late, so she wants you there for as much of it as can be managed."

"Why Eliza isn't good enough for that, I don't know," Diana said. "You'll have to ask your sister."

He arched a brow. "So you'll be accompanying Mrs. Pierce, me, and Rosy in a few short hours?"

"Yes. Well, not entirely, since there are two carriages, and you and my sister will be in the other one." Her stomach knotted up. "And I know what you're thinking."

"Do you? Pray do enlighten me, then."

"You're thinking I planned this for my own purposes."

He gave her a blank look. "What purposes would those be?"

She swallowed hard. If he hadn't already thought she might be scheming to be around him, she certainly wasn't going to make him think it. "You tell me."

"I haven't a clue. I'm merely surprised you're willing to sit in a carriage for what could be hours waiting for us."

He *should* be surprised that a lady with Eliza's family situation was accepted as a sponsor. Diana certainly was. Because one of the requirements was fairly specific: *No member of a family touched by scandal is received at court.*

Diana could only assume that the no-scandal rule didn't apply to sponsors. How else had Eliza been accepted? Or perhaps it wasn't *her* they were accepting but Lady Rosabel, sister to a newly minted duke. Perhaps they were purposely overlooking Eliza's family scandal.

Then another thought occurred to Diana. "Rosy may be hoping to have an ally if something goes wrong and she has to make a quick escape."

"If that happened," he drawled, "would you help her?"

"It depends on why she wants to escape. And how far she got into the presentation." She drew a deep breath. "I would probably urge her to go back. Verity . . . had a bit of a mishap at her own début. Ever since, she has steadfastly refused to attend the Queen's Drawing Room again, and I would hate to see Rosy have any such permanent reaction to it."

His eyes narrowed on her. "What sort of mishap?"

"It wasn't Verity's fault, I swear." She pulled him farther down the hall from Rosy's bedchamber. "And you cannot tell Rosy or she'll be terribly self-conscious about it, and then it could happen to her, too. The mind can act against us sometimes."

"*What* could happen to her, too, for God's sake?"

"The ladies have to curtsy very low to the queen. Queen Charlotte either kisses their foreheads, if they're children of peers, or she gives them her hand to kiss, for everybody else. Then they have to back out of the presentation room without tripping over their trains."

"I take it that Verity tripped?"

Diana winced. "Actually, it was worse. She sneezed just as Her Majesty bent to kiss her forehead."

Grenwood laughed, the devil. But when he saw her expression he sobered. "You realize that could happen to anyone."

"Especially to my sister because many things make her sneeze, particularly feathers. But we were taught to hold in any coughs or sneezes or other untoward bodily . . . sounds, no matter what. Sneezing in Her Majesty's face is considered unacceptable behavior."

"God help us all if that's what passes for unacceptable these days," he muttered.

She ignored his remark. "We of course have schooled

Rosy the same way we were schooled. And we've had her practice walking backward with a train multiple times a day. It's harder than you may think."

"Trust me, I can only imagine how hard it must be."

Pasting a reassuring smile on her lips, she patted his arm. "But everything will be fine. Rosy is a quick study. I'm sure she will make a great impression."

He covered her hand before she could pull it away from his arm. "Earlier, you were worried."

She wasn't worried now, not with his large, warm hand encompassing hers. She was trying not to read too much into his kind gesture. "I'm always worried. Ask my sisters. I get fidgety on the day of the presentation. And I don't want Rosy to lose her confidence."

Sliding her hand from beneath his, she curled her fingers into her palm, trying to keep his touch somehow in her grasp. "You must go. You'll barely have time to do what you require."

"I thought the Queen's Drawing Room didn't begin until two."

"Yes, but there will be a dreadful line of carriages, so it's best to go early."

He arched an eyebrow. "How early?"

"Noon?"

He groaned. "I shall see you then."

"No, earlier than that, because you must change clothes."

"Fine. Eleven."

She beamed at him. "Perfect!"

When she turned to go, he stopped her with one hand. "You may have to dress me after all, Diana. Because you're right, that barely leaves me time to do what I must."

She looked down her nose at him. "Then you'd best hurry, Your Grace, hadn't you?" And resisting the urge to watch his reaction to that, she walked away smiling.

Chapter Seven

Standing next to his friend Foxstead, Geoffrey watched for Rosy from a corner of the Blue Drawing Room. He'd already had his fill of St. James's Palace. Too many strangers, too many odd looks from people wondering who he was, too many feathers, and definitely too many glittering diamonds. He simply didn't belong here.

Worse yet, Lady Diana was alone in the first of the two carriages he'd been forced to bring to accommodate two women in hoop skirts. He told himself there was no safer place in London at present than the streets around the palace. But it still nagged at him that he'd left the lady alone.

As if reading his mind, Lord Foxstead said, "You know, you no longer have to stay. No one does. The ladies will be quite a while, judging from the long line of them waiting in the corridor as I came in. I'm leaving myself. You could join me at White's for a glass of brandy. It's close enough to walk, and I'm sure Mrs. Pierce has matters well in hand with Lady Rosabel. The widow will make certain your sister arrives home in plenty of time for the dinner."

Bloody hell. He'd forgotten there was still to be a

dinner at Grenwood House tonight, with thirty guests and dancing afterward. *Intimate dinner entertainment, my arse.*

"Thank you, Foxstead," he told the earl. "But I think I'll wait for my sister in the carriage." *With Lady Diana. Whom you ought to be avoiding. And who draws you to her as a lodestone draws iron.*

"As you wish. Either way, I'll see you this evening. But if you change your mind about joining me at White's, simply tell the porter you're a guest of mine and he'll show you right in."

They walked out together, talking about plans for the Teddington Lock. Fortunately, Foxstead would pass nowhere near Geoffrey's carriages, so the man wouldn't see Geoffrey joining Lady Diana. Geoffrey wasn't certain why it bothered him to think of her being seen, except that he didn't want tongues wagging about him and her when nothing more than an innocent kiss lay between them.

Right. Completely innocent.

Geoffrey sighed. He'd best find a way to keep from ruining her. He wasn't entirely aware of the details, but he felt fairly certain that sitting alone with a man in a carriage was a sure way for a woman to find herself taken off the rolls of society. If not for Elegant Occasions, she'd already be banished from society completely, so he didn't want to destroy her business as well.

He and Foxstead parted, and he went on to the carriage where Diana was awaiting her sister. As he approached and the footman leaped down from his perch, Geoffrey signaled to the man to stay where he was. Geoffrey wanted to catch Diana unawares. She seemed always to be in control and he wanted to see the real Diana.

Alas, he was doomed to be disappointed. When he peered inside the coach, she was reading what looked like a magazine, with the windows fully open. Her back was straight, not a hair was out of place, and even her skirts were unruffled.

Then she licked her finger and turned the page, and his lust for her reared its ugly head. Literally. Damn. He should leave before she saw him.

He didn't. "You should at least close the windows. If only for safety's sake."

Her head whipped around, and she blushed as she shoved the journal under a shawl he'd assumed was Rosy's. "I should think with so many footmen about and half the palace guard nearby, it would be safe."

"I suppose," he said. "What were you reading?"

"Oh, nothing of consequence."

"You seemed very engrossed." Before she could stop him, he reached through the open window to whisk the magazine out from under the shawl.

She set her lips in a prim line. "You have a bad habit of sneaking up on people and stealing their things."

He smiled. "Not people. You. I'm still trying to figure you out." Then he focused on the magazine. Or rather, the *Journal of Civil Engineering*. No wonder she blushed. He lifted his gaze to her. "Admit it. You were reading my article."

"I have no reason to deny it. I'm still trying to figure *you* out," she said, eyes gleaming.

Leave it to Diana to throw his own words back at him. "And have you?"

"Hardly. I don't understand half of what you wrote. But I can tell you're passionate about it."

"As passionate as you are about how to navigate the Season. I have to ask—who helped *you* navigate the Season? Or were you born knowing all those rules?"

He'd hoped to make her laugh, but she glanced out the other window instead and then turned to look past him, too, as if to make sure no one was around on either side of the carriage to listen in. Then she smoothed her skirts. "Eliza helped me, fortunately."

"Not your mother?"

She shrugged. "Mama was too . . . busy."

He leaned on the open window. "To manage her own daughter's début?"

A great sigh escaped her. "Yes. If you must know, she and Papa were more engrossed in their ongoing quarrels at the time."

"What were they quarreling over?"

She sniffed. "And you claim that only people in society gossip."

"Trust me, I'm not planning to tell anyone. And it's not gossip if I get it from the source itself."

"True. But the answer is complicated. They quarreled over whether he had a mistress. Whether she had a lover. Anything they could find to argue about, to be honest. Papa would go to his club, then not return home until dawn, which infuriated Mama, who was sure he was seeing his mistress. So Mama would disappear for days without telling him where *she* was going. It drove Papa mad, not knowing where she was. Which is probably why she did it."

"It must have driven you and Lady Verity mad, too. After all, there's a reason gentlemen are supposed to be discreet with their paramours, and ladies are supposed to pretend they don't have any themselves. To avoid upsetting the children. Or so I'm told anyway."

Her gaze met his. "We got used to it. Eliza was already married by then, but she started coming by our house in Grosvenor Square just to see how Verity and I were managing and to make sure neither Papa nor Mama had killed each other. That would be quite a scandal, you know. Our family supposedly disapproves of scandal."

So did his, especially the sort of scandal that might break about them if he wasn't careful. "I can't blame your family for that. Scandal spawns gossip and makes matters uncomfortable for you in society."

"Papa generally managed to keep their battles quiet, but not always. It got so the rafters fairly rang with their shouting. Since my own presentation to the queen had just happened, Eliza took me to every event she attended, just to get me out of the house and give me some semblance of a début in society. She was very good at ignoring what was occurring at our home so she could help me—and Verity, during her Season—to make important connections and find friends."

He shook his head. "Your mother should have been doing that for you, from what I understand."

"She should have . . . but Mama was never interested in being a mother." Her tone betrayed a cynicism he didn't usually hear from her. "Mama is interested in two things these days—having fun and annoying Papa. It was only after she pushed him to the edge by running off with the major-general that Papa decided to sue for divorce."

"I'm not surprised. Her behavior must have broken his heart."

"Not really. He just never could stand to let Mama get the better of him."

Tired of standing outside one of his own carriages, he put the step down and opened the carriage door. Before he could climb in, the footman raced to his side. "Your Grace, you cannot enter!"

"Why not?" he asked irritably, still holding the door open. "It's my carriage. I should like to sit in it. And perhaps—unfeeling creature that I am—even *ride* in it."

Diana seemed to be fighting a laugh as she gazed at Geoffrey. "Thomas is concerned about my reputation. A lady isn't supposed to be alone in a closed carriage with a man. It could ruin her."

Geoffrey gestured to the row of carriages, each of which had at least one footman lounging about, not to mention the coachman. "I hardly consider us 'alone.' Nor is it a closed carriage. You've got every window and curtain open, and it's broad daylight besides."

"It's all right, Thomas," she said to *his* damned footman. "I came prepared for this." She reached behind her bonnet to tug a veil over it, which fell like a shroud about her features.

"Oh, for God's sake," he muttered under his breath as he pulled up the step and shut the carriage door. "I'll stand out here."

"If you wish," she said lightly. "I certainly wouldn't want to do anything that might make you uncomfortable."

"Right." He gestured to her bonnet. "You can unveil yourself now." He disliked not being able to see her expressions.

"Oh, I wouldn't dream of it," she said with clear amusement in her voice. "I find it best to be prepared."

Suddenly, the carriage shuddered, then crawled forward. "What the hell?" he cried. "You're moving!" But as he walked alongside, he noticed it only rolled forward a carriage length before halting again.

"We're in line, you know," she said.

"I did not know. If you'll recall, I've been in that torture chamber for the past hour waiting for Rosy, who still hasn't emerged."

"That's because she was seventeenth on the list. The line is moving periodically because the carriages are positioned in that same numerical order. And why was it a 'torture chamber'?"

"Let's see." He began ticking things off on his fingers. "My wig itched and I couldn't move without my sword catching on something."

Before he could go on, she had the audacity to chuckle. "I see I should have given you the same lessons on walking at Drawing Rooms that I gave your sister."

"Perhaps so." He eyed her closely. "Or perhaps you should just have found me a different sword."

"That did what? Disappeared when you were done with it?"

"Preferably. Speaking of that—" He removed the sword and scabbard and handed it up to the coachman. "Do you have room to stow that beneath your perch?"

"Certainly, Your Grace," the coachman said as he took it.

"See there?" she teased. "You found a way to make it disappear all on your own."

He laughed. Then coughed. "God help me, my mouth is bone dry. And that's another thing. If you'd warned me that the Queen's Drawing Room didn't include refreshments of any kind, I would have slid a flask into my pocket before I left Grenwood House."

"That would hardly have worked. Your coat is much too well-fitted to allow for a flask that wouldn't give you away at once." She thrust her head out the window. "Thomas, could you bring His Grace some refreshments?"

When the footman answered in the affirmative, Geoffrey wondered what the fellow could possibly have on hand. The damn woman already ran Geoffrey's household better than he could run it himself. Then again, he'd been ducking out every day to avoid seeing her, so he'd hardly left her any choice.

As he was leaning on the window, the carriage moved again.

"That's it," he grumbled after it stopped. Opening the carriage door, he climbed inside and settled into the seat across from her. "I might as well get comfortable now that you've made yourself anonymous."

He stretched out his legs and collided with hers, which were draped in some sheer fabric but were still distinguishable. This and the other carriage behind it were the largest his coachman had been able to produce from the depths of Grenwood House's carriage house, the only ones capable of carrying a woman in a hoop skirt and her companion.

But he hadn't been expecting to be in the same one with *her*, even only for a short while. Diana had ridden here with Rosy, while he'd come in the other carriage with Mrs. Pierce. So he hadn't had the chance to make adjustments for the fact that both he and Diana had long legs.

He had the chance now, however, because he sat directly opposite her. Instead of taking it, he shifted position so that his thinly clad knee brushed hers, and a bolt of desire shot through him. Clearly, he'd acted in error.

For a moment she froze, her breasts rising and falling more rapidly than usual. He couldn't wait to see them more fully in an evening gown tonight. Her present dress was of some purple fabric that stretched from her toes to just under her chin, where it met the lavender ribbons of her straw bonnet. It was far too unrevealing for his liking.

Then she straightened, to move her knee away. Damn. This was precisely why an unmarried couple wasn't supposed to be alone together in a carriage.

"Admit it," she said, her voice strained. "You simply don't want to eat while chasing down a carriage."

That provided a suitable distraction, thank God. "You brought food, too?" His stomach rumbled, as if echoing his question.

"I could hardly let a fellow of your stature go without sustenance for too long. You might have fainted, and even with Thomas's help, we would never have been able to lift you."

"I'll have you know I've never fainted in my life."

"Thank heavens. You might have crushed someone. But you're looking a bit peaked at the moment. That's all I'm saying."

Crossing his arms over his chest, he snorted. That was ludicrous. He never looked "peaked" either. Or if he did, it was because he was thirsty and starving.

Thomas approached the window on Geoffrey's side of the carriage and slid a small picnic basket through it. Geoffrey practically snatched it from him, then rummaged through its contents. "What the devil are these?" he asked, picking up a miniature pear too small to be real.

"Marzipan pears."

His mouth watered. "Marzipan is my favorite," he said, then eyed her suspiciously. "You asked Mother what I like to eat."

"And drink, yes. I also asked what your mother and Rosy liked. In my opinion, one should always have *some* food at one's own party that one truly enjoys. Don't you agree?"

He nodded, his mouth too full of marzipan to speak. When he swallowed his last bite, he dug around in the basket until he found some rather small sandwiches. Holding one up, he said, "Please tell me these aren't marzipan, too."

She laughed. "No. Those are ham and cheddar, cucumber and butter, and roast beef and mustard sandwiches. The mustard is Verity's own special recipe. She won't even tell me or Eliza how she makes it or what's in it, but it's delicious."

Geoffrey tried that first, then closed his eyes in sheer bliss. "God, that's good." He picked up one of the cucumber sandwiches while also pointing to what looked like small tarts. "What are those?"

"Lemon, jam, and Bakewell tartlets. Oh, and miniature mincemeat pies." As he reached for the mincemeat, also his favorite, she added, "We're serving all these at the ball supper in two weeks. What do you think?"

"I think you should give Lady Verity a much higher percentage of your profits."

She eyed him askance. "If you don't mind, I shall keep that our little secret. Verity already has a very big head."

"So do I, as it happens. That's why I always have trouble

finding hats." He polished off a lemon tartlet. "I don't suppose there's anything to drink with this."

"Oh! I forgot completely!" She thrust her head out of the window. "Thomas? We're ready for the claret."

"Of course, my lady."

Thomas had to wait while the carriage moved up again, but as soon as it halted, he poured two glasses of claret for them and handed them in through the window. Geoffrey stared at his. It looked like a decent enough wine. And there was something to be said for having a woman manage matters in his household, even considering the high cost of Elegant Occasions.

Don't become too comfortable with that. The only woman who'll be managing your household for a long while is Mother. At least until I'm sure it's safe to marry.

Diana told Thomas, "You may start icing the champagne now. We're about five carriages back, right?"

"Four, my lady."

As Thomas left the window, she lifted her veil to sip her claret, and Geoffrey watched her cautiously. "What's the champagne for?"

"To celebrate your sister's success, of course."

"You're that sure of her?"

"I'm that sure of Eliza's ability to guide her through this. And yes, that sure of Rosy, too. Your sister has come a long way in the past few weeks. She's determined to do well."

He swallowed some claret. "Then I hope you're right. Because if you're wrong, tonight will be a disaster."

"But as my other clients know, I'm always correct in matters like these."

"And modest, too," he drawled.

"Of course. Being otherwise would be gauche."

The carriage moved again, jostling his glass. "*Showing* otherwise would be gauche. *Being* otherwise is another thing entirely. I happen to be well aware of my own abilities, and I'm beginning to think you are as well."

She smiled and sipped more claret. "Aware of yours or aware of mine?"

"Both, I would imagine." He'd best change the subject. "You've got me curious now about your mother. What happened between her and her paramour?"

Diana waved her hand dismissively. "Oh, they married. For a time, the scandal made it impossible for him to serve in the army, but eventually he went to the Continent and took up his sword and rifle again."

"And your mother? Did she go with him?"

"She did. For about four months. But war isn't pretty, as you might guess, and the major-general finally packed her off home to wait for him on his estate in Cumberland."

"I can understand why he— Wait, he has an *estate*?"

"He does. After he married Mama, his father died, so he inherited his father's viscountcy." She pursed her lips. "I suppose we should stop calling him the major-general, but we simply cannot. It's too vexing to realize that after he and Mama upended our lives, he became Lord Rumridge through no effort of his own and in spite of his involvement in an adulterous affair. And Mama became Lady Rumridge and is now holding court in Cumberland."

"I've been to Cumberland. It's hardly a place to hold court."

"I wouldn't know. We sisters have not yet been invited."

The palpable pain in her voice made him ache on her behalf. He could hardly believe what she was telling him. What grown man and woman . . . no, *children* behaved like this to their offspring? The offspring were more adult than the parents, for God's sake.

She straightened her shoulders and set her chin. "So, you'll undoubtedly understand why I am reluctant to marry. Watching my rather theatrical parents parry and thrust my whole life has made me . . . Can we *please* change the subject?"

"Of course." For a moment, he was at a loss for what to say. Then he ventured, "So, is this always how matters progress with débuts? You sit in the carriage while the young lady is presented, sponsored by your sister?"

She uttered a rueful laugh. "Nothing about this is how matters generally progress. I'm not usually present, and the young lady's mother is her sponsor, so Eliza is rarely present either. As I told you already, Rosy asked me to come."

"Right, to buck up her courage, so to speak."

Her lips tightened. "Do you not believe me?"

"Of course I believe you. Especially because Rosy confirmed it." Although Diana had said this morning that he probably thought she'd planned it for her own reasons. She'd never answered him as to what reasons she might be referencing. He was on the verge of pressing her on the matter when the carriage moved forward. "What number are we on now?"

"I'm not sure. I wasn't paying attention."

He was. Not to the carriage, but to the little glimpses he got of her mouth every time she lifted the veil.

The footman looked in. "The young ladies are coming. Shall I open the champagne, my lady?"

"Certainly," she said.

Geoffrey stared out the window and spotted them at once. Mrs. Pierce was smiling proudly, and Rosy's steps quickened as she floated to the carriage in her hoop skirt. Diana hadn't been lying about that gown. It looked *exactly* like a dollop of whipped cream. Or perhaps a hot-air balloon. But, to his surprise, Rosy was maneuvering it masterfully.

As the two ladies approached, Geoffrey jumped out to help them in and then belatedly remembered that he and Rosy would be in the other carriage. Neither of these carriages were built to hold more than *one* lady in a hoop-skirt and headdress with overreaching feathers. So his conversation with Diana would remain unfinished. What a pity. He still hadn't asked her about their morning conversation.

"It was wonderful, Diana!" Rosy gushed as she hurried up to them. "The queen asked me how I was liking London, and I said what you told me to—that I liked all the sights, but I missed being at home, where I could be comfortable. Then she kissed my forehead and said I would do well in the Season and that she would make sure of it!"

"That's quite a coup!" Diana said. "We're so proud of you, aren't we, Eliza?"

"We are, indeed." Eliza turned to Geoffrey. "You should have seen her, Your Grace. She held her head high and didn't once falter in her steps." Eliza smiled approvingly at his sister. "And she's already made her first conquest: Devonshire's heir, the Marquess of Hartington." She flashed Diana a knowing look. "A handsome and well-spoken young man only a year or two older than Rosy."

Rosy blushed, as she should, given that Hartington was as wealthy as sin, and probably was sin's boon companion to boot. Hartington was definitely the Prince Regent's friend, an alarming connection in itself.

"Rosy, I should caution you—" he began.

"Let her have her triumph for today, will you?" Diana whispered. "Tomorrow you may do all the cautioning you like."

He saw Rosy staring at him with hopeful eyes, waiting for him to impart some wisdom. Damn. Much as he hated to admit it, Diana had the right of it. "I should caution you not to wear that gown when next you meet him. You might very easily knock him over."

Rosy laughed gaily and touched his arm with her fan. "La, you are so silly sometimes, Geoffrey. My hoops are not as formidable as all that."

How he wished they were. Then he wouldn't even have to worry about her suitors.

"They're coming to tell us we must go," Mrs. Pierce said, "so we should probably enter our respective carriages and leave."

"Of course." He held out his arm to Rosy. "Shall we?"

"I want to ride with Diana. I haven't finished telling her all about how it went."

A long-suffering sigh escaped him. He'd already shared his equipage with Mrs. Pierce once. Must he do so again?

Then it dawned on him. He could ask her about Diana now that he knew more about the sisters' situation.

And why would you want to do that?

Damn. He didn't need to focus on Diana right now. He needed to focus on Rosy. "You can tell *me* all about how it went."

She cocked her head, and her plumed tiara threatened to fall off. "You'll really listen?"

"Of course." He was paying for this nonsense; he might as well learn if he'd received his money's worth. "Besides, you'll have to tell Mother everything anyway, so just make sure Lady Diana is around when you do."

That was the only way he got her into the carriage.

Chapter Eight

"How was she, really?" Diana asked Eliza as the carriage set off. "We went over a few things on the way to the palace, but I wasn't sure if she'd remember everything."

"You prepared her expertly. There were a few girls waiting in line who snubbed her because they didn't know who she was, but after the queen showed her such marked attention, those selfsame girls wanted to ask her a hundred questions."

"And you told them you were sorry, but Lady Rosabel had to go prepare for her début dinner tonight. Because they weren't invited, they are now all the more eager to find out who this upstart is, and why she warrants the attention of Elegant Occasions. Everyone knows by now how particular we are about whom we accept as clients."

"What they don't know is that we err on the side of preferring ones who are interesting and pleasant to work for," Eliza said.

"And who pay attention," Diana said.

"Precisely." Eliza grinned. "To be honest, I think the queen was impressed that Rosy could curtsy so well. *I* was impressed. That girl gave the perfect curtsy—her back straight, her head lowered in deference, and her two feet precisely placed to allow the correct dip. The only person I've seen do it better was Verity. If not for her sneeze . . ."

"I know. It was such a shame. It has made Verity so skittish."

"In any case, you would have been very proud of Rosy."

"Which is how I always wish to feel when everything is said and done. That's why I like clients who pay attention."

"So why, exactly, if not that you fancy him, did you take on the intractable duke's education in proper behavior?"

Diana struggled not to reveal her feelings. "He's *not* intractable. He's just . . . overconfident. And dismissive of the things we value." She could feel Eliza searching her face. "Besides, *you* were the one who said he was important. That we should most certainly treat him well."

"Is that why you allowed him to sit in this carriage with you at risk to your reputation?"

"What risk? There were scores of footmen around and every window of the carriage was open. Besides, he was only in it for a few minutes. And it is *his* carriage, after all."

Wonderful. Now she was parroting the duke's words and stretching the truth with her sister.

"Diana," Eliza said in a low voice, "be careful. Don't let his lack of ability to be a courtier fool you. Grenwood isn't a typical lord in any respect. There's . . . a darkness in him that worries me. He has secrets."

Yes, he did. Even Diana knew that. "Everyone has

secrets. Or have you forgotten Papa's temper when he's drinking, or Mama's many flirtations meant to make Papa jealous? None of us is perfect." When Eliza said nothing, she added, in as light a tone as she could muster, "And in any case, there's nothing going on between us." *Not yet anyway.*

"Very well." Eliza reached past her hoops, which were rather constraining, to pat Diana's hand. "Just remember, if you need me, I am there, no matter what."

Diana squeezed her hand. "Of course."

As for secrets, Diana would have to keep her plans to seduce Grenwood very, very private. Eliza wouldn't approve of her plans and might even tell Papa. Diana wasn't as sure about Verity, but Verity might tell Eliza, and then it would be the same result as if Diana told Eliza herself.

And Diana *did* want to seduce Grenwood. When he'd kissed her, she'd felt such stirrings in her blood that she could only imagine how much more she would feel if he went beyond kissing. That is, *if* he were susceptible to seduction. He *did* look at her with interest—she couldn't deny that. So she hoped he'd be amenable to bedding her.

Oh, that sounded very naughty, didn't it? But she couldn't help it—she wanted to be naughty with the duke. She just wasn't entirely sure how to go about enticing him into her bed.

Should she drop flirtatious hints and leave him to make his own conclusions?

No, he might think she wanted to trap him into marriage and then avoid her even more than he had the last three weeks. He was, after all, a gentleman.

Should she offer herself and let him do the rest?

No, because if he turned her down, she would be forever mortified. And what if he told someone? Good Lord, but she would never be able to raise her head in public again.

Honestly, she didn't know the best way to proceed. She'd simply have to think about it more. There must be a way to convey her interest to him without sending him running from the room as he had after their first—their *only*—kiss.

But she had no more time to ponder it. Eliza wanted to discuss some last-minute issues about the music to be played after dinner. Then they arrived at Grenwood House, and from that moment on, everything involved Rosy's début dinner.

As usual, Eliza spent a great deal of time talking to the quartet of musicians about the pieces to be played. Verity was in the kitchen making sure the wine, port, and flavored waters were ready, along with the dinner itself. That left Diana to oversee everything else, what felt like a hundred last-minute details with the dining room and Rosy's attire.

At last she ended up in the dining room, making sure the china and silverware she'd chosen for the dinner had been correctly placed.

"I see you've chosen to have the dinner inside after all."

She jumped, having not expected the duke to be roaming around quite yet. "You really enjoy keeping me on my toes, don't you?"

"That's only fair," he grumbled. "You enjoy making me pay for things I would normally never buy."

"Like what?" she asked, turning to face him.

My oh my, what a mistake. He looked unbearably handsome in his tailcoat of jet superfine wool, his waistcoat of a blue silk so pale it appeared almost white, and his tight pantaloons of jet kerseymere. If she'd been a less hardy female, she would have swooned.

Instead, she dragged in a calming breath. "What exactly have I forced you to pay for?"

"Having the ballroom floor chalked for tonight, for one thing. And Argand lamps installed in the dining room and drawing room, for another."

"The chalking of the ballroom floor is for the ball and not for tonight. Trust me, it is—"

"Very expensive," he put in. "And what the devil is chalking anyway, that it costs so much? I assume you put chalk on the floor to keep people from slipping around when they dance, but even so, chalk is cheap."

She wondered if the play on words was intentional. Probably, judging from the gleam in his eyes. "In the case of Rosy's début ball, it's more than that. Certain artists chalk floors by creating chalk images: figures dancing, landscapes, pretty designs . . . things of that nature. I haven't met with the chalking fellow yet, but I thought we could have him create a design in honor of the bridges you build. Wouldn't that be lovely?"

He narrowed his gaze on her. "I suppose, but it would also be gone within an hour of the ball's beginning."

"That's the point. Have you never heard it said that people 'danced out' the chalk? It's special precisely because it doesn't last. It would be like . . ." She tried to think of an example. "Like having someone sing a song at a musicale. Once it's sung, that particular rendition of the song is gone, too, is it not? This is the same idea, but with art. It will make a grand impression—chalk images on ballroom floors are very popular with eligible young men and women at present." When he winced, she added, "But only if you approve. Although if you don't, you should say so now, before I meet with the chalking fellow tomorrow."

After a bit, he muttered a curse under his breath. "If it's just for the ball, I suppose it's all right."

"It's just for the ball," she echoed him. "Tonight we're using only the formal drawing room for dancing, so there will be no chalking. And the drawing room is more intimate for dancing anyway."

"Intimate! Thirty people have accepted the invitation to this 'intimate dinner entertainment.'"

"We've invited two hundred to Rosy's ball in a couple of weeks."

He gaped at her. "You're joking."

"Not a bit. The ball needs to be a crush if Rosy is to become the toast of London, and your ballroom easily holds a hundred and fifty." She narrowed her gaze on him. "Your mother said you had approved the number to invite."

"If I did, I don't remember." He paused, as if to reconsider. "I do vaguely recall agreeing to the Argand lamps."

"On your way out to some meeting of bridge investors, no doubt," she said archly. "But you won't regret the purchase. Have you been in to look at the drawing room now that the lamps have been lit?" When he shook his head no, she said, "They make it so much brighter than it was. And once they light them in here, you'll be able to see your food clearly for a change."

"I don't need to see it clearly as long as it's edible."

Trying not to laugh, she shook her head. "You're hopeless."

"So you say." He squared his shoulders and tried to look snobbish. "Yet nearly every person invited to this intimate dinner entertainment accepted the invitation, and given that *I* was the one officially sending out the invitations . . ."

"Before all those acceptances swell your head too greatly," she said, "I should tell you that Verity's meals are rapidly becoming legendary. She knows precisely how to make the food come out at its peak of perfection, and how to choose food and drink that gentlemen of a certain age enjoy. *That* is why they're all attending."

"Gentlemen of a certain age?"

"Married fathers of titled and wealthy gentlemen."

"And they prefer a certain sort of food?"

"Not all of them. But you must admit younger men are willing to try exotic dishes or eat tartlets and such without needing a full meal, mostly because they're busy drinking. And dancing, of course. But men of a certain age want their joint of beef or mutton and some nice potatoes."

He started to protest that, then realized she was right. Even his own father became very stodgy about food as he aged. And Geoffrey's grandfather . . . a joint of beef or mutton and potatoes was all the man ever ate for dinner.

Diana added, "So, if they are catered to sufficiently at this dinner, they will make sure their sons attend the ball later. The mothers are unpredictable—we can't necessarily count on them—but because the way to a man's heart apparently really *is* through his stomach, we'll have to count on Verity's menus. The rest is up to Rosy, and from what I heard of how she fared at the Queen's Drawing Room, she should be able to impress them all quite handily."

Grenwood frowned. "But I don't *want* her just to marry a titled, wealthy man. I want her to marry someone who'll make her happy, too."

To keep from biting his head off, she counted to ten before speaking. "Whom, pray tell? A military officer who will go off to war and get killed like my brother-in-law? A banker who'll be focused on her fortune? A penniless student? Can you give me *some* idea of who you think would be perfect for her? Because when I was choosing whom to invite, you were sadly unavailable to instruct me."

That seemed to fluster him. "I don't know. I'll recognize the chap when I meet him."

"Listen to me, Your Grace. You could pick the perfect fellow for Lady Rosabel and she might feel nothing for him. She has to want the fellow herself in order to be happy. The best you can do—*we* can do—is invite a nice assortment of respectable gentlemen and see if any of them make her heart race."

"Fine," he said through gritted teeth. "But I swear, if she ends up with some fellow who keeps a mistress and makes her miserable, *I* will not be happy."

"Nor will I. My father made my mother miserable, and it wasn't pleasant for any of us."

"My father did the same to my mother, so I sympathize."

"Good." She now wished he would return to ignoring what was going on in his household.

"Good," he replied. "So long as we understand each other."

He started to walk away, when a thought occurred to her. "You say your father made your mother miserable, but she never says that herself. Whenever she talks about him, she's effusive in her praise."

"I know." He sighed. "What is that saying about absence making the heart grow fonder? When my father was happy, she was radiant. He made her laugh with his witty remarks, and he quoted Shakespearean sonnets about comparing her to 'summer days' and the like. That's who she remembers, not the brooding fellow who drank too much."

"Ah. That's utterly different from *my* father. He tried to keep Mama under his thumb, and he did, still does, have a mistress even though he remarried. I somehow think that your father's brand of creating misery might have been more palatable than *my* father's."

"Perhaps," he said, but his eyes hinted at those dark secrets Eliza glimpsed. One day Diana fully intended to find out what they were.

Again, he began to leave, but this time he chose to return himself. "Tell me something. Are you planning to wear that gown tonight?"

"Yes. Why?"

"You wore it to St. James's today. I thought ladies wore different gowns at night."

She blinked. Then awareness dawned. "Don't you remember? I told you we won't be here as guests. I'm not *attending* the dinner, you understand. I'm not even the hostess. Your mother has that position, but unofficially, because she's in mourning. I will be darting around behind the scenes, helping your housekeeper deal with problems, making sure the footmen have their orders, and the like."

"But do you have to?" He paused to pin her with an assessing look. "Surely by this point my servants know what to do, and whatever emergencies arise can be handled by your sisters."

"Are you saying you *want* me to attend the dinner?" she asked, trying not to show how inordinately pleased she was by that.

"Not me so much as . . . well . . . Rosy seems to rely on you, and even Mother looks to you for advice." He groaned. "Not that I *wouldn't* want you there, but it's more for the sake of my sister and Mother. That is, I don't *need* . . ."

"I understand. And you mustn't worry. I never expected to attend, so I am not insulted by . . . whatever it is you're trying to say."

He sighed. "No one who heard me talking so clumsily about this would believe I can command an audience of fifty gentlemen and convince them to invest in a project they can barely imagine as feasible."

"I would believe it," she said softly. "I read your article after all. I didn't understand much of it, mind you, but I could tell you were explaining it cogently for the people who did."

He arched a brow. "You 'could tell,' could you?"

"Yes." She drew in an unsteady breath. "If I am to attend—purely for the sake of your sister and mother, of course—I will need a dinner gown, and I have none here."

After pulling out his pocket watch, he checked the time and said, "You have at least an hour and a half, and you don't live that far away. Send a servant for it. Surely there's a footman you can spare."

The duke had no idea how long it could take a woman to dress and have her hair put up. But Diana could probably manage it if she kept the gown simple. "I . . . suppose."

"Excellent." He stuck his finger inside his cravat and tugged, apparently trying to loosen it.

"Don't do that," she said, reaching up to straighten the now-crooked knot. "You'll ruin all your valet's hard work."

"How old are you anyway?"

She tugged this way and that. "You know it's rude to ask a woman her age."

"Yes, but judging from how you're fussing over my cravat, I would guess you to be my mother's age." When she eyed him askance, he laughed. "Come now, tell me. Or I'll ruin my cravat again."

"If you must know, I'm twenty-four."

"You behave like a woman much older," he said.

"Thank you?" She smoothed a wrinkle. "There. Now leave it be, Your Grace, if you can."

He got that intense look in his eyes that sent an answering tremor down her bones every time. "For your sake I will, but only if you stop calling me 'Your Grace.' It makes you seem like a servant, and you're not."

He was right, of course, but no other client had ever suggested such a thing. A lump formed in her throat as she patted his cravat knot to make it bulge less. "So what am I to call you? Duke? Grenwood?"

"Geoffrey. Call me Geoffrey."

"I cannot call you by your Christian name in front of anyone," she stepped back to say. "They will assume we are . . . up to something together." Especially if anyone caught sight of her fixing his cravat as a wife would do. And while she wanted to be "up to something" with him, she didn't want anyone else to know about it. It had to remain absolutely private.

"Right. I see." He ran his fingers through his hair, thoroughly mussing what his valet must have taken a while to achieve. "Then call me Grenwood or Duke in front of others, but no 'Your Grace' this and 'His Grace' that. And call me Geoffrey in private."

In private. That was encouraging. "Very well. *Geoffrey*, I have much to do before the dinner begins, especially if I am to attend, too."

"Go," he said with an imperious wave that showed him to be more of a duke than he realized. "Go and do what you must. I'll have a whisky and settle down to wait for the evening to start."

She laughed at that. "Then do it in your study, will you? That will give one of us a chance to retie your cravat, if necessary, and make sure you haven't thrashed your hair into wildness." Then she flew off to find a footman who could fetch her appropriate clothing for dinner.

The duke—Geoffrey—could be maddening sometimes, but all in all he might be exactly the sort of man she needed for a seduction. Now if only she could figure out how best to seduce him . . .

Geoffrey watched her go with great interest, noting that when she hurried, she lifted her skirts slightly for ease of motion, which inevitably gave him a glimpse of her ankles. They were pretty, finely shaped ankles, albeit shrouded in white silk stockings. He imagined moving his hands up her legs to her garters, which he would untie so he could drag her stockings down and off. From there, well . . .

God help him, he was going to embarrass himself if he didn't stop that train of thought.

"Where's Rosy?" came the voice of his mother from behind him.

Damn, he hoped Mother hadn't seen him salivating over Diana. He turned to find her looking a bit frantic. "I haven't seen her," he said. "Have you looked in her dressing room?"

"Of course." Worry etched lines in her brow. "But none of the ladies there had seen her either, not since they'd finished helping her dress. They said she'd gone down to talk to Eliza about her hair, but I passed Eliza on the stairs and she said she was looking for your sister, too. Could Rosy be hiding? You know how she gets when she panics over an upcoming social occasion."

"Yes, but I can't see her doing that tonight. Judging from how she gushed about meeting the queen all the way back to Grenwood House a few hours ago, Rosy wasn't at all worried about the dinner."

Mother scanned the dining room. "If she saw all the chairs in here, it might have made her reconsider."

In strolled his sister, as if on cue. "Mama, someone told me you were looking for me. Is everything all right?"

The worry drained from his mother's face. "It's all right now that you're here." She kissed Rosy's cheeks in turn, then frowned and took her hands. "You're awfully cold, my dear. Have you been outside?"

"On this blustery day?" Rosy countered. "I would be mad to go out there. It has already taken two hours of dressing to meet Diana's strict requirements for my appearance tonight. One step in the outdoors and the wind would wreak havoc on the drape of this gown, not to mention turn my hair into a rat's nest, or more of one than it already is anyway. Why do you think we decided to hold the dinner inside?"

That did make sense. "So where were you?" Geoffrey asked. "No one could find you."

"That's because I went into the conservatory to cut *this*." She produced a burgundy rosebud from behind her back. "Isn't it perfect? I thought you could wear it as a boutonniere." She came up to tuck it in his buttonhole. "There. It makes you look quite dashing. I shall have to claim at least one dance with you before the other ladies demand all the rest."

Alarm seized him. But before he could say a word, Mother said, "Don't be silly, Rosy. A man cannot dance with his sister. It's against the rules."

Thank God, Geoffrey nearly said aloud before he caught himself. "I'm sorry, poppet. Perhaps another time, when no one is around to legislate our dances."

"Now go, my dear," Mother said. "Eliza is waiting for you upstairs so you can have your hair done to perfection."

Rosy laughed. "To perfection, is it? I daresay I've never had anything on my person done to perfection. But my hair certainly needs taming before I can be displayed to our dinner guests."

Just as Geoffrey was about to pay her a compliment,

she darted off. "We have a conservatory?" he asked his mother.

"Of course," she said lightly, although she seemed distracted. "Don't all dukes have them?"

"I don't know. Haven't yet met any other dukes. I suspect they're hiding in their houses from the hordes of women who want to snag them as lovers or husbands." He shook his head. "Do you know that in the past few weeks, every time I show up at a meeting, some fellow I met while speaking somewhere else is waiting to introduce me to his sister or cousin or even his mother? How old do the chaps think I am anyway?"

His mother said nothing, staring off into space. "I didn't think we *had* any roses in the conservatory. I believe I shall go check."

"Wait a moment, Mother. What time is it?" Geoffrey pulled out his favorite pocket watch, which his grandfather had given him upon his coming of age. "Excellent. We have an hour or more, so you have time to go hunting for roses, and I have time to drink a whisky." *And Diana has time to dress.*

He hoped she did anyway. His insistence that she join them for dinner wasn't intended to add to her worries over how everything was transpiring.

"It's fine," Mother said. "I'll look for the roses after dinner is over. It isn't as if they'd escape the conservatory on their own."

"True," he said with a laugh.

Geoffrey spent the next hour in blissful solitude in his study. None of the servants dared disturb him there, and no one other than Mother and Diana knew where he was. That was something to be said for being a duke. At least he was accorded some measure of quiet, especially in a house this large. In Newcastle, they lived in a nice house, but modestly sized, so quiet had been hard-won.

That was probably why Mother kept asking when they would move from Newcastle to the ducal estate, Castle Grenwood, situated on the River Ouse in Yorkshire. His answer was always, "When Rosy marries." But the move might have to happen sooner, so they could establish themselves in the town before the gossip in Newcastle followed them.

A knock sounded at the door to his study. He sighed. It must be time for dinner.

When he said, "Enter," it proved to be Diana. But no Diana he'd hitherto seen.

"Your mother sent me to fetch you. . . ."

She trailed off as he sprang to his feet. He couldn't help staring at her. Her golden dress glittered even in the candlelight, turning her into a goddess. The requisite puffy short sleeves barely clung to her shoulders, and the black trim of the bodice seemed to emphasize the fullness of her breasts. It would be so easy to pull those sleeves all the way off her shoulders and lift her breasts out of their hiding place so he could—

Bloody hell. He had to stop gawking at them, but it was hard. *He* was growing hard, and that would not do. Swiftly, he shifted his gaze up to her auburn curls, which for some reason drew his attention to her full and winsome mouth. He wanted to kiss it so badly he could taste it. Taste *her*.

"Will this gown do?" she asked nervously when he continued to be silent.

"Most certainly," was all he managed to eke out. At

her frown, he hastily added, "You look as beautiful as your namesake." *You steal my breath. You weaken my resolve. You are more dangerous to me than a bridge crumbling.*

No, he mustn't say any of that. She would consider it encouragement.

And now she was looking at him oddly. "My namesake is my great-aunt Diana."

"I was referring to the namesake of all Dianas: the Roman goddess of the hunt."

She smiled coyly. "I wouldn't have taken you for a classicist."

"Newcastle-upon-Tyne Academy, remember? I did absorb *some* of that education beyond mathematics or physics. Besides, for a while my father had a particularly good oil painting in his study of Diana bathing. You could have been her twin."

She arched one brow. "Let me guess—she was half-undressed."

"Not at all. She was *fully* undressed." He grinned. "Which, for some reason, my mother found utterly appalling."

"What a surprise." She was obviously struggling not to laugh. "I believe my father has a similar painting in *his* study. The subject seems to be a favorite among gentlemen. Very classical."

"So your father is a classicist, too?"

"In much the same way you are, I would imagine," she said dryly.

At that moment, he realized he'd as much as said he'd imagined her without clothes. To which any gently bred woman would take offense.

That he had indeed imagined her without clothes wasn't

the point. He had to move this conversation into tamer waters. "Perhaps I should start over with a more gentlemanly approach. Lady Diana, you look very beautiful in that gown."

"Thank you, kind sir," she said with a curtsy. "And you look quite handsome, Duke. Somehow you even managed not to wrinkle your cravat. Beau Brummell would be proud."

"Who's that?" he asked.

"Doesn't matter. You wouldn't like him. I certainly don't."

"Sadly, I fear my hair is probably still 'thrashed into wildness.'"

"True," she said, approaching to smooth a lock here and a curl there. "Although the look of it is growing on me, actually."

God, but she tempted him. If the door weren't open and if his mother hadn't sent her here, he might have given in to temptation and kissed her again. Her eyes meeting his told him she might actually want him to.

But when he did no such thing, she colored and turned for the door. "In any case, pay me no mind when it comes to fashionable hair. That's Eliza's purview. And speaking of Eliza, she would like to see you, your mother, and Rosy all together, to make sure your attire is harmonious."

He followed her out of the study. "God forbid our attire not be harmonious."

"All I can say is Eliza has some idea that families should have harmonious attire, especially for important occasions like this one. She says it leads to harmonious family relations. She's convinced that the lack of it is what tore our family apart years ago."

"And not the multiple mistresses, I take it?"

Diana shrugged. "I've been told my parents were on speaking terms once, long ago. So she might have the right of it. Who really knows?"

"Who really knows, indeed."

Certainly he was no expert in how to hold a family together. Father had seemed to argue with Mother as often as he'd shown her affection. Grandfather and Mother were always at odds over Father. And lately he and Rosy . . .

No, *that* relationship was improving, thanks to Elegant Occasions. So he would watch her being launched into high society and applaud her all the way. Because getting her and Mother well-settled would at least set them on the path to harmonious family relations.

And take a hell of a large load off his mind.

Chapter Nine

Why had she insisted on touching him, not once but twice? It made no sense. Men didn't usually have such a profound effect on her. Only *him* . . . and his talk of undressed goddesses and the way he'd tried to make it better by starting over and the wit that surprised her every time. She knew no one like him.

That must be his appeal. He was different. A duke, but not really a duke. A gentleman, but not always a gentleman. How could she *not* want to touch him? His size alone made her feel safe from all the sneering nobles and their gossipy wives.

So she sought to put him from her mind . . . at least until she had time to ponder him further. For now, she had to make sure everyone followed the rules of precedence in seating, that Verity had remembered to arrange the little marzipan swans on the mirror to mimic them swimming on a pure mountain lake, and that someone had put an extra seat at the table for her. By some miracle, one of the ladies expected to be in attendance had bowed out due to an illness, so Diana could actually join the dinner without destroying the ratio of men to women.

Geoffrey didn't look terribly happy to be seated between a widowed marchioness and the young daughter of a duke, but the rules of precedence had dictated that.

Diana had dictated who was invited. Having heard that the aging marchioness's eldest grandson was of an age to marry, Diana had hastened to add the widow. Meanwhile, the duke's daughter had a favorite brother who was heir to her father. Short of marrying a duke or a marquess, Rosy could do no better than to marry the heir to one of those, and sadly, there weren't many heirs to dukes and marquesses running around.

Still, Diana now regretted inviting the duke's daughter, because the girl looked so adoringly at Geoffrey that Diana wished she could shove the chit's face into her bowl of chilled Russian soup.

"Have you tried the duck?" her dinner companion to the right asked. "It's better than I expected of a dinner thrown by a duke who is rumored to have no breeding whatsoever."

A strangely fierce urge to defend Geoffrey seized her. "You do realize that in addition to his father's prestigious line, His Grace is also descended from the Newcastle Stock-dons on his mother's side? His breeding was forged at that old and very expensive school—Newcastle-upon-Tyne Academy. Her Majesty is considering sending one of her grandsons there."

The fellow nodded as she spoke, as if she weren't telling the most blatant lie of her life. She doubted he would ever know the truth anyway. And the ne'er-do-well had sparked her temper, which was generally hard to do. He deserved to feel cut out of the general flow of gossip.

After a second such conversation with her dinner companion on the left, she was more than happy to see the dessert course arrive, a massive endeavor involving a sugar paste castle, marzipan swans on a mountain lake, and piles of nonpareil-covered chocolate drops for the snowy foothills surrounding the castle. On either end of the centerpiece were sugar paste bowls of marzipan fruit and assorted biscuits. From the way the other diners oohed and aahed, she wasn't the only person impressed with Verity's handiwork.

When the ladies withdrew to Mrs. Brookhouse's boudoir to let the gentlemen have their port, Diana took the opportunity to pull Rosy aside. "How are you, my dear?" Diana asked. "Are you enjoying yourself?"

"Yes. But the guests are all so *old.*"

"They are, indeed. But because none of them were eligible gentlemen, did you find them easier to talk to?"

"Well . . . yes, but how am I to find a husband if I never meet eligible men?"

"You'll meet them at your début ball in two weeks, which their parents, who are here now, will encourage them to attend after finding you to be the lovely eligible woman you are. And I'm sure the parents will invite you to any events they have in the interim, so you might even meet the gentlemen sooner. For tonight, I thought you might find it less taxing to converse with older people."

Rosy's eyes went wide. "Oh! It *is* much less taxing."

"Now, the question is, will you wish to dance with the gentlemen who are here? Because it will be very good practice for when there are men who are more your age."

"I'm always happy to dance as long as someone asks me."

Diana patted her shoulder. "Trust me, being asked won't

be an issue. The couples here are all fine dancers who enjoy a lively reel or two."

"What a coincidence. So do I!"

Rosy had said it in all earnestness. Diana could only nod and smile. The young lady wasn't much like her brother, was she? He seized whatever he needed, and Rosy waited for someone to offer it to her. Perhaps it was a matter of differences between the sexes. Or perhaps it was the gap in their ages. At nineteen, Rosy wasn't very worldly, but she would catch up eventually. Diana didn't know Geoffrey's precise age, but she would guess him to be in his late twenties.

"I never thought to ask," Diana said, "but how old is your brother?" Diana regretted the question when Rosy got a speculative glint in her eyes.

"He's thirty," Rosy said. "And very eligible, I believe."

Diana fought not to betray her interest in him. "Sadly, there are few eligible ladies here, but I will certainly make sure to invite some to your ball on his behalf."

Then, before she could give away any of her true feelings, she went to the boudoir to make sure the women were comfortable. She sat a while, enjoying the chatter of the ladies, most of whom were kind and intelligent, which was why they were invited to Elegant Occasions' affairs.

Before long, the sounds of music being played wafted to the boudoir. Lured by the lilting tune of "Monymusk," the dinner guests rose and surged toward the formal drawing room. By the time Diana got there, nearly everyone had found a partner and joined the dance.

Except for Geoffrey. He stood near the door, drinking

a glass of port and watching his guests twirl around the floor . . . particularly his sister.

She approached him. "Rosy is doing well, don't you think? She definitely has more confidence than she showed a few weeks ago."

"True. She dances nicely, too. But then, once she learned, she took to it readily."

"And I see she had no trouble whatsoever gaining a partner."

He smiled to himself. "I didn't expect her to do otherwise. She's going to break a number of gentlemen's hearts, I daresay."

"No doubt."

He looked at her. "Why aren't *you* dancing? I was surprised to see you weren't already on the floor."

"Perhaps I'm waiting to be asked," she said coyly, hoping that was a broad enough hint for him.

"I can find you a partner, if that's what you need," he said, sweeping the room with his gaze.

She sighed. "I suppose I should find *you* a partner. Your dinner companion, perhaps?"

"The marchioness? I don't think so. Besides, I see her there dancing with some nimble chap already."

"I meant your other dinner companion," she clipped out, fighting to hide the jealousy in her voice.

"No, indeed. That chit yammered at me long enough at dinner—nothing but inane gossip about people I'd never heard of. Why do I care if some earl got into trouble with his wife over some bet he placed in White's betting book?"

Thank heavens he had no interest in the duke's daughter. Diana was relieved, though she wasn't sure why. She doubted he would marry any woman whose whole existence was tied up in a business so foreign to his own.

"You could always dance with *me*," she said, as coolly as she could manage.

"No, I couldn't," he said belligerently, then followed his refusal with a large swallow of port.

She tamped down her hurt, but couldn't resist asking, "Why not?"

"I can't dance."

"But why? It seems to me—"

"I *can't dance*." He glared at her. "I don't know how."

That caught her completely off guard. "How can that be? Didn't you ever dance at parties or assemblies in New-castle?"

He snorted. "When I wasn't attending my all-male academy, my grandfather was taking me to various engineering projects and showing me how things work at Stockdon and Sons. Once I was old enough to travel with him, I was away from home half the time." He turned defensive. "I didn't mind not learning to dance. It wasn't as if I could guess that one day I'd have a use for the ability."

"Didn't your mother care that you were gone so much? How old were you?"

"Twelve. And I was glad to go. At home . . ." He shrugged. "Mother had Rosy and Father. And she knew I was in good hands with Grandfather."

Just when she thought she was beginning to understand him, she found out something that threw everything else into disarray. "All right, but after your grandfather and father died, why didn't you take dancing lessons when you got them for your sister?"

"Because I was overseeing the building of a canal. Because I had no idea I was going to be handed a dukedom in a matter of months. And because . . ." He hesitated, his dark brows bent in a scowl. "I don't think I'd be very good at dancing. I'd feel like an elephant trying to perform a minuet."

"I once saw an elephant dancing at the Tower Menagerie. Despite its size, it danced quite nimbly. Besides, you're no elephant. Your size doesn't prevent you from being light on your feet." She looked out over the other dancers. "And anyone who can balance atop half-finished bridges and locks, as I assume you do routinely, is perfectly capable of dancing. You might even find you enjoy it."

"I highly doubt that."

"Then why don't we prove it? Let's slip out to the terrace and I'll give you your first dancing lesson. We can hear the music easily enough out there, and it has turned cold again, so no one else will want to be out there."

He stared hard at her, as if trying to determine why she wanted to do this. She wasn't entirely sure herself. All she knew was that she needed to explore this tenuous connection between them, and she had to do it more privately than in a room full of people.

While she merely waited for his answer, he nodded and gestured for her to precede him out of the drawing room into the hall rather than the terrace. "This way no one will jump to any conclusions," he explained. "You and I are just going to take care of an emergency somewhere in the house." He led her through the now-empty boudoir and then out onto the terrace.

She hadn't been out here much. She'd inspected it as a possible place to set up tables if they had their dinner outside, but the cool, foggy weather had made that unwise. So, once they were out there, Geoffrey took the lead, guiding her down the steps to the outer perimeter of the terrace, where they could still hear the music but could not easily be seen in the darkness.

But the darkness might actually hamper them. It was hard to demonstrate a dance step if your companion couldn't see you. As if for their benefit, the clouds broke just then, and the full moon shone bright enough for them to make their way. Ahead of them, a low brick wall encircled the terrace. At least it gave them some boundaries to work within.

He halted and faced her with a serious expression. "I'm all yours, Diana. Do as you will with me."

"Don't tempt me," she said with a laugh. "I hardly think dancing lessons require such devotion. But you will have to be the judge of that. Is there a specific step you wish to learn, or is it all beyond your abilities?"

"I should like to learn the trotting step," he said, and when she eyed him in confusion, he added, "Of course it's 'all beyond my abilities'! If I can't dance, that means, by its very definition, that I don't know any of it, or even what the steps are called!"

"All right, all right," she grumbled. "You don't have to be snippy about it." So she began the same way her own dancing master had begun. "Have you ever learned to skip?"

He looked perplexed. "Can you demonstrate what you mean?"

So she did, hoping he could see well enough in the moonlight and the light of the Argand lamps in the drawing room to pick up what she was doing. "Now you try it," she said.

"I actually do know this from when I was a boy," he said as he skipped back and forth. "I just never knew what it was called."

"Wonderful! So now we'll join hands and skip together."

That went well, so she started expanding on the skipping to turn it into a chassé step. Then she made him practice it several times. She could almost see his engineer's brain taking apart what she did and applying it to himself.

She'd been right about his ability to balance beautifully, not to mention his agility. He definitely was *not* an elephant in any way, except that he wasn't terribly aware of his own strength or even his own weight. If he ever trod on her foot, he would probably break it.

So she would simply have to make sure that never happened.

The music had changed inside, signaling that the dance was changing as well. They ought to go in, just in case someone had noticed they were both missing, but she didn't suggest that and neither did he.

Then came the moment when she tried to teach him how to join their right hands above their heads while they slowly turned. Somewhere they lost track of the turning.

Someone initiated the kiss—probably him. Later she couldn't say whether it had been the moonlight or the close proximity or even the scent of jasmine in the air. All she knew was that when he kissed her, it seemed utterly natural.

This time she wasn't surprised by how he thrust his

tongue into her mouth to advance and retreat, much as they had done in the dance. With flagrant abandon, she gave herself up to the act of intimate kissing. Before long, they had stopped moving their feet, so they could move their hands, their heads, their *mouths*. So they could concentrate on the excitement building between them.

The way he kissed was glorious. Taking her by surprise, he backed her up against the low terrace wall, not even stopping his kissing of her, and lifted her up onto it. She'd thought she'd imagined how good it felt to be with a man, sharing an intimate moment like this, but no. It was him. *He* made her want . . . and yearn . . . and burn. All day, they'd been avoiding this moment, so it felt incredible to be kissing again at last. She loved that they were . . . they could finally . . .

Heaven help her. She'd never known kisses like these. The lazy sweeps of his tongue. The taste of port on his lips. The very scent of him, bergamot and musk. The way he made her feel, so . . . so like a woman . . . as he delved over and over inside her mouth.

As his kisses grew more needy, more frenzied, he cupped her head in his hands, enticing her into doing the same to him. Then he swept his large hands down to her shoulders and trailed kisses from her mouth to her neck and throat, then lower to nuzzle the tops of her breasts.

"Ohhh, yes," she whispered as he ran his lips along the edge of her bodice. She craved his hands on her, caressing her breasts, kissing them and kneading them the way she'd imagined in her dreams. "Touch me," she said, then froze when she realized she'd said it aloud and not in her head.

He pulled back just enough to cover her clothed breast with one hand as if he'd read her mind. "Here?" he rasped.

"Yes. *Please*."

"Whatever the lady wants," he murmured, his eyes shining in the moonlight as he filled his hands with her breasts.

She closed her eyes and clung to his shoulders, letting the exotic sensations wash over her. For a man of his strength, he was oddly gentle with her. Knowing he was being careful excited her beyond measure.

And when he thumbed her nipples through her gown, she nearly leaped out of her skin. She'd had no idea that a man could make . . . could do something so . . . so . . .

"Can I suck them?" he asked hoarsely.

"Heavens, yes," she said, before realizing he meant to bare them. "But won't . . . someone see?"

A harsh laugh escaped him. "Not unless they can see through me." He pulled her cap sleeves from her shoulders and down her arms. That enabled him to drag down her bodice and the top of her corset enough to free one breast, then the other.

He made some guttural sound, befitting of a wild beast, then knelt on one knee to take her breast in his mouth. This time the lashings of his tongue roused something deeper, fiercer in her. Like a boat at sea, she'd lost her moorings. Because nothing like this had ever happened to her before.

"Geoffrey . . . oh, *Geoffrey*, that feels . . . that's so . . ."

"Yes. And you, my dear goddess, taste like heaven."

He lightly seized the tip of her nipple between his teeth, and she moaned, so eager for more that she pushed her breast into his mouth. That prompted him to use his hand to caress the other breast, going back and forth between them with a hungry growl.

She buried her hands in his thrashed-into-wildness hair, and thrashed it even more as she clung to him, pulled him into her, swayed forward. Just as she felt herself sliding off the wall, he rose to catch her about the waist.

"Careful there, sweetling." He kissed her deeply once more, but this time too briefly for her liking before he lifted her fully off the wall and set her on the terrace floor. "Forgive me, I went too far. It was wrong of me to—"

"Not one word more." Already feeling the shift in him from heat to guilt, she pressed her finger to his lips. "I don't regret it, so why should you?"

"Because we aren't married." He attempted to pull her gown into place, but he was making a hash of it, so she took it over. "Because I'm not even free to marry."

Her hands froze on her bodice. She couldn't look at him. "You're engaged to be married?"

"Not exactly, but—"

"But you're not free." That meant only one thing—some woman was waiting for him somewhere. She pushed past him. "I have to go. Eliza and Verity will be looking for me."

"Diana . . ."

"No, I don't want to hear your excuses." She hurried away, fighting back tears, struggling to straighten her gown, and praying that no one had seen them.

A pox on the big oaf. She wasn't about to become involved with a man who'd already made a commitment to another woman. She'd seen how badly it had hurt Mama every time Papa had gone off with his mistress. She couldn't endure that pain herself. She'd always refused to be some man's mistress, and that had not changed.

Because being either party in that situation inevitably led to disaster. And the last thing she needed in her life right now was more disaster.

Chapter Ten

Geoffrey debated going after her, then thought better of it. For one thing, it was safer for the two of them to enter the drawing room through separate doors at separate times, so no one would guess what they'd been up to. For another thing . . .

He groaned. One look at his breeches right now, and they'd know precisely what he and Diana had been up to. Despite how the encounter had ended, he was still so aroused, he couldn't think.

If he had his way, he'd leave the dinner, go upstairs to his bedchamber, and take matters into his own hands . . . or hand, as the case may be. But Diana would probably chide him more for running away from the dinner than for his blatant misbehavior with her.

If she would even speak to him again.

Bloody hell! He dared not tell her she'd had it all wrong about a fiancée, or she would keep pressing until he revealed the real reason he'd said he wasn't free. Then she might tell someone else. Like his mother or sister.

No, there was too much at stake to involve her. Besides, she and her sisters had already weathered one scandal—

they couldn't weather two. So he should focus on getting Rosabel a kind, respectable husband and making sure his mother wasn't suspected of anything untoward or subjected to public shaming. And *those* two things were contingent on Father's secret not coming out.

What did Diana want from him anyway? To marry him? To bed him? He supposed he could have misread the level of her intimate experience.

That was impossible. Their first kiss had definitely been tentative on her part. And their encounter just now had shown her to be eager but unsophisticated. Hell, the only reason he knew what to do himself was that he'd had a certain lusty friendship with a merry widow in Newcastle. She'd taught him a great deal before she'd figured out he was only fourteen. At that point, she'd transferred her affections to a man who wasn't still a green lad.

The widow wasn't the first to assume he was older than he was either. Geoffrey had sprouted up so tall and quick that women had often assumed him to be a man in his prime. For a while, Geoffrey had taken advantage of their assumptions. What young man didn't want to bed as many women as he could?

Then Father had sat him down and warned him about the perils of disease or getting a woman with child. Father had said that one day Geoffrey would marry, and he would hate to have the activities of his salad days hanging over his head.

Geoffrey had been mostly celibate ever since. With women. But not with his hand.

"What are you doing lurking about out here?" a female voice asked.

"Damn, Rosy, don't surprise me like that! I just needed

a breath of fresh air." Thankfully, he'd lost the bulge in his breeches. For the moment anyway.

"Well," she said, "Diana sent me to fetch you. Everyone is asking about you."

"Fine. I'll come back in." His heart raced. Diana wanted to see him. To refuse to be involved any further with him and his family? Had he mucked matters up beyond his ability to fix them? "Did she say what she wanted?"

Rosy gazed up at him. "For you to come in, so people stop asking about you. Or at least that's what I assumed. She didn't really say."

Damn. His sister was no help at all. As they walked together toward one of the doors into the house, he asked, "Are you enjoying the dinner and the dancing?"

"I am indeed! Thank you for pushing me into having a Season. So far, it's been grand." She paused just inside the door. "Oh, and I danced with one of your friends—Lord Foxstead. He seemed very nice. I didn't know you had any friends in the nobility."

"And now you do." Foxstead. Damn. The man might have a title and wealth, but his reputation for wenching was almost as bad as Lord Winston's.

Geoffrey might know better than to voice his honest opinion to Rosy. But that needn't stop him from having a word with Foxstead—asking about the man's intentions, making sure Foxstead knew what he was getting into and all that rot. For God's sake, the man was a full nine years her senior!

You're six years Diana's senior. Besides which, you're taking advantage of her every chance you get. Yet

you're ready to throttle Foxstead for merely dancing with
your sister? Don't be a hypocritical arse.

Geoffrey really *was* a hypocritical arse, and he didn't
care. Diana had begun to dominate his thoughts, and he
wasn't sure how to handle that. He'd better figure it out
soon, though. Otherwise, he would find himself on the
outs with the very woman who could spin a golden future
for Rosy. Mother and Rosy would never forgive him for
that.

He would kick himself from here to Hades if his own
hasty and unwise behavior caused him to lose the help of
Diana and her sisters permanently.

The only reason Diana had sent for Geoffrey was to
reinforce the guests' illusion that he and she hadn't been
alone together on the terrace. She certainly hadn't done
it because she wanted to see the duplicitous scoundrel.
No, indeed. Which was also why she had sent Rosy to
fetch him. That way Diana wouldn't have to be alone with
the great lummox.

Once he arrived, she would remind him that as soon
as he was ready for the dinner entertainment to conclude,
he should toast Rosy to give a celebratory end to the
evening. After giving him that reminder, Diana would flee
as fast as she could.

While waiting for him, she paced the empty boudoir,
working herself up into quite the fit of anger. Then Rosy
showed up without Geoffrey.

"I thought you were fetching your brother," Diana

said . . . a little too sharply, judging from Rosy's widened gaze.

"I was, but he told me he had to take care of a matter in the drawing room first and he would return shortly."

Right. This was Geoffrey's way of running off, the same way he had the first time he'd kissed her. Wasn't that just dandy? "Tell me something," she said to Rosy. "Why didn't any of you mention that Geoffrey . . . that your brother has a fiancée?"

Rosy blinked. "Because he doesn't."

The reply bewildered her. Surely Rosy wouldn't lie for her brother. As far as Diana could tell, the young woman was generally quite honest. Then again . . . "He told me earlier today that he wasn't free to marry."

"I can't imagine why he'd say such a thing. He's a very eligible bachelor in Newcastle. At least now that he's a duke, that is." Rosy's face lit up. "Wait, were you two discussing *marriage*?"

That caught Diana off guard. A pox on him! Now he had her revealing things that she shouldn't. "To each other? Don't be silly." She scrambled to come up with a reasonable explanation. "We were merely discussing how to find a wife for him once he does decide to marry. That's when he said he wasn't free to marry at present."

"I see," Rosy said, clearly not convinced.

Good Lord, this lying had to stop. Diana didn't like it, and she was bad at it, besides. "Has he *ever* had a fiancée? Someone he might still be in love with?" If the Prince of Wales could have a not-so-secret wife, Geoffrey certainly could have a fiancée, or even a wife, whom he kept secret from his family.

Rosy laughed, then took a look at Diana's face and

sobered. "As far as I know, Geoffrey hasn't even courted anyone. Ever. His bridges and tunnels and canals seem to be his only love. Could he have meant *them*? Could you perhaps have misunderstood him?"

"Oh, trust me, he was quite clear on the matter." Her breath started to falter. *Had* he been clear? She repeated the conversation in her head, and although he'd said very firmly he wasn't "even free to marry," he hadn't necessarily said it had anything to do with another woman.

Or was she just grasping at straws? Either way, he'd been decidedly unforthcoming about whatever he'd meant. "Your brother can be so infuriating sometimes."

"Not *sometimes*," Rosy said. "Most of the time. I am often tempted to box his ears. And I would, too, if I could reach them."

"How am I supposed to help him when I don't know what he means and he won't explain?" Diana hadn't stayed long enough to let him explain, but that was neither here nor there. He'd probably known exactly how she would interpret his words, and he'd let them stand, the arrogant scoundrel.

Rosy watched her with a troubled expression. "I should probably warn you that Geoffrey tends not to explain himself to anyone, and he's just as bad about it with me and Mama as he is with anyone else. Honestly, he's never said anything to us about marriage one way or the other. Or about when we're moving to Castle Grenwood. Or what Papa might have said on his death bed, if he even said anything. Not a word."

"And you don't *demand* that he tell you?"

"Geoffrey doesn't do well with demands. He's very . . . er . . . independent."

"Determined to have his own way, you mean. I did notice *that*." Diana planted her hands on her hips. "And you have no idea what he meant when he said he wasn't free to marry?"

"None whatsoever. Perhaps he was referring to how he's been trying to sell Grandpapa's business? After our grandfather died, Geoffrey ran Stockdon and Sons by himself for years. Papa never had any interest in it, so nothing changed when *he* died. But after Geoffrey inherited the dukedom and all . . ."

Rosy crossed her arms over her waist. "He and Mama want us three to move to Castle Grenwood, the family seat, in Yorkshire, so he can set about putting the estate to rights. But I hate leaving my friends behind. I only have two, but still . . ."

"I understand," Diana said kindly. "Female friends are essential to any life in society."

"Yes! You do understand." Rosy chewed on her lower lip. "You have sisters, though. A mother, no matter how wonderful she is, cannot take the place of sisters."

"True," Diana said, a lump forming in her throat. But sisters couldn't entirely take the place of a mother either.

It had been weeks since she'd last seen Mama. During the Season, they were all so busy. Still, Diana missed her. Stripped of the anger Mama had felt against Papa, their mother had changed, had become easier to deal with somehow, happy for any crumbs of affection her daughters could offer her. Could it be that Mama had acted the way she did during the marriage solely because of Papa's adulterous affairs?

Not that it mattered anymore. Regardless of what had

caused the rift between Mama and Papa, their marriage wasn't the best illustration of a successful union.

Geoffrey's secrecy didn't bode well for marriage either. Oh, why was she even thinking about him in terms of marriage? He would make an awful husband. Everything would always be *his* way, and she'd already had enough of that with Papa. Besides, he'd made it perfectly clear that marriage wasn't something he sought.

Unless it was just *her* he disapproved of, *her* he didn't wish to marry. Did he think her a wanton because of her behavior? If so, a pox on him. It wasn't as if she'd forced him into anything.

He probably thought she was angling to snag him. That might explain why he'd lied to her about his reasons for not marrying. For pity's sake, she hadn't even mentioned marriage—how and why he'd jumped to whatever conclusions he'd made was beyond her. But she was not to blame for it. And she would tell him that once she saw him.

Just not tonight.

"Should I go back to the dancing?" Rosy glanced at the door. "I don't know what has happened to Geoffrey."

"Yes, go back. You deserve to enjoy the dinner entertainment. It's for you after all. But if you'd first find Eliza and send her here, I would vastly appreciate it."

"And send Geoffrey, too, if I see him?"

"No." Diana wasn't staying. And she was too tired and angry to deal with him at the moment. She needed to figure out an approach.

By the time Eliza arrived, Diana was ready to be done with the whole Brookhouse family. But she knew better than to act hastily in her present mood. So she merely asked her sister to remind Geoffrey about how he should handle the end of the dinner entertainment.

Eliza's gaze narrowed on her. "You've been doing most of the discussions with His Grace today. What has changed?"

Diana cast her sister a weary smile and lied for all she was worth. "It's nothing to do with him or his family. I merely have a horrendous headache. And I can't take another moment of being around people. You understand." She grabbed her sister's hand. "But if you need me to stay, I will absolutely do that."

"No, no, of course not." Eliza cradled Diana's hand in both of her own. "You have had a very long day—"

"So have you," Diana said.

"But I haven't been going neck or nothing for the last three weeks the way you have been. Go home. Besides, you know as well as I do that Verity and I have more than once asked to be allowed to slip off before the end of a social occasion. You never have. So I'm sure Verity would heartily agree it's your turn."

"Thank you, Eliza," Diana said softly and kissed her cheek. "I won't forget this."

"I won't let you," Eliza said, then laughed. "Now, go on with you. I must find our grumpy client and make sure he does his duty by his sister."

Eliza left, and Diana went to fetch her work bag, wherein lay the dress she'd worn earlier, her hussif, with its sewing implements, and assorted scraps of fabric for repairing Rosy's gown and reticule. Diana had stashed the bag behind a sofa, knowing no one would notice it there. But just as she'd retrieved it, she heard a man clear his throat.

When she whirled to see who it was, she found the duke himself in the doorway.

The sight of him briefly caught her off guard. Then she dropped into a deep curtsy. "Your Grace. Did you require something?"

He flinched. "Diana . . ." he said and came toward her.

She backed up a step.

That seemed to give him pause, for he stiffened. "I was told you needed to speak to me."

"Not any longer. Not now that I know you deliberately misled me earlier, and let me believe a lie." She picked up her bag and waited for him to step aside. "I suppose Eliza has already told you what to do for the remainder of the evening. If not, she will. For myself, I have naught to say to you, *Your Grace,* so if you could please stop blocking the doorway . . ."

He advanced into the room, but didn't exactly move out of her way. "Forgive me, Diana. I didn't mean to imply earlier that I was betrothed. I misspoke."

"Misspoke." She snorted. "After your sister expressed surprise when hearing of your fiancée, I gathered that you *misspoke*. So you aren't officially engaged. Are you *secretly* engaged? Secretly married?"

"I can hardly keep an ordinary secret from my sister and mother. I certainly couldn't keep *that* sort of secret."

That opened the floodgates for some reason, and her hurt and mortification came pouring out. "I don't know which is worse: fearing I was enjoying the attentions of a man who's actually engaged to another or knowing that the self-same man deliberately chose to let my misapprehension stand rather than admit the truth of why he doesn't wish to involve himself with me."

"The truth!" He turned to look out the door before closing it. "What truth would that be, pray tell?"

At the moment, she was too frustrated to care that her reputation would suffer if she were found alone with him in here with the door closed. "I have no idea. You didn't say, remember? But I've considered a number of possibilities. Were you offended by my wanton behavior on the terrace, even though you were the one to instigate it? Did you think me too lofty to marry a man who once worked for a living? Did you perhaps find my red hair appalling?"

"None of those, good God!" he protested. "Wait, there are men who find your red hair appalling? What is wrong with them?"

"Do *not* change the subject!" she cried. "If none of those reasons is the correct one, perhaps you would have the decency to tell me what the correct one is. And why would you even assume I *wanted* to marry you when I have never said anything of the kind?"

"I was just . . . I didn't consider . . ."

"No, you didn't consider my feelings one whit. You could have just told me you weren't interested in any sort of dalliance between the two of us." She swallowed hard. "Trust me, that would have ended matters right there. You may not realize this, but I have never before muddied the waters with a client by changing our business arrangement into a personal one. If that made you uncomfortable, all you had to do was say so. Whatever you may think of me, I'm not the sort of woman to engage in underhanded tactics to entice a man into marriage."

"I never thought you were. Our encounter caught me

by surprise, that's all. I'm not used to . . . dealing with women of the fashionable set, as you must have noticed by now."

"Oh, I have *definitely* noticed that," she said dryly. "Everyone around you has noticed that. The queen herself has probably noticed that. But I also took you for the honorable gentleman you claimed to be, not one who would let a woman assume she's been dallying with the fiancé of another woman."

"I know. You're right. I shouldn't have done that."

"No, you shouldn't have."

He dragged his hand through his hair. He had a bad habit of mussing his hair, and she hated that she found it so endearing. "The thing is," he said, "I can't tell you why I'm not free to marry, beyond saying I'm drowning in responsibilities at present. Between learning the rules for ducal behavior, settling the properties of my late predecessor, trying to manage Stockdon and Sons and my current projects, and making sure Rosy and my mother end up in a good situation, I am at my wit's end."

"I have a similar set of weighty responsibilities," she said. "Yet I did not imply I was 'not free to marry.' Indeed, have I once said anything about marriage to you at all?"

"No," he said gruffly. "But most women—"

"Even you will agree I am not most women," she said before he could say anything to make her even angrier at him than she already was. She would be sorely tempted to brain him with her bag if he did.

Not that it would do any good. He had much too thick a skull for anything to penetrate.

"And to think," she said, as she walked past him toward the door, "I actually considered having you tutor me in the ways of passion, so I could decide whether I *did* wish to marry someday. Obviously, that would have been a huge mistake." She opened the door and paused to look back at him. "I suppose I'll have to find some other man to tutor me. Do let me know if you have anyone to recommend for the post."

She had the enormous satisfaction of seeing his jaw drop before she marched off down the hall. So he'd thought to mislead her, had he? Well, he would never do that again. She would make sure of it.

Chapter Eleven

Geoffrey walked out the door to stare after Diana as she hurried away. Had she really said what he'd thought? Or had his fevered imaginings of her in his bed finally taken charge of his mind?

"What sort of post is she looking to fill?"

Geoffrey turned so fast he nearly knocked over his friend Foxstead and the glass of champagne the man was clutching. Good God, how much had the fellow overheard? "I beg your pardon?"

Foxstead nodded at Diana's disappearing figure. "Sorry for eavesdropping, old boy, but I heard Lady Diana ask you for recommendations. I'm merely wondering what post she's trying to fill. If it's anything I can help with—"

"It isn't," Geoffrey snapped. Friend or no, if Foxstead thought for one minute he could bed Diana—

"All right," the earl said. "No need to be testy. I merely thought I'd offer."

That was when Geoffrey noticed the confusion on his friend's face. Then the light dawned. Foxstead thought

Geoffrey and Diana had been talking about a post for a servant or a tradesman or something equally innocuous.

Damn. He'd better watch himself or the whole world would figure out that the woman was starting to rattle him. "Forgive me, Foxstead. I'm just a bit short-tempered right now. I'm not used to being the host of anything. Hell, I'm not used to any of this."

"Well, you chose the right people to arrange it."

Geoffrey wasn't so sure. He would have preferred having "people"—one in particular—who didn't tempt him quite so much. "Speaking of Elegant Occasions, I am curious about one thing. You move in the upper echelons of society a great deal. What do you think of Lady Diana and her sisters? For that matter, what is your opinion about three women of rank running a business?"

Foxstead drank deeply of his champagne. "I think that through no fault of their own, they found themselves at the mercy of the gossipmongers four years ago. So they chose to build a business for themselves that put them entirely outside high society, rather than sit around waiting for society to accept them . . . or waiting for their parents to behave like adults." He shook his head. "Which, from what I understand, was never going to happen."

"Yes, but the two ladies who were unmarried could have taken husbands instead."

Foxstead gave a harsh laugh. "First of all, Lady Verity already had a serious suitor, a scoundrel who diverted his attentions to some other lady once news of the parents' divorce broke."

"That's unconscionable!"

"I agree. But that's London society. All it takes is a

whiff of scandal to send everyone running. When the sisters started their business, the divorce had just begun to be litigated. No mother or father wanted their sons anywhere near the taint of something so scandalous. So even if Lady Diana and Lady Verity could have found men to ignore all that, they would undoubtedly have had to marry far beneath them. Society was pretty rigid then concerning how it felt about divorce. Still is, come to think of it."

That seemed enormously unfair. No wonder Diana was angry at him. She believed him to be accusing her of luring him into a situation where he had to marry her. Geoffrey knew she would never do such a thing. So why had he even hinted that she might?

Because he was too busy hiding his own secrets to think about how the act of hiding them could affect her. Next time—assuming there was one—he would do better. "So how is she . . . how are *they* regarded in society these days? Their business does seem to be successful."

"Given that they turn away more clients than they accept, I would say they're *very* successful. The high sticklers who disapprove of them are still around, but Elegant Occasions has enough supporters and people clamoring for their aid to keep them busy. Because they don't themselves appear at the events, they're able to walk a fine line between providing a service and being nominally in society."

"Nominally? Surely by now the divorce business has been forgotten. They're the daughters of an earl, for God's sake!"

"And the daughters of an adulterous mother who ran

off with her lover. That would give any prospective suitor pause."

"That's ridiculous," Geoffrey muttered. "It's not as if bad character is inherited."

"I agree with you, but you and I are men of science. The average members of high society are creatures of superstition, with a flagrant disregard for facts and evidence. I'd take Lady Diana over half the chits in London any day, but the fact remains that you and I aren't typical."

Geoffrey's stomach twisted into knots. "Do you have your eye on Lady Diana?" Geoffrey asked. "As a possible wife, I mean."

"I don't have my eye on anyone. I'm not finished sowing my wild oats." Foxstead regarded him closely. "But you seem inordinately interested in the woman for a man who'd previously stated he had no plans to marry anytime soon."

"I still don't. I merely think she . . . is a fascinating woman, that's all."

"Damn, Grenwood. You're smitten, aren't you?"

Geoffrey scoffed at that. "No more smitten than you are with your glass of champagne there."

"Ah, you're such a romantic fellow, comparing a woman to champagne. Then again, this is bloody good champagne."

"As well I know," Geoffrey said, "because I paid for it."

Foxstead let him change the subject, thankfully. "I could use another glass. Will you join me?"

"Certainly." Geoffrey sighed. "I have to make a toast to Rosy, so I might as well do it with champagne."

Geoffrey's mention of Rosy seemed to give the earl pause. "I assure you I took your lecture to heart earlier. I won't do more in future than dance respectably with your sister, I swear." Foxstead broke into a grin. "Although I understand she has a fortune, which is always an asset. Besides which, she is a fine-looking female, if I do say so myself."

"I recommend that you *not* say so yourself in *my* hearing," Geoffrey growled. "And whoever offers for her had better not be doing so only because of her fortune, or I will end the betrothal before it's begun."

Foxstead laughed. "Duly noted."

The rest of the evening was a blur . . . partly because Geoffrey had for once drunk a bit too much champagne with Foxstead, who'd stayed well past midnight. And partly because Diana's words about passion kept ricocheting through his brain, not to mention through certain other parts of him.

Geoffrey dragged himself to bed shortly after Foxstead left, but didn't fall asleep right away. Instead, he lay staring up at the canopy of his four-poster bed in his impressive master bedchamber while he futilely attempted not to imagine Diana lying in it with him.

The fantasy tantalized him—of her naked beneath him, beckoning him down atop her, while he planted his knees between her thighs, and savored the look and feel of her plump breasts, there for the taking, as he had his wicked way with her. He fell asleep to that glorious image.

Somewhere in the wee hours of the morning, he awoke from a vivid dream of her, just long enough to frig and fall back to sleep. When next he awoke, the sun was high.

Fortunately, everyone else in the house had slept as late as he had. Now he understood why the ladies of Elegant Occasions had been so sluggish and ill-tempered the first morning he'd met them. There was no way in hell he'd be able to attend any meetings at ten a.m. today. Thank God he'd had the foresight to cancel them.

He debated whether he should show up at Mrs. Pierce's, given how angry Diana had been with him last night. But how else was he to gauge the depths of her anger? How else was he to determine whether she was just tormenting him by mentioning having him tutor her in "the ways of passion"? Or whether she really had considered that? And if so, if she might consider it again?

Because God knew he would find it impossible to get any work done when the thought of her in his bed filled his mind. So either he needed to clarify her willingness on that score. Or wash his hands of her entirely and let Mother and Rosy deal with Elegant Occasions without him from now on.

With that decided, he downed his new valet's cure for being cropsick—a nasty concoction of sage tea, Epsom salts, vinegar, and sack-whey—and headed downstairs to see what the ladies would be up to today. He wasn't too terribly cropsick, thank God, because his valet's cure, while banishing his headache, was only increasing his nausea.

He found his mother and Rosy at breakfast, dressed well enough to impress. After pouring himself a cup of coffee, he joined them at the table. "You two look very nice this morning. Where are you off to?"

"The dressmaker," Rosy said, loudly enough to make him wince. "Our gowns for my ball are ready, so we're off to try them on. Then Diana is taking us shopping for suitable reticules, shoes, and gloves to go with them."

"Among other things," Mother said, and exchanged

a glance with Rosy that had them both giggling like schoolgirls.

"Do I dare ask what the 'other things' are?" he drawled.

"No," Mother said. "You don't have to know *everything*, Geoffrey."

"Fine. If you don't want to tell me, don't. But perhaps I will join you for the shopping." Which might give him a chance to talk to Diana alone. "I could use gloves and shoes myself."

"You most certainly could." Rosy peeked under the table. "The Hessians you have on now are marginally presentable, but they will not do for Almack's, where boots aren't allowed. And you can't wear the same shoes you wore last night to my début ball. You must have fancier ones."

He blinked at her. Elegant Occasions already had her talking like them. "I had no idea my sister had become such an expert on men's boots. I do hope no cobblers have been courting you in secret. I'll have to put my foot down."

Rosy laughed gaily. "The only cobblers I've met are either old or recently married, with jealous wives standing by as they measure my feet. So they'd hardly make suitable husbands."

"Especially not the married ones," Geoffrey said.

"And what Rosy means when she says you need 'fancier' shoes," Mother said, "is you need dancing shoes. The shoes you wore last night weren't really for dancing."

He stifled a groan. Exactly when did his mother learn the difference between dancing shoes and regular ones? They'd better not expect him to dance. One short lesson given to him on a dark terrace with Diana in his arms had hardly made him an expert.

"I will be very glad once the balls and fêtes and Almack's vouchers stop dictating how we spend our days," he groused. "Or my money."

"So will I," said a lilting voice from the doorway. "Because it will mean *you*, Your Grace, will no longer be dictating how we do either one. Rosy's *husband* will. And I won't have anything to do with that, thankfully."

Diana was here. Good. At least he could settle this once and for all.

He rose to his feet like a proper gentleman and gave a proper bow. But as he straightened, he couldn't resist saying, "Aren't you the one who says that discussing money is boorish?"

"Were we discussing money?" Diana pulled off her gloves one finger at a time. "I don't recall saying the word 'money.' You were the one who did that."

"She's got you there, Geoffrey," Rosy said with a bit too much glee.

"Yes, she does." Geoffrey let his gaze trail down from her regrettably buttoned-up, dark-brown spencer to her gown of spotted muslin. "Would you like to join us for breakfast, my lady?"

"I've eaten. Although I could use a strong cup of tea, if you have it. And honey, perhaps?"

He gestured to the footman, who nodded and hurried off to fetch what she required.

She sat down beside Rosy and began detailing where they'd be going after they left the dressmaker's shop.

"Oh, and Geoffrey is going with us today," Rosy said innocently. "He needs gloves and . . . What else was it you wanted, Geoffrey?"

He stared at Diana. "Shoes. Particularly *dancing* shoes."

She didn't so much as blush at his mention of dancing. Perhaps she was as "cold" as she said she was.

He doubted that. "I hope to be doing a great deal of *dancing* at Almack's next Wednesday. Did I happen to mention, Lady Diana, that I acquired the requisite vouchers for me, Mother, and Rosy? Apparently, the Patronesses there appreciate the opportunity to engage with a duke socially."

"A properly dressed duke," she clipped out. "Shoes rather than boots, breeches rather than trousers, a white cravat, and a chapeau bras."

He cocked up one brow. "Do you really think they'd turn me away for leaving off any of those?"

"I know they would. They've done it before."

"To a duke?"

"To an earl. Ask your friend Lord Foxstead, who tried to get in with trousers."

That sounded like Foxstead. He shook his head. "Fine. I will attend as a 'properly dressed duke.' Thank God I have all those things."

"Thank *heavens* you do." The footman brought her tea, and she rose to take it from him, then set it down on the table. "Your Grace, might we speak a moment in private? There are some things regarding your account that I must go over."

He nodded. "Let's go to my study, then."

They had barely reached it before she exploded. "Why on earth, after days of avoiding me, do you all of a sudden mean to ruin me by referring to our 'dancing'—"

"First of all, I did not refer to 'our' dancing. I wouldn't do that to you. Which is why my sister and mother took my reference to dancing as completely innocuous. Second of all, I could think of no other way to speak to you alone. To tell you that I would like nothing better than to 'tutor you in the ways of . . . passion.'"

"And as I told *you* last night—that would be a huge mistake. I see that now. I have no desire to engage in an affair with a man heartless enough to mislead a woman because he lacked the courage to admit *why* he can't marry."

"I have reasons for my secrecy, for my reluctance to marry, that I dare not explain, to you or anyone else. But it's not because I lack courage or compassion. I have plenty of both."

"I've seen no evidence of it."

"Fine. Then I'll give you evidence of it. So much evidence you will grow sick of it."

"That's your prerogative. It doesn't mean I will change my mind. Or at least not without a fight, Your Grace."

"I'd expect no less of my goddess of the hunt, Lady Diana."

"*Your* goddess of the hunt, sir? Bold words for a man lacking proof. You're cocky, I'll give you that."

He came near enough to smell her strawberry scent. He wanted so badly to taste her, but not here, where they risked being seen. He would not embroil her in scandal if he could help it. She'd suffered enough of that already. "You haven't yet seen me cocky, my lady. But you will."

"You haven't yet seen me stubborn, Your Grace. But you will."

With that, she turned and walked back toward the breakfast room. He chuckled. What she truly hadn't seen was him hanging about all the time.

That first day they'd met, she'd insisted on making him a more presentable duke. Fine, let her do so.

Because every time she started working on him, they ended up kissing. Or "dancing." So he would just let her keep at it until they both landed in his bed.

Chapter Twelve

A week of Geoffrey "escorting" them everywhere had made Diana realize a few things. There was something to be said for having a large duke at one's beck and call. Any supposed gentleman who'd made nasty remarks to them before thought twice about it when they saw Geoffrey glowering at them. Any supposed lady who generally snubbed them reconsidered doing so when they had a duke with them.

Geoffrey had even managed to get them vouchers to Almack's along with tickets for tonight's ball, and not because he was a duke either. The Lady Patronesses were known for turning down people of the highest ranks.

In the past, Elegant Occasions had only been able to gain vouchers if they agreed to do a favor for one of the Lady Patronesses—either to provide one of their services free of fee or to spread some important tidbit of gossip among their connections. Elegant Occasions could always refuse . . . but that meant the Patronesses could refuse them entry. Because she and her sisters declined to be blackmailed, they were rarely given vouchers, and with no voucher, there was no ticket. Not to mention the added stigma of being barred from entering that holiest of holies.

Somehow Geoffrey had circumvented all that. So now she and her sisters were at Eliza's, choosing the accessories they meant to wear with their new gowns for their sojourn to Almack's that evening. So far, Geoffrey *had* shown her his courage. Because anyone who could take on the Lady Patronesses of Almack's had fire in his soul.

And to take them on and win? That almost never happened. She'd been trying very hard ever since not to show she was impressed. When next she saw him, she would ask how he'd done it.

"Where's your suitor this afternoon?" Verity asked Diana.

"What suitor?" Diana asked, trying for a tone of nonchalance.

"Grenwood," Eliza said. "And don't be coy with us."

Diana forced a laugh. "Then don't be silly. Grenwood is not my suitor. He has no intention of marrying and neither do I, so by definition he can't be a suitor."

"Bodyguard, then?" Verity asked. "Pet tiger? Good luck charm? Do stop me when I hit on the right description."

"Friend and client," Diana said firmly. "That is all." Though he was rapidly becoming less of an annoyance during the day and more of a potent temptation at night. "And duke, of course. Which precludes him from being any of those things you said." She held a violet-hued shawl up to her face. "What do you think? This one or the ivory one?"

"It precludes me? Really?" said a male voice from the door.

With her heart jumping into her throat, she whirled on Geoffrey. "You simply must stop convincing our poor butler to let you in unannounced."

"Why? Norris thinks it's a lark."

She cocked her head and eyed him with pure disbelief. "*Our* Mr. Norris? Stodgy, disapproving Mr. Norris?"

"All right, so he doesn't approve, but he still lets me in." He winked as he approached her. "As for my title precluding me from anything, I rather like the idea of being your bodyguard. But the pet tiger . . . I don't think so."

"Why not?" Verity asked.

"Because he wants *me* to be the pet," Diana said coolly. "It would make it easier for him to keep me under his thumb."

"On the contrary," Geoffrey said, "I have no desire to own a pet of any kind, and certainly not a tigress. But I do like the sound of being your good luck charm."

Geoffrey looked her over thoroughly enough to make her want to smile. But she dared not, or he'd become even cockier than he already was.

"You should wear the purple shawl," he said.

"Why?" she asked, narrowing her gaze on him.

"Because I like it."

"The ivory one it is," she said.

He laughed heartily. "I knew you would do that. That's why I chose the purple."

"It's violet." She eyed him askance. "And I know *you*, too. You would never choose ivory. Your tastes run to the more . . . garish."

"Are you saying that one of your choices of shawl was 'garish' to begin with? Tsk-tsk. Here I thought you were the queen of fashion."

She bristled. "I have never said that I—"

"That's what Rosy calls you."

"Oh." Diana melted. "Well, that's very sweet of her."

He folded his arms over his ever-impressive chest.

"Why is it that when I call you the queen of fashion, you are insulted, but when she does, it's 'sweet'?"

"Because you're never sweet." *Liar. You've seen him sweet with Rosy and his mother plenty of times.*

"Now *I'm* insulted." He held up some pieces of paper and waved them at her. "Perhaps, because I'm never sweet, I should get rid of these tickets to tonight's ball."

Before Diana could even react, Eliza walked over and snatched them. "Don't you dare. I shall not let our tickets to Almack's become salvos in whatever battle you two are fighting."

"Battle?" Geoffrey stared hard at Diana. "We're not fighting any battles, are we, my lady?"

"Not at all," Diana said with the biggest smile she could muster. "I can't imagine what they're thinking, Your Grace."

"Watch out, Eliza," Verity said sotto voce. "Once they start with the 'my lady' and 'Your Grace,' you'd better prepare to duck."

Diana decided it was best she change the subject. "Where is Rosy, sir? I thought she was planning to join us all here."

"She and Mother should arrive any minute. They took the carriage down to pick up something at the glover's, and I had them leave me here first. I've had enough of shopping these past few weeks to last me a lifetime."

"I can well imagine," Eliza said with a chuckle. "My late husband would never have endured as long as you have."

The truth of Eliza's words hit Diana hard. She'd been so caught up in her resentment of Geoffrey's evasiveness that she'd deliberately ignored his finer qualities, shown by his behavior to his sister and mother.

And by the fact that he was willing to try things and change. Somewhat. "You might have tired of shopping," Diana said, "but the improvement in your . . . attire demonstrates that all your shopping has borne fruit. You're dressed perfectly for tonight's ball. Those black silk breeches are new, are they not? And you must have settled in with your new valet, for he has knotted your cravat most appealingly."

"Thank you. I'll pass on your compliment. He will be thrilled to hear it, for he, too, thinks you the queen of fashion." Then Geoffrey cleared his throat and turned to her sisters. "Oh, one other thing. Yesterday I decided to heed Lady Verity's advice and stop in at Gunter's to look over the menu for the ball supper."

"What did you think of it?" Verity asked.

"In my opinion, you made excellent choices. I didn't change a single item." Then he broadened his gaze to include them all. "I did, however, learn something interesting from Mr. Gunter. He said that you ladies use part of your fees to support two charities. Is that true?"

"It is," Diana said, wondering if he were thinking to push for a lower fee that didn't include supporting charity. If he was, he would have a bigger fight on his hands. And she would take back every generous opinion of him she'd just formed.

"In that case," he said, "I feel it is wrong to expect the three of you to give up any portion of your fee to charity." As all three ladies started to protest, he spoke louder to be heard over them. "Which is why I'm donating my own funds to your charities, so that you can keep your fees for yourselves."

The three of them were stunned into silence. Especially

Diana. He'd now shown both courage *and* compassion. Not that it changed anything. He still hadn't given her any reason for not marrying. Although honestly she couldn't demand such a thing of him because she herself had no desire to marry. Really, she didn't. She'd told him that very firmly.

He handed three envelopes to Diana, fixing her with a speaking look. "I don't know whom to approach," he went on, "so I'd prefer you give the charities these donations on my behalf. If you don't mind."

Why would she mind? She stared down at the envelopes he'd handed her and noticed that while the top two were addressed to the charities, the third was addressed to her. Ohhh. That was why she might mind. Because he was attempting to give her a private message, which was very improper.

He continued to stare steadily at her, clearly aware of the choice she was making. She could always hand the suspect envelope back to him, after all, with some excuse. But her curiosity overcame her propriety, so she slipped all three envelopes into her apron pocket.

"Thank you, Your Grace," she said. "It is most kind of you, and I know they'll be glad to receive the donations."

"I hope so." When her sisters looked at him oddly, he added hastily, "I mean, I hope it's enough to make up for the money Elegant Occasions would normally give them."

"Any gift will help," Eliza said. "We'll make sure they get them."

At that moment, Mr. Norris appeared in the doorway. "Mrs. Brookhouse and Lady Rosabel, here to see Lady Diana."

"Show them in, Mr. Norris," Diana said.

Once those two entered the room, the noise tripled. Rosy was excited, and so were Diana's sisters, and everyone was talking at once. Diana thought it safe for her to leave for a few minutes.

She should have known better. Just as she was about to pass through the door that led to their private drawing room, Eliza called out, "Where are you going?"

Fortunately, Diana had an answer ready. "I just remembered something I wanted to offer Rosy to use with her new gown. I'll be right back."

As soon as she'd cleared the door and shut it behind her, she hurried to the window and unsealed all of the envelopes Geoffrey had given her. The donations were so incredibly generous that they quite took her breath away. Then, bracing herself for anything, she read the letter in the third envelope:

Dear Lady Diana,

Tonight I wish to meet with you alone. Whether you choose to do so is entirely up to you. But I do believe I have shown you what I promised: that I am neither heartless nor a coward. Please allow me to state my case in person, in private, so we are not overheard. I can think of no other way to explain myself.

If you agree, accept this copy of the floor plan for the building on King Street. I have marked a meeting spot inside. If you can meet me there at 10 p.m., I would be honored.

D

A floor plan? She shook her head. Only Geoffrey the Engineer would offer a floor plan. And who was "D" supposed to be?

Duke. Ohh. She read the note again and realized that if it fell into someone else's hands, no one would know it was him or what it was about. It could just as easily be a former client of Elegant Occasions or a friend. It didn't even have to be a man. The care he'd taken to protect her caught her by surprise. She had to admit, he really *could* be sweet sometimes.

Not that she would let his efforts be in vain. His note was going right into the fire. But the floor plan . . . she would keep that. Because she, too, wanted to meet alone, if only to see if he meant to tell her more about his situation.

On second thought, she might have a better use for his note. She found a pencil and scribbled a message below his, writing it to D and signing it ML for "My Lady." Then she tore off the top part, threw it in the fire, turned the envelope sheet inside out, placed her note inside, and secured it with her personal wax. To be extra careful, she left the envelope blank.

She headed for the door, then realized she'd forgotten one thing. Grabbing the reticule she'd actually intended to use for herself, she hurried out into the larger room, where the noise had begun to die down.

First, she approached Geoffrey. "Your Grace, I believe you included a piece of your own mail by mistake with the two donations." When his face fell to see her holding out what must look like his original, she said in a lower voice, "Perhaps you should open it. It might be important."

His eyes glinted in the fading daylight. "Very well." A smile broke over his face when he read the contents. "Thank you, Diana. It was important after all."

After she shot him a secretive smile, she walked over to Rosy. "Now, here's the reticule I was thinking of for you. . . ."

The rest of the afternoon faded quickly into evening as they made their final preparations for Almack's. Mrs. Brookhouse was so proud of her son and daughter that she asked again if she couldn't attend.

"I'll simply stand to the side," Mrs. Brookhouse said. "They'll hardly even know I'm there."

"You're still in mourning," Diana explained patiently. "It would forever color how people regard you . . . and Rosy, too. You don't want them to see you as disrespectful of your husband's memory. It's one thing when the event is in your son's home, but at Almack's—"

"It's quite another," Eliza broke in. "People are unkind. Bad enough that those who consider an Almack's voucher the holy grail tend to pick apart the clothes and behavior of everyone who attends, but they will be especially critical of the three of you. Which is the only reason the three of us are wanting to attend. We can act as a barrier between them and your son and daughter."

"No need to act as a barrier for me," Geoffrey said coldly. "I assure you, I know exactly what to say to anyone who is cutting to me or my sister."

Diana flashed him a pleading glance. "You mustn't say a word. Anything defensive will make them even more cruel. You must appear bored by the whole experience. You, too, Rosy. That wide-eyed awe of yours was appropriate at

St. James's Palace, but at Almack's it marks you as a mushroom."

Geoffrey frowned. "The *fungus*? In what way could my sister ever be a fungus?"

"Not an actual mushroom," Diana said. "It's a word for someone who springs up to great prominence overnight."

"That does describe us fairly well," Geoffrey said. "And also mushrooms."

"Hence the term. But more importantly, it's an insult. If anyone calls you a mushroom, they mean it unkindly."

Geoffrey crossed his arms over his chest. "All this is making me wonder why I fought so hard for those vouchers and tickets in the first place."

"Because having them marks you as one of the chosen few," Verity explained. "If Rosy succeeds at Almack's, she will have her pick of the men."

"So how is she to succeed?" Mrs. Brookhouse asked. "What must she do?"

"Act bored and self-assured," Diana said. "We will go in as a group, and all behave as if we hold the lot of them in contempt."

"That should be easy," Geoffrey drawled. "I already do."

"I'm not worried about *you*," Diana said dryly. "I'm worried about Rosy."

Rosy frowned. "Perhaps we shouldn't go after all."

The cry of outrage from everyone startled her.

"All right, all right, I'll go," she said. "Heavens, but you lot place too much faith in me."

"Too much?" Diana said. "Nonsense. You're worthy of it. Just stay close to me and everything will be fine. Besides, you're sure to see some of the ladies you know from your presentation to the queen, or even your dinner. If you get bored with talking to us, you can talk to them— anything to make it appear as if you're perfectly comfortable at Almack's. I've already asked Lord Foxstead to save his first dance for you, so that will start you off in an enviable position."

She could already see Geoffrey drawing himself up to protest. "And don't you even think about trying to forbid it, Duke. Your friend Foxstead will behave. He *is* a gentleman, after all."

Geoffrey snorted in obvious disbelief. But he said nothing more.

Diana turned to his mother. "Would you rather stay here until we return? Or should one of us bring you to Grenwood House?"

"No, indeed, it's far out of the way. I'd rather wait here for your return. I brought a book to read, so I'll be quite comfy."

"Very well." Diana surveyed the rest of them. "Are we ready to invade Almack's?" When everyone nodded, she said, "Excellent. Our carriages await."

Chapter Thirteen

After they arrived, it took some time to get inside. Both the vouchers and the tickets had to be presented at the doors. They'd shown up at the same time as a number of other guests, so entering the rooms meant waiting in long lines.

Once they were in, Geoffrey surveyed the ballroom, trying to figure out why people fought to be here. "So, this is Almack's. I'm afraid I don't see the appeal."

"Nor do I," Diana said. "But others do, and thus my sisters and I must play the game." She looked up at him. "I haven't yet thanked you for gaining the vouchers and tickets. However did you manage it?"

He grinned at her. "You didn't think me capable of acquiring such a thing?"

"It has naught to do with you or your abilities. I just happen to know that the Lady Patronesses can be haughty to the point of cruelty."

That took the grin off his face. "I assume you're speaking from personal experience."

Diana shrugged. "My parents' scandalous marriage had a long-reaching effect. When a club like this makes respectability its key virtue, no one who's had an ounce of scandal in their lives is safe. We haven't been able to get a voucher for Almack's in some time." She eyed him closely. "How *did* you get those vouchers and tickets anyway? Somehow I can't see you cozying up to the Lady Patronesses for them."

"That's because everyone does that, according to Foxstead, and it rarely works. Perhaps if I'd been someone else . . . but I knew those women would pay me no mind." He shuddered. "So I figured 'cozying up to' the Lady Patronesses' husbands made more sense. Their husbands— a couple of whom invest in the same projects I do—were a bit keener to help me."

"Why, you sly dog, you," she said. "You're learning to twist the rules so you can get what you want on your own terms."

"Precisely."

"And you're a man, so you're used to getting around women."

"Of course." It dawned on him how his explanation must have sounded. "I mean, I wasn't . . ."

Diana laughed. "I'm teasing you. At least you're using your power for the good of your sister, which is admirable." She stared across the room to where some Lady Patronesses were gathered. "And you couldn't have picked a more deserving group of women to get around or overlook."

He relaxed. "I gathered as much from what you said earlier."

"My father has been trying to get Sarah into Almack's for the past couple of years and hasn't managed it yet. He's . . . er . . . difficult, so I understand why they won't give *him* a voucher. But she's perfectly lovely and about as respectable as a widow can be."

"Who's *Sarah*?" he asked. "Is there a fourth Harper sister who didn't want to be part of the business?"

"Oh! No. Sorry." Diana drew him over to the area under the musician's balcony, which wasn't as crowded or noisy. "She's our . . . stepmother, I guess you'd call her. She was a widow with children when Papa married her. But she's only a bit older than we are, so we tend to call her by her given name. I suppose we should be calling her Lady Holtbury, but that's confusing to us because then we think one of us is talking about Mama."

"Your father certainly wasted no time in getting re-married." If Geoffrey hadn't already hated what the man's actions had done to his daughters, this would have convinced him to do so.

She shrugged. "Papa needs an heir. Sometimes I wonder if he'd merely been waiting for an excuse to divorce Mama so he could try again with some other woman because Mama had given him only daughters."

That sent a chill through Geoffrey. "If you're right, his behavior is loathsome. There's more to a marriage than siring an heir, no matter what the aristocracy believes."

"You really need to stop talking as if you're not part of the aristocracy," she said with a shake of her head. "You're a duke and will be expected to sire an heir."

"I don't feel like a duke."

"But surely you have had time to get used to the possibility."

"Actually, I have not." He probably should at least tell her about that, so she could better understand his situation. "Rosy wasn't lying about Father's family cutting him off when he married my mother. After that, they were all dead to him—it was a mutual disinheriting, if there's any such thing. So Father didn't keep up with the lineages, assuming he was way down on the list to become duke. He died still believing he was sixth in line and I was seventh."

"But he was wrong."

"Yes." Geoffrey blinked at her. "Wait, how did you know?"

Diana gave him a sheepish smile. "I probably shouldn't tell you this, but after we took you on as a client, we traced the family connections. They're very twisted."

"To say the least. My predecessor lived so long, he not only outlasted his three sons, none of whom had possessed male heirs, but also a couple of cousins who'd outlasted their own sons. By the time my predecessor died, the College of Arms had already traced the dukedom, at his request, up through several ancestors to the original title-holder and then come down a completely different branch of the family to find me. Fortunately—or unfortunately, depending on how you look at it—by then my father's two brothers had died without male issue."

"If your father had lived, he would have been duke before you."

"And Viscount Brookhouse. Yes." Perhaps Father wouldn't have died quite so soon either. Because his rotten relatives would have embraced him with open arms, and he wouldn't have been so sunk into melancholy that he'd disappeared into a bottle. Or bottles, as it were.

Then again, he'd hated his relatives, so perhaps not.

A thought occurred to him. "Why did you and your sisters trace my line of inheritance?"

She shrugged. "So we would know who your relations were if we needed to invite them to any of our social occasions for you."

He shot her a dark look. "You didn't invite them to Rosy's ball, did you?"

"No, indeed. Your mother made it quite clear they weren't to be invited to anything ever. Besides, I gather that your most immediate relations—your grandparents on your father's side—are deceased."

"If you say so. I never knew or cared. They washed their hands of Father once he married Mother. If I could have refused the dukedom and the viscountcy, too, I would have, but aside from the fact that it's mine whether I want it or not, Mother pointed out that actually claiming the title might help with some of my projects down the line. God knows, the Duke of Bridgewater has certainly benefited from his title."

Diana cocked her head. "I don't know who that is."

"That's because he never took part in politics and almost never came to London. Spent all his time building canals." The Duke of Bridgewater was a man after Geoffrey's own heart.

"Oh, right—the one they call 'the Canal Duke.' Who was *his* heir?"

"Nobody. He never married and had no relations to inherit."

"Like you."

"I suppose." Geoffrey hadn't considered that before.

"There is no supposing involved. We traced all your relations. You are the last Duke of Grenwood."

He crossed his arms over his chest. "Until I marry and have a son."

She eyed him askance. "First of all, I seem to recall you saying you don't wish to marry."

"That's not true. I do. One day. Many years into the future."

"Even if—" At his scowl, she quickly amended her statement. "*When* you marry, there's no guarantee you'll have a son."

"True." But he would damned well enjoy trying to sire one. With her, the only woman he'd ever thought he'd like to marry. Then, realizing he was heading into dangerous territory, he changed the subject. "Do you mean to dance this evening?"

She stared up at him with a raised brow. "If I'm asked."

"Don't look at me," he warned. "That one lesson you gave me wasn't nearly enough for me to be able to dance in public."

She chuckled. "Then clearly we shall have to get you more lessons before Rosy's ball next week. You simply *must* dance at your sister's ball, even if not with her."

"If you insist." He glanced up to see that the clock said nine. After looking around to make sure no one stood nearby, he lowered his voice. "You do mean to meet me in an hour, I hope."

"I said I would, didn't I?"

"Not exactly. Your note implied that you would, but 'I can' wasn't as clear an answer as I was looking for."

She sniffed. "If you will recall what you wrote, 'I can' is a direct answer to your last line about whether I can meet you."

"Ah. I take it you will do anything to keep your reputation safe."

"Not 'anything,' obviously, because I've agreed to

meet privately with you. But you went to such great lengths to hide *your* identity in the note that I thought it only fair I do the same." She drew herself up. "I don't wish to ruin you, sir."

He laughed. "Why sign the note ML?"

"'My lady.'"

"Ohhh. I'm afraid I missed that."

She flashed him a rueful smile. "It took me a while to figure out what 'D' stood for. When it hit me, I felt like a dunce. Perhaps I should have signed my note 'D' as well, for dunce."

"Or 'Diana.' If anyone ever saw the note, they would assume you were writing to yourself."

Her smile warmed him.

"Were you able to understand the floor plan?" he asked.

"I didn't have time to study it." She shook her head. "Leave it to you to include a floor plan."

"What do you expect from an engineer? I request floor plans routinely. Besides which, I wasn't familiar with the building, so I needed one."

"Well, I'll try to look it over before ten."

"Better yet, do you know where the ladies' retiring room is?"

"If you're looking for privacy," she whispered, "that is not the place to get it."

He rolled his eyes. "I realize that. But there's a stairwell right past the ladies' retiring room door. If you pass up the retiring room around ten o'clock and go to the stairwell, I'll meet you inside and take you to where we're going. Just make sure not to be seen by anyone."

"I shall do my best."

At that moment, Lord Foxstead approached. She moved aside, apparently assuming that the earl wanted to talk to Geoffrey. But the rascal stopped in front of *her* and bowed. "Lady Diana, will you give me the pleasure of dancing with you?"

She shot Geoffrey a veiled look. "I . . . I would be honored, sir. Thank you."

Geoffrey glowered at Foxstead, which did nothing but make the chap smirk. They went off together, leaving Geoffrey to seethe. He wasn't angry with Diana—he'd learned through the course of Rosy's instruction that only very special situations allowed a woman to refuse to dance with a man. Hell, even if she *could* refuse Foxstead, Geoffrey understood why she might not. From what he'd seen, Diana and her sisters got few opportunities to dance.

No, it was Foxstead whose neck he wanted to wring. The man had picked Diana just to annoy Geoffrey, because Foxstead assumed he was jealous.

Geoffrey wasn't jealous. Not one whit.

Keep repeating it to yourself, and it might become true.

He scowled. Why would he be jealous of Foxstead? In less than two hours, Geoffrey hopefully would be the one holding Diana, kissing Diana . . . giving Diana the pleasure she obviously craved *and* deserved. The pleasure she would have gained if her father hadn't driven her mother to leave and thus ruined Diana's chance at a more conventional life.

That was what Geoffrey had come to believe had happened. The veiled—and not so veiled—comments of Diana and her sisters had implied as much. But there was no reason Diana should have to spend the rest of her life as some chaste acolyte of high society. He meant to make certain she didn't. He might not be in a position to marry her himself at present, but he damned well wanted her to experience what marriage could be like, so that if Geoffrey did become free, or a man like Foxstead offered . . .

No, not Foxstead. The man couldn't be trusted to be faithful to her, and neither could the likes of Lord Winston, the only other bachelor he knew in her world.

Well, that part of it she would have to decide. But now that he had the idea of marriage to her in his head, he couldn't get it out. What if he were just to . . .

That wouldn't work. He needed to do as he'd originally planned. The rest he'd have to leave up to her.

To Diana's surprise, Foxstead wasn't the only gentleman to ask her to dance. Two others followed him. Perhaps her performance with the earl had reminded them she'd been known for her dancing before the Incident had brought her and Verity's romantic lives to a screeching halt. The men were both polite, so she felt certain they weren't merely angling to gain something sordid from her.

Only Geoffrey is doing that.

Was he? She didn't think so. Geoffrey wasn't like any of them. Or at least she hoped he wasn't. But it was ridiculous that she was finally at Almack's, with a perfectly lovely gentleman walking her back to Eliza, and she could only think of Geoffrey and their assignation later on. She looked at the large clock again. Ten more minutes.

"Diana?" said a low voice.

Whirling around, she broke into a grin. "Winston!"

Diana introduced her dance partner to her second

cousin, and her partner considerately bowed and moved away, leaving her to speak to Winston alone. Casting a furtive glance around to make sure Geoffrey wasn't close enough to overhear them, she smiled. "It's so good to see you."

"I was hoping you'd be here." He nodded to where Rosy was happily dancing with another gentleman. "I don't suppose her brother would allow her to dance with me. Grenwood has to be around someplace."

Lord Winston had been a handsome man at twenty—with black eyes, raven hair, and a tall, lean figure. But at only twenty-eight he'd begun to look more . . . hardened, as if he'd been to the well so many times that his thirst couldn't be quenched by mere water. Tonight, however, under Almack's famous wax candles, he appeared more youthful.

Diana stared hard at him. "What is your interest in Rosy?"

"She's . . . different from all the other girls having their débuts."

She eyed him askance. "How would you even know? You met with her only once before."

"Romeo met Juliet only once and fell in love."

"And died for it, not a fate I'd wish on either of you." She lowered her voice. "Are you saying you're in love with Rosy?"

"I don't know. I can't even explain it, because I don't understand it myself."

Diana sighed. "You don't need to explain." She looked for Geoffrey but didn't see him. He must have already gone to the stairwell. "Rosy and her brother are both different from people you and I are likely to meet in society."

"They don't belong." He continued to gaze at Rosy, the way an artist might assess how to paint a portrait. "More importantly, they don't *want* to belong. It's rather . . ."

"Intoxicating."

"Disturbing." He cast her a rueful look. "Throws everything one believes into question."

"That it does." The clock began to ring the hour. "Forgive me, Winston, but I was just on my way to the retiring room. We should have a chat sometime soon, however."

"Of course," he said with a nod.

She started to hurry off, then paused. "If you wish to dance with Rosy, now would be the time to ask her. I . . . um . . . heard Grenwood say he was going to the tearoom."

When Winston brightened before hurrying away, she wondered if she'd been unwise to encourage him. But she didn't stay to find out. Besides, his interest in Rosy helped her as much as him, because it meant he could truthfully tell prying people she had gone to the retiring room and Geoffrey to the tearoom.

If anyone happened to notice, which they probably wouldn't anyway.

She went out toward the retiring room, thankful she saw no one in the hall. Passing by its entrance, she headed for the stairwell and managed to slip into it before anyone saw her. She'd barely entered when Geoffrey melted from out of the dim light to hold his finger to her lips. Then he led her downstairs and through a door to a part of the building she'd never been in before.

While she knew the building was home not only to Almack's assembly rooms but to various lodgings, she hadn't thought about what they must be like, so she was surprised when he unlocked the door to one and led her inside.

The room was fully furnished, which took her by surprise. "Whose lodgings are these?"

"Mine. That's how I got the floor plan of the building. I told the owner I wanted to rent a furnished room for a private gathering of my bachelor friends next week, and he insisted upon my renting it for a month. So here we are."

"But you can't . . . I don't think . . . Doesn't anybody know you've rented it?"

"No one but you and me. And the owner, of course, who's delighted to have a duke as a tenant." He took her gloved hand and kissed it, which somehow felt more intimate than when he'd kissed her lips before. The lighting was low, and they were alone. It was wonderfully forbidden.

And when he kissed his way up her arm to the bend in her elbow, it became even more so. He tasted her there . . . actually *tasted* her with his tongue, and that shot a current of excitement through her.

"Geoffrey," she said in a soft voice. "I–I thought we could . . . talk."

"Later," he rasped.

Later? Oh dear.

Now he was holding her loosely about the waist so he could kiss the part of her breasts showing above her bodice, and she couldn't breathe for the thrill of it.

But if they were caught . . . "How much later? We . . .

we have to return before eleven . . . when they serve supper."

"I heard the supper isn't that good," he murmured, thumbing her nipple through her gown.

Oh. My. Word. "That's n–not the point." When he ran kisses up her throat to her ear while also kneading her breast, she moaned. It felt *so* good, *so* wicked. "At least one of us . . . must be there, or people will . . . notice . . . So we have to leave . . . well before then."

"And we will. But that still gives me plenty of time to feast on you," he whispered, then nipped her ear as if he literally meant to devour her.

"What do you . . . mean?"

"I'll show you." He pulled back to stare at her, eyes glittering like blue flames in the lamplight. "It finally dawned on me that I can introduce you to pleasure without ruining you. You'll walk out of here as chaste as when you came in." Dragging up her skirts, he backed her toward a sofa, then settled her down upon it as gently as a bird settling onto her nest. "And then you'll know . . . whether it's worth marrying for."

The mention of marriage confused her. He didn't want to marry—he'd told her so. Had he changed his mind? Had *she*?

Heedless of her fixing on that word, he pushed her gown up to her waist, exposing every part of her below. When she started to close her legs, he murmured, "No, no," and pushed them carefully apart. "I want to taste you here . . ." He licked her inner thigh. "And here . . ." He licked her other inner thigh. "And then I want to sip your honey."

Good Lord, what did *that* mean? The "fallen females"

had said naught of sipping honey when they'd tried to explain what lying with a man entailed.

Then his hot mouth covered her mons and his tongue flicked her soft folds, and she nearly lost her mind. So *that's* what he meant by "honey."

But he wasn't exactly . . . sipping it. He was stroking and flicking and *caressing* her tender flesh with his mouth and tongue so exquisitely that she grabbed for his head to press him closer. He chuckled against her, then resumed lashing her most deliciously with his tongue.

Now he was thrusting his tongue *inside* her. Oh . . . *Lord.* The most scandalous sensations rocketed through her. She pushed against his mouth, and he pressed his thumb over a place she'd found it pleasant to rub herself in the past. Except that when *he* did it . . .

"Yes," she choked out. "Like that . . . good heavens . . ."

His tongue drove into her, harder, faster, and his thumb worked her in perfect accord, until she felt as if an invisible string pulled her up into the air and she thought she might fly . . . or die . . . or quite well *explode.*

And then she did, her back arching, her hands clutching his head, her body shattering around his tongue and thumb.

Then she sank back depleted. Her senses were still vibrating as if the plucking of the invisible string still reverberated inside her. How . . . marvelous.

"That, my dear Diana," Geoffrey said softly, "is passion."

Well, well. She had been missing out on more than she realized. She lay back a moment, savoring the feeling, wishing she could tell someone how magical it was. She could only tell *him.* And judging from the cocky smile on his face, he already knew. She wasn't sure how, but he *knew*.

Then something awful occurred to her. She sat up and pulled her skirts down to cover her delightfully sated flesh. "What about you? Don't you want to feel pleasure, too?"

"I got my pleasure from watching you get yours," he said smoothly as he rose to sit beside her. He was still breathing heavily, as if his exertions had tired him.

"I may not be quite a woman of the world," she said, "but even I know that's not how it works. You may have noticed that one of the charities we support is for 'fallen females.' Some of them are quite forthcoming about the process of becoming 'fallen.'"

"Are they now?" he said, cocking up one brow.

"You know perfectly well they are. They even told me where to buy sponges to keep me from bearing a child and how to use them." She nodded at the bulge outlined beautifully by the black silk of his breeches. "That's how I know you are not as . . . shall we say, *satisfied*, by our encounter as I am."

"Doesn't matter." A frown etched lines in his brow as he pulled out his watch. "By your own terms, you should leave here in fifteen minutes if you mean to preserve your reputation. So, we can either talk. Or you can pleasure me. Your choice."

Frustrated by how he always created situations where he couldn't go as far as she wanted, she stood up and smoothed her skirts. "I don't want to pleasure you. I don't want you to pleasure me. I want *us* to have a mutual enjoyment of pleasure the way married people do, which is clearly something you have no interest in."

As she started to move away, he caught her hand. "It's not that I don't want to. But I dare not marry until I'm sure of . . . certain matters."

"I'm not saying you should marry me. I've never said that. I'm *saying* I want to experience the same love-making that married people do. Because as wonderful as your pleasuring me *was*, it doesn't tell me if sharing a bed with a man is equally as enjoyable." She tugged her hand from his. "I've heard it can be painful for a woman."

"So I'm told." He rose, his face reddening. "But mainly, I'm trying not to ruin you."

"I don't care if you ruin me! Besides, if a man has relations with some widow he's just met, why do other men nudge and nod and congratulate him, but if a woman does the same with some man she actually knows, she's ruined?" She began brushing her skirts, trying to smooth them so no trace of their enjoyment . . . of *her* enjoyment remained. "I reject the idea that it ruins me in any way."

"So do I!" he said. "But the very care you're taking not to be seen with me demonstrates that you do accept the idea. Hell, at this very moment you're trying to hide what we did. You have no more choice in the matter than I do. Unfortunately, you and I don't run the world. We don't even run Great Britain."

She tipped up her chin. "Well, we should. We'd do a better job of it."

"I'll go tell the king at once," he said dryly. "I'm sure he and his ministers will step right down and allow us to take the throne."

Diana swallowed the tears gathering in her throat. "I should like to see that." She patted her hair, hoping it hadn't become too disheveled. She wanted to cry but knew she didn't dare. Showing up in a ballroom with red eyes and a red nose would get all the tongues to wagging.

Which just proved his point, curse him!

Geoffrey pulled her into his embrace. "If you really wish to share my bed, I will not say no. What man would? We could do it here. But we'll have to come up with a way to meet that won't attract notice."

She sighed. "I'll think on it. I'm sure I can figure out something."

"If anyone can, it's you." He glanced at his watch. "You'd better go. I'll need some time to . . . deal with my bulging breeches."

That made her smile. "How exactly do you mean to—"

"Never you mind," he grumbled. "You'll find out soon enough."

"Then I'll see you at supper."

"I've already had my supper," he said in a husky voice, his eyes alight. "Quite a good one, actually."

"Oh, dear, I know *that* look," she said. "I'd best leave."

Thankfully, she was able to slip out of the room, climb the stairs, and dash toward the retiring room before anyone saw her. But as she walked into the room to find it empty save for one dozing lady, she couldn't help wondering why he still wouldn't tell her the source of his reluctance to marry. It made no sense to her.

One thing at a time, Diana, she told herself. *One thing at a time*.

Chapter Fourteen

They all left Almack's at two a.m. As soon as Geoffrey and Rosy picked up their mother at Grosvenor Square and headed for home, he started unknotting the draconian torture device called a fashionable cravat.

"Geoffrey!" Mother said. "You should at least leave it on until we get to Grenwood House. What if we have an accident and someone sees you like that?"

"If we have an accident," he said, "everyone will be far more concerned about the carriage shaft sticking out of my chest than whether I'm wearing a cravat."

"Heavens!" his mother said. "How gruesome!"

"Very well. The carriage shaft sticking out of my—"

"That's enough about carriage shafts sticking out of one's body," she said with a roll of her eyes. Then she turned to Rosy. "I want to hear all about the ball."

Good God, not again. He'd heard more than enough about it on the way from Almack's to Grosvenor Square. "I can tell it to you in one minute," Geoffrey said. "Rosy danced nearly every dance. She went in to supper—which, by the way, was as awful as I'd heard—on the arm of an earl. She was the toast of the ball."

"Not the toast, Geoffrey," Rosy said. "But I do think I got on pretty well with most people."

He laughed. "Poppet, that's the understatement of the century. You got on well with everyone . . . because you were your usual self—kind and considerate, not joining in the nastiness of the gossips." He looked at his mother. "During the only dance Rosy had no partner, she chatted with a woman who, as chance would have it, was the aging mother of a Lady Patroness, who, of course, took an instant liking to Rosy. Later, my sister put some bashful young fellow at ease enough for him to ask her to dance. It turned out his father was a foreign prince. Both he and his son were most grateful."

He shook his head. "After that, even the most hardened society dowagers looked on her with approval." His sister had a habit of wandering where angels feared to tread and coming out on the other side triumphant. He only hoped her luck stood her in good stead if the family scandal ever broke. Once one had been tarred and feathered in the court of public opinion, it was virtually impossible to become completely clean again.

"So far, that all sounds *wonderful*!" Mother said, then turned back to Rosy. "But I need details. With whom did you dance? How many times? Do I know any of them?"

Geoffrey groaned. Why did women always want details?

Like Diana. She kept pushing him to explain, to do

more . . . to take her innocence. And God, how he wanted to. If he could have a wife, she would be his first choice.

But he couldn't, not yet. Not if he meant to protect his sister and mother from disaster. Perhaps once enough time had lapsed, and the chatter in Newcastle about the manner of Father's death had settled down, Geoffrey could settle down, too.

He sighed. If anything, that chatter would grow now that he'd inherited the dukedom. No, he couldn't expose any fine lady to that, especially not Diana, who'd endured plenty of scandal already. Bad enough that his sister and mother might suffer through it, too.

"What has you so quiet, Son?" Mother asked.

He forced a smile. "Nothing, why?"

Rosy nudged their mother. "He went missing for nearly an hour before we went in to supper."

"Did he, now?" Mother arched one brow.

"Foxstead and I went out to get some food and drink we'd stashed in his carriage," Geoffrey said.

"That's ridiculous," Rosy said. "Foxstead was dancing with Verity. I remember it quite clearly because I was dancing with . . ."

When she paused, he narrowed his gaze on her.

Then she waved her hand dismissively. "Oh, I can't remember his name. Some lord or other. As you can imagine, I found him quite dull."

That didn't sound like his sister, but a bit of society haughtiness might have rubbed off on her. The fellow would have had to be *very* dull for her to have mentioned it. She tended to be more generous with her descriptions.

"So where were you?" Mother asked Geoffrey.

Damn it. She'd sniffed something suspicious and wouldn't let go unless he gave her a believable tale.

Or a patently unbelievable one. "I sneaked out to seduce one of the Lady Patronesses," he said with a straight face.

"Geoffrey Arthur Brookhouse!" his mother exclaimed.

"You did not," Rosy said with a worldly air. "None of the Lady Patronesses were terribly happy to see you there. And they're all married anyway."

"Hence the need to sneak out," he said.

"I swear," his mother said, "one of these days you're going to make up an outrageous story and there will be just enough truth in it to make people believe you did something, whether you did it or not."

That was precisely what he was afraid of.

They arrived home, and he said good night to the ladies, even though he had no intention of going to bed yet. Instead, he headed to his study to have his first whisky of the night. Almack's was notorious for not providing spirits or wine because the Lady Patronesses wanted the men to be sober. How they expected a man, especially one who couldn't dance, to endure that place sober was anyone's guess. He'd begun to wish he'd brought a flask.

After pouring his glass of whisky, he collapsed in the comfortable chair he'd had transported from Newcastle. Good God, how he hated the round of parties, musicales, balls, fêtes, and whatever other nonsense London high society could dream up to plague him with. But he would keep doing it for Rosy.

Like a dog licking a sore, he got up and went to unlock the top desk drawer. For a moment, he just stared down at the letter. Then he drew it out, handling it carefully because he never wanted his repeated readings to damage it. He might one day need it, after all.

He'd read the damned thing a hundred times, but had still never found a solution to the dilemma Father had put him in. Not that his father had meant the letter to be a solution. No, indeed. His father had intended it to be insurance. Instead, it had become a two-edged sword that could slice Geoffrey's life to ribbons no matter which way it cut.

Staring down at it, he realized he wasn't in the right frame of mind to look at it tonight. He would much rather go to bed and dream of the lovely Diana, and her insistence that he and she find a way to swive.

He chuckled. The woman was quite the adventurer. After downing the rest of his whisky, he went upstairs to his bedchamber and undressed himself, because he'd given his valet the night off. Diana was the only good thing about this round of social nonsense. She made him laugh. She enticed him in a way no woman had ever done. He couldn't believe that Englishmen had considered her unacceptable as a prospective wife because of some silly scandal that wasn't even half as awful as the one he was hoping to spare her from enduring. But he was beginning to learn that aristocrats didn't always make sense.

Her willingness to give her virtue to him made no sense either. Still, he was more than ready to instruct her in the bedroom arts, as long as he could do it without ruining her. She might not accept the idea that a chaste woman could be ruined, but it existed all the same, and he would do his damnedest to make sure that rumors of her desire to be deflowered never got out. He owed her that, at least.

The idea of her in his bed . . . Bloody hell, it made him hard again. He could still smell her, still feel her coming beneath his mouth, still hear the sweet little sounds of satisfaction she made. He couldn't wait to have her in full.

Now he just had to figure out how to meet with her privately without raising anyone's suspicion. It wasn't as easy as it might seem. She had nosy sisters, and he had a nosy sister and mother both.

He lay in his bed, staring up at the canopy. The design was flowers of all sorts on a creamy background. He recognized the roses, geraniums, and daisies, but the other blooms were not as easy to tease out. It didn't help that he knew little about gardening. He'd given the gardener for Grenwood House carte blanche to do anything with it so long as his sister approved. She was the gardener of the family.

Now he wondered if Diana liked gardens. She'd been keen to have the dinner outside, before the weather had turned too chilly. God knows there was plenty of acreage for it, even here in the midst of London. There were parts of the extensive gardens so private that . . .

That was it! He knew precisely how to get Diana alone without alerting any of their nosy family members or servants to what they were doing. He'd have to rise early, though. He needed to prepare.

He fell asleep still staring up at the canopy with a smile on his lips.

Late the next morning, Diana lay in bed, reliving every moment of her interaction with Geoffrey at the lodgings he had rented in the Almack's building. But it wasn't enough for her. She wanted to experience everything.

Ooh, it was so infuriating! A woman like her ought to be able to enjoy certain things without being branded for life. But as Geoffrey had said, that was the way the world worked, and no one was going to make an exception for her.

Frustrated, she rose and dressed, then headed downstairs for breakfast. She wasn't surprised to find herself alone at the table. After being out late last night, everyone was sleeping until noon at least. Except her. Because she couldn't sleep for thinking of how to see him privately again.

If she left the house alone, she'd have to take a footman for propriety's sake—for *safety's* sake, to be honest—and footmen weren't as discreet as they should be. At the very least, the servant would tell her sisters about her jaunt if she went anywhere but to Grenwood House for an appointment.

Very well. Then she'd go to Grenwood House. And if she left while everyone was still abed here, she wouldn't have to endure an onslaught of questions about why and where she was going. Not to mention her sisters' endless teasing about her and the duke, whom they were convinced was on the verge of marrying her or ruining her. Which one they chose depended on the day, the time, the weather, and Lord knew what else, probably which way the wind blew.

She would merely leave a note saying she'd gone to Grenwood House to consult with Geoffrey's mother about Rosy's upcoming ball. That was vague enough, wasn't it?

She hurried about and was surprised she was able to be off fairly quickly. That was what happened when you didn't have to manage two drowsy sisters. It was nearly noon by the time she arrived at Grenwood House. Unfortunately, she wasn't quite sure what she meant to do now that she was there.

Fortunately, Geoffrey practically met her at the door. "I see you got my message."

"Your message?"

"Never mind." He cast a veiled glance at the various servants hovering close by, eager to see any confrontation between him and Diana. "You're here. That's all that matters. Do walk with me. I had an epiphany about your idea of having the ball supper outdoors, weather permitting. The date for the ball coincides with the full moon, you know."

"I do know. That's why we picked it." When had she ever considered having the ball supper outdoors? Because whenever that was, she'd been daft or foxed to think it. Everyone's dancing shoes would be like paper on the gravel garden paths. The only reason it would have worked for last week's dinner was they could have confined it to the terrace, which had a smooth marble surface.

But with two hundred guests, that wouldn't be possible. The terrace simply wasn't large enough.

"This way, Lady Diana," he said, offering her his arm. "I'll have to show you."

She took his arm readily. She did have to admit it was a gorgeous day for walking in the gardens. The sun was shining, the robins flying, the starlings warbling, and the roses blooming. Who could say no to that?

The minute they left the house, however, he wanted to talk. "Do you still want a lesson in . . . er . . . marital bliss?"

Her heart began pounding. "Why? Have you thought of a way to do it without being caught by any of our relations?"

"Or the servants." He gave her a smoldering look. "Yes."

That was when the truth occurred to her. "This isn't about serving the ball supper outdoors at all."

"Of course not. In fact, when I said that, I was worried you might protest the very idea."

She chuckled. "I would have, but I was curious to hear your argument. Besides which, it's too lovely a day to pass up a visit to the garden."

"I hate to disappoint you, but we're not actually visiting the garden. It's far too close to the house. We're going to a little building at the other end."

Her pulse quickened, and, when he covered her hand with his, grew positively frenzied. "Is it anything I've seen? I've been too busy inside your house to wander that far afield."

"It's not very big, to be honest. But I came out this morning to see if it's usable, and it's in better shape than I thought."

"That sounds ominous. What kind of building is this?"

"You'll see in a moment." His voice grew husky. "I mean to seduce you, dear Diana. Assuming that is still what you want."

She gazed up at him, her blood racing to see how hungrily he regarded her. "Most assuredly."

He rounded a bend in the path, and at the end, nearly surrounded by birches and lime trees, was a small stone building with a chimney and a large open window. It was as tall as some of the trees and bore no resemblance to the main house.

"That is . . . the oddest building I've seen in London, I think, and that's saying something. What is it?"

He stopped, as if bracing himself for her protests. "It's a laboratory."

She pulled away, then planted her hands on her hips. "You want to make love to me in a laboratory."

"It's not a laboratory anymore. And even when it was, I doubt my predecessor used it much. He had it built because his wife didn't want him playing around with chemicals inside the house."

"Clever woman," Diana said.

"It's not perfect for our purposes, I daresay, but sadly, everyone will notice if we disappear into my private quarters. And you may not *want* to care about being ruined, but we both know that you do."

She sighed. "I wouldn't wish my sisters to suffer any embarrassment."

"How about this?" he said, tugging her by one arm toward the little building. "Just look at it. No one ever comes back here, and my predecessor wasn't a very good scientist, apparently, so it doesn't even smell of chemicals. Much. I've had the window and door open all morning so the scents of the flowers can waft through it. As a matter of fact . . ." He hurried ahead of her to go inside, then came out with his arms full of lilies. "I set these in there hoping to help the smell even more."

"Flowers for the deflowering?" she quipped.

"Something like that," he said, his eyes intent on watching her reaction when he handed them to her.

She couldn't help but soften. She did love lilies. She sniffed the blooms as he urged her toward the door. Once she entered, she caught her breath. In one corner were several plush cushions of assorted sizes, fabrics, and colors, obviously all placed there in anticipation of their rendezvous.

"Please tell me the servants didn't bring those out here for you," she said.

"I carried them all out myself. And made sure no one saw me doing it."

She shook her head and laughed. "Yes, I'm sure they didn't notice His Grace hauling a pile of cushions out to the garden."

"The back of the garden. Where no one ever goes." He took the lilies from her and placed them on a marble tabletop right behind her, a maneuver that crowded her in until she was standing right up against the table's edge. Not that she minded having him this close. He smelled downright fragrant today.

"Don't lie to me," she said. "You *are* wearing Hungary water, aren't you?"

"I wondered if you would notice," he said with a grin. "After you mentioned it, I thought that if you liked it, it might not be too bad. But the scent is making me hungry. For food, I mean."

"I daresay you're always hungry for food, but in this

case, the rosemary and thyme in it may be sharpening your appetite."

"Perhaps. Not to mention the wine the rosemary and thyme are soaked in. Which reminds me . . ." He reached under the table and pulled out a bottle and two glasses, then set them down behind her. "This place has another advantage. The marble and the darkness keep the champagne cool. Do you want some?"

I'd like some of everything you have to give me, sir. "Champagne? Of course. I have a weakness for champagne, I confess."

Wearing a sly expression, he opened the bottle and poured two glasses while she took off her bonnet and laid it on the table. The window was directly behind them, letting in a cool breeze.

"So, if I pour enough of it," he said as he handed her a glass, "you'll let me have my wicked way with you?"

After they'd each had a couple of swallows, she put her glass to the side. "Or you'll let *me* have my wicked way with *you,*" she said, and started unknotting his cravat. "I mean to seduce you, dear Duke, assuming that's still what you want."

"I've been wanting that since the day we met," he said roughly.

She faltered. "The day we met? That long ago? You hid it well."

"I don't know how I managed to hide anything, honestly." His gaze dropped to her bodice, where her fichu-cravate was loosely tied. He began to untie it. "Every time you stuck that damned pencil in your mouth, I found myself wondering what it would be like to . . .

thrust my tongue in your mouth. To be your pencil, as it were."

She burst into laughter, which clearly startled him. "I couldn't figure out why you kept staring at my pencil! Oh, Lord, I should have realized it was something . . . naughty."

He'd finally worked loose her fichu-cravate and taken it off, apparently not even aware when he'd dropped it on the floor in his eagerness to look at what she wore beneath it. "Now, *this* is naughty," he said. Her gown was perfectly presentable with the fichu and very definitely *not* presentable without. "Did you wear this for me?" he rasped, as he ran a finger along her low-cut bodice.

"Of course," she said in what she hoped was a sufficiently seductive voice. "It's the only gown I have that unfastens in the front."

Even as his gaze burned into her, he groaned. "You're a bit of a tease, aren't you, my lady?"

"If you say so." She tugged off his cravat and draped it around the champagne bottle. "I don't really know what I'm doing."

"You know all right. You just don't know you know."

While she was trying to make that one out, he walked over to the pile of cushions, picked up a nice fat one, and brought it back to toss onto the table. Then he examined her gown. "I can't figure out where it unfastens."

She could understand that. Men rarely understood the mysteries of female garments, and telling him it was an apron-front gown would be about as informative to him as calling it a dress in Chinese. "Just watch." She unfastened the two decorative buttons on her shoulders and let the front drop down.

Before she could do more than that, he'd unpinned the part covering her corset and shift, then unfastened the ties that kept the skirt in place, allowing the entire business to fall open from her neck to her pelvis.

"Well!" she said. "It didn't take you long to figure out how *that* worked once I got it started."

"I keep telling you, I'm an engineer. I'm a quick study at things like figuring out how something is put together." His gaze skimmed her in a provocative sweep meant to entice her. "And now I wish to figure out how *you're* put together." With that, he lifted her up and set her down on the cushion.

"What do you think you're doing?" she cried. "There's a window behind me!"

"I'm aware." He stretched past her to close the window. "But it's in full sun, so I'll see anyone approaching long before they see you. Besides which, this clever gown of yours will look perfectly respectable from behind." His eyes burned into hers. "But erotic as hell from the front."

The thrill that his words gave her seared her from her head to her privates, making her squirm a bit on the cushion. "Geoffrey—"

His kiss cut her off. It was hard and fierce and somehow lavish, too, like a working sword in an ornamental scabbard. He took his time kissing her as he pulled down her corset, then untied her shift and maneuvered it until it lay beneath her bare breasts, lifting them a bit for his gaze. Next thing she knew, he'd kissed his way down to her nipples, so he could suck and tease them in turn, sending frissons through her that had her trembling with need.

Raking his hair back with her fingers, she found the collar of his coat and hooked it with her thumbs on either side so she could tug it off. Or try futilely to, anyway, until he realized what she was doing and shrugged it off for her before tossing it over onto the cushions.

But when she unbuttoned his waistcoat, he wouldn't let her push that off, too. "If your family comes looking for you," he warned, "we must be able to dress quickly. But if you're looking for a way to occupy those deft hands of yours . . ." He swiftly unbuttoned the fall of his pantaloon trousers, then lowered the falls to expose his drawers.

They were expanding rather impressively. As she stared at them, they seemed to expand even more.

He chuckled. "As I said, a tease." He tugged her hand down to cover him there. "But I don't mind, as long as I get what I want in the end."

"And what is that?" she asked in a breathy whisper.

"The two of us intimately joined." He bent close. "But first, rub me . . . *please*. You have no idea how many times I've dreamed of having my . . . er . . . pencil in your hand."

It was her turn to laugh. "I've never heard it called that by the 'fallen females.'" She stroked his aroused flesh through his drawers, marveling at how he responded so readily to her touch. "And this is quite a bit more . . . substantial than a pencil."

"I'm trying to be . . . a gentleman," he choked out. "But

that's probably fruitless . . . I have no self-control where you're concerned." He grabbed her hand. "God, enough." He undid his drawers, then shoved both his pantaloon trousers and his drawers down below his behind. "I need to be inside you, sweetling."

Inside. She was trying to decide if she still wanted that. Because what she could see of his . . . interesting equipment was rather daunting. The rod of flesh, jutting out as if seeking company, and the red bollocks. This was the moment. He meant to enter her with that. Would it hurt *too* very much? Or would it be like so many other things—something that didn't live up to its reputation?

"Try not to worry," he rasped, his gaze centered on her. How had he guessed? Was she that transparent?

"You know how this works?" he asked. "Your 'fallen females' told you?"

"They did. Although I had a hard time believing it at first."

This second mention of the "fallen females" reminded her—she hadn't thought to bring her sponge! But she wasn't about to risk telling him and having him stop now. Besides, how likely was it that she would find herself with child from one encounter?

"I will take it very slowly, I swear." He fingered her between her legs until she moaned low in her throat. "Do you trust me?"

"Of course." She grabbed his arms. "I want this, too, you know." Partly to emphasize that and partly just because she ached for more, she pushed her mons against his hand, prompting him to fondle her more. "Oh, yes, that's *splendid*."

"Then let's get you a bit more comfortable," he said with a cheeky grin, and shoved her skirts to the top of her thighs. When he lifted her off the cushion enough to push the fabric up around her waist so her bare bottom sat on the cushion, she couldn't help marveling at his strength.

He pulled up her knees on either side of him. His motions were so swift that she had a moment of panic. Then he used his hand to continue arousing her, waiting until she relaxed some before he oh so slowly pushed his aroused flesh into her.

Well! That was interesting. It didn't so much hurt as seem like an intrusion. A rather large intrusion in a rather tight place.

"Are you . . . all right?" he asked, as if hesitant to hear her answer.

"As soon as I adjust to it, I will be." She hoped. She prayed, although it was probably blasphemous to pray for God to make her fornication more comfortable.

Oh, she didn't want to think about that. So she pulled down his head, placed his free hand on her breast, and kissed him with all the wantonness she could muster. If she must be a sinner, she would make sure to be good at it.

"You feel . . . glorious," he whispered against her mouth. "Wet and sweet and capable of bringing me to my knees, I fear." Then he began to move in and out below. He shifted his hand from her breast to the small of her back so he could pull her into him. "Lock your legs behind my arse."

"Language, Geoffrey," she teased him, but did what he'd ordered.

Good heavens, but *that* certainly made a difference. Her body shifted marvelously to meet his forward motion, and suddenly each of his thrusts thrummed a very sensitive part of her privates, starting a sort of pleasurable hum between her legs that got stronger by the thrust.

Soon they were in a rocking motion, with her nearly half off the table as he drove into her in thundering, silken plunges that took her by surprise. So very hot . . . and raw . . . and *wonderful*.

It wasn't magical or mystical or any of those soft, hazy feelings. It was earthy, like rain and lightning, like river water rushing over rocks. They were gasping for air together, panting hard, until she didn't know whose breath was whose.

"Geoffrey . . . *Geoffrey* . . ." she said hoarsely, her body wrapped around him, clinging to him so he could show her the way.

"Whatever you want . . . is yours . . . my goddess Diana. . . ."

For a man who said he didn't wish to marry, he certainly was possessive.

Now she felt as if he were dangling fruit above her, urging her to reach for it, grab for it. She had to have it, a sheer, unadulterated need for it taking her over more and more by the minute. Her pleasure seemed just beyond reach. She jumped, stretched toward it, had to have it, had to have *him,* faster and harder, pushing her higher so maybe she could . . . just . . . get it. . . .

"Oh my," she whispered as her ache for it rose to a fever pitch within her that spurred her that last inch up. "That's . . . quite . . . Oh, God, Geoffrey . . . Geoffrey . . . yes!"

And with that she finally tasted her fruit of paradise.

Chapter Fifteen

The words *Oh, God, Geoffrey* rang in his ears as he felt Diana's muscles clench repeatedly around his cock, cuing his own release. He should have pulled out, but he couldn't bring himself to leave the delicious warmth of her satin flesh, the place he wished to stay forever. So instead he poured his seed into her and prayed it didn't take root.

"Sweetling . . . you . . . you . . . slay me," he whispered as he felt his cock dying, shrinking, now that he'd come.

He had never understood why the French called an orgasm *la petite mort*, "the little death." Until now. Having to leave her, to slip out of her and know that this might be the last time he was inside her was a kind of death.

Especially with Diana. She said she only wanted to experience pleasure with him. But what if she didn't want only that? Did he dare risk her future by marrying her? Dragging her into the family scandal that still might come any day? She'd lived through scandal once. Why would she want to go through it again? Especially when it could lead to something far worse. That would spell death to their marriage.

She was still shaking in his arms, which only made him want to hold her closer. Then she lifted her lips to his ear and murmured, "I forgot my sponge. But to be fair, I didn't know we would be doing this . . . so soon."

"Marry me," he answered, surprising himself. Hadn't he just been thinking of why they couldn't marry?

Then, realizing it was more a command than a question, he drew back and kissed her squarely on the lips before announcing, "We should marry."

Her eyes went wide. Then she slid off the table and averted her gaze as she began to fix her clothes. "Why? Because we had an enjoyable time together?"

"Because . . ." *Because I want you again and again. Because every day I look forward to when I'll see you. Because you are the one bright thing getting me through the endless dark aftermath of Father's death.*

He said none of those things. They would be too telling. Instead, he pulled up his drawers and pantaloon trousers to cover himself, then picked up the bloodied cushion and handed it to her. "I took your innocence. That's why."

Flinching at the words, she handed the cushion back to him. "I told you before, our . . . swiving isn't and never was about trapping you into marriage. It was about determining if I could find the physical part of marriage appealing. And I learned what I needed to know."

Did he dare ask? "And what did you decide?"

"I don't know if I should tell you," she said archly, though she kept restoring her clothes, tying here, buttoning there. "Your head is already twice the size it should be."

He laughed. "I come from a long line of bigheaded chaps." He buttoned his drawers and then his trousers. "Just ask my mother."

"I'd rather not. I wouldn't be able to do so without blushing, I fear." When he said nothing to that, she released a long breath. "Let's just say I can now understand why sharing a bed with a man has its . . . attractions."

"But?"

Her head jerked up. "What makes you think there's a 'but'?"

"Because you're resisting my offer of marriage when any other woman would be begging me to wed her now that I've deflowered her." He stared her down, daring her to answer him.

"If you'd been in my position for the past four years, don't you think you'd prefer spinsterhood to marriage, too?"

"The past four—" He paused. "Oh. Right. Your parents." And how could he have been such an arse as to forget that?

"I've seen what a bad marriage looks like. It's not pretty, and it affects more than just the married couple— it affects the children, too." She found her fichu and looped it around her neck before tying it much the same way a man might knot a cravat. "I'd like to think I would handle it better than my mother and certainly better than Papa, but who knows? Until I have my own children, there's no way to be sure."

"Speaking of children," he said, "what if you find yourself—"

"I would marry you, yes. A child should never have

to suffer. And let me say again that I'm very sorry I forgot my sponge."

"Don't be. I could have brought a French letter just as easily. I should have, just to be safe. But then I would have had to purchase one, because I have none with me in London."

She cocked her head. "What good would a letter do, in French or any other language?"

He chuckled. She always had this odd mixture of innocence and worldly knowing about her. Perhaps that was what drew him to her. He never knew what to expect. "I'm speaking of a condom."

"Oh! I've heard of those." The expression of dawning awareness on her face was comical. "So *that's* how they work. When the fallen females showed me one, all flat and limp, I couldn't conceive of its being very effective, but I guess it wasn't filled up." To cover her sudden blush, she said, "And it's called a French letter, too? Why?"

"Hell, I have no idea." When she opened her mouth, he added, "Don't you dare say, 'Language, Geoffrey.' My mother says that, and I won't have a wife who does, too."

"Then stop cursing," she said primly. "And anyway, I haven't agreed to *be* your wife, not that you were serious in your offer."

"I *was* serious."

"Really?" She crossed her arms over her now respectably covered chest, which reminded him that he'd best finish dressing himself, before someone came along. "So you've suddenly changed your mind about marrying? Now you want a wife?"

"No . . . I mean, yes, but . . ."

"You see?" She put on her bonnet, tying the ribbons under her chin. "You have a 'but,' too."

"I suppose I do." He buttoned up his waistcoat with a sigh. "Tell me this. Do you believe a man should protect his family? Make sure no harm comes to them, even if it means he has to deny himself something?" *Like the woman he wants?*

"If his family can't protect themselves, I suppose. But that's not the issue here. The issue is that you wanted to know all my reasons for being reluctant to marry, but you don't want to share any of yours."

He came up close to her. "Your reasons can't ruin anyone. Your reasons won't have repercussions for years to come, decades possibly, if you choose to share them with the wrong person."

Her gaze narrowed on him. "And I suppose you think I could be the wrong person."

Damn, he shouldn't have put it that way. "I didn't say that."

"You didn't have to." She turned to leave, then stopped to look back at him. "You won't trust me with your secrets, and perhaps I can understand why." He'd just started to relax, to feel relief that she *did* accept his reasons for keeping things private, when her tone turned sarcastic. "After all, we've only known each other a month. And only a short while ago, you were *inside me.*"

He winced at that.

But she scarcely noticed. "I've heard every intimate secret of your sister's and your mother's—apparently *they* trust me. How do you know they haven't already told me what you're hiding so closely?"

"Because *they* don't know it. And I'd prefer to keep it that way. Hence my refusal to tell *you*."

"You haven't—" She gaped at him. "Good heavens! If I were them, I'd never forgive you. Why do men always assume that women can't keep important secrets? They can and do, all the time, especially where their families are concerned. Besides, if I had a mind to ruin you, I could do so just by accusing you of . . . of seducing me, or of injuring my sisters or any number of things."

"You could," he said, irritated by her refusal to recognize that he wasn't ready to tell her these things. "But then I wouldn't pay you and your sisters what you're owed."

She stared him down. "You're an arse, do you know that?"

"Language, Diana," he said as he retied his cravat. He could see from her reddening face that those words really set her off. But then, she was setting *him* off right now.

"Ohhh, you are so . . . you make me . . . Ooh! Why in the world I would ever even *want* to marry you is beyond me." She tipped up her chin. "Thank you for the lesson in lovemaking, Your Grace. It was most enjoyable. But what happened afterward was enough to give me a sense of how marriage to you would be, and I do believe I can do without that experience, thank you very much!"

She marched out of the laboratory and up the path through the gardens, heedless of the blow she'd struck to his heart.

No, not *heart*. This wasn't anything absurd like that. Because if it were, he would be in a world of trouble. He watched her until she disappeared around the corner of the house. Then he started roaming the room, throwing cushions, and in general behaving like a child.

Or an arse. He halted to stare at the wall. God, she was right. He *was* an arse. But she made him insane when she . . . demanded things he couldn't give her.

Like your trust?

"Shut up!" he shouted at his conscience. "Why do you have to jump on my every little error and rub my face in it?"

"Excuse me," said a female voice from the doorway. "Is this a bad time? Should I come back?"

With a scowl, he rounded on Verity, who was looking furtively about the room as if wondering to whom he was speaking. "Yes," he snapped. "It's a bad time. But come in anyway. Why not?"

Now even more wary than before, Verity edged her way into the building. "I met Diana as she was coming across the lawn. She said you'd been showing her a self-contained laboratory? Is this it?"

"It is." He forced himself to calm down, to hide the truth of what he and Diana had been doing in here. "Forgive me for being short with you. I'm a bit concerned about the upcoming ball, as you might imagine." He nearly choked on the lie. He doubted he'd ever be concerned about any ball, but he had to give *some* reason for raging aloud at his conscience.

"Not nearly as concerned as I am," she said. "Your cook is inexperienced with food for ball suppers. I gather that your predecessor rarely entertained."

"He died at the age of ninety-one, so I doubt he'd done so in decades."

"I think you're right. I never heard that he had any parties."

Silence fell between them. He liked Verity generally,

although she was a bit *too* artistic for his tastes. Diana at least had a sensible head on her shoulders.

"May I ask a question?" Verity said, then went on without waiting for his answer. "What are the cushions for? Does it have something to do with this being a former laboratory?"

It has to do with your damned sister sending you back here to torment me while she made good her escape.

No, he couldn't say that, of course. He probably should go on with the ruse he'd created with Diana earlier, despite how ridiculous it had made him seem. "I was trying to convince Diana that we should have the ball supper outside under the moonlight. The moon is supposed to be full that night, you know."

"I do. That's why we picked that date."

God, she sounded so much like her sister, it was maddening. "Anyway, I was thinking that the cooks could be back here using the hearth for whatever was needed, and the footmen could grab the trays of champagne glasses through the window."

Verity lifted an eyebrow. "One window. For enough trays of champagne to serve two hundred people."

He feigned a sigh. "Your sister didn't like the idea either."

"Even after you plied her with champagne?" Verity nodded to the two glasses sitting there with the bottle.

He was starting to get testy again. "I just wanted her to taste it before I ordered enough for the ball."

Verity walked over and swigged some right out of the bottle. "Even after being uncorked, that champagne tastes very expensive, Your Grace. I don't think you have any idea how much this particular champagne for that many guests would cost you."

"Oh, I think I do." He crossed his arms over his chest. "Which is why we settled on a slightly less expensive one."

Verity smiled brightly. "Excellent. That's one thing off my list." She nodded toward the corner. "And the cushions?"

Damn, he should just tell the woman he'd been seducing her sister. It would be easier and make him look less like a dolt.

And more like a . . . well . . . seducer. Not to mention that Diana would have his head if he did. "Those were here when I came. I think the footmen store the extra cushions in here."

"Right. Instead of in a closet or attic, away from the weather but easy to access from inside the house."

She laughed and turned for the door. Then she paused, as if thinking, before she faced him again, this time looking quite sober. "Honestly, Your Grace, the next time you and my sister wish to steal a moment or two to kiss or—" She held up one hand. "I don't want to know. But you'd better let her come up with the lies. Because you are very bad at them. I mean, if Eliza had been the one to come in here, she wouldn't even have let you past the part about the champagne before she started blistering your ears."

"And you?" he asked. "Are you going to blister my ears?"

"I'll do more than that if you dare to hurt Diana. For now, I'll wait and see. I know she likes you. Just see that you don't take advantage of that. We may not have a father or husband in our house to protect us, but we do have Mr. Norris, and I understand he is a crack shot."

"Norris?" he scoffed. "You're joking."

"Not one bit. He was in the Royal Navy. I believe he was with Admiral Nelson at Trafalgar. But after that engagement, he sold his commission. Too much blood and death, he said. So, have a care with my sister's heart. Or you'll see how much he still remembers about how to cause blood and death."

And with that final salvo, she left.

Bloody hell, those Harper sisters were not to be trifled with, were they? No wonder they were able to pick and choose their clients. Not only did they know what they were talking about when it came to society, but as sisters they stood together.

He had a sneaking suspicion he had just lost this particular battle, and on two fronts. He would have to be more clever next time.

Diana was in the drawing room of Grenwood House trying to figure out how they should arrange the furniture for the ball when her sister waltzed in.

"Good Lord, Diana, what the devil have you done to that man?" Verity said as she plopped down on the sofa. "You should have heard the ridiculous tale the duke just spun me."

With a scowl, Diana walked over to examine the fire screen. "About what?"

"What the two of you were doing in the laboratory."

Her heart froze in her chest. She whirled to face her sister. "You can't believe a word he says."

"Oh, I don't. Not for a moment do I think he took you

back there to convince you that the ball supper should be held outside."

Diana nearly collapsed with relief. "Actually, he did suggest it." Sort of. And because the servants had overheard him doing so, Verity would hear nothing to gainsay that.

"Did he also suggest you should have the footmen fetching their serving trays of champagne through that one window?"

"He did mention it." *A pox on you, Geoffrey Brookhouse. Couldn't you have come up with something more believable?* "Of course, I told him that would never work."

Verity narrowed her gaze on Diana. "Did he tell you that the cushions were stored there as a general rule?"

Diana returned to looking over the fire screen for imaginary flaws. "Well, no. He didn't say that to me. That would be absurd."

"That's what I said. To him, I mean."

Diana could feel her sister's gaze boring into her back. "What do you want to know?"

"I want to hear *your* version of what you two were doing there."

"That's none of your concern," Diana snapped.

Verity came up behind her to slip her arms about Diana's waist. "Don't be angry. I just don't want to see you hurt."

Diana turned to hug her sister. "I know. And he's not going to hurt me. He's just . . . Sometimes he can be . . ."

"An arse?"

Diana laughed. "Yes. Precisely." She drew back to look at her sister. "But the rest of the time, he turns me into mush when he looks at me. Did Lord Minton ever do that to you?"

Verity sighed. "Very rarely."

"Well, then, I'm glad he showed his true dastardly character by jilting you."

"Me too."

"Because someone else will come along who will make your heart race and your knees buckle, and thanks to Lord Minton's cowardice, you will be free to marry *that* man."

Verity eyed her askance. "Now you're just being absurd."

"Not a bit! I think—"

Someone cleared their throat in the doorway. Diana and Verity both turned to find Rosy standing there.

"Diana? Could I talk to you? Privately?"

Diana forced a smile. "Of course."

With a nod, Verity murmured something about consulting with Cook in the kitchen and left the room.

Diana took a seat on the sofa, then patted the place beside her. "You can talk to me about anything you like any time you like, Rosy. We're friends."

"Thank you." Rosy sat down stiffly next to Diana on the sofa. "There's no sense in mincing words. What's laudanum?"

Diana blinked. She'd assumed that Rosy wanted to talk about something involving her début. Not medicines, and certainly not one as powerful—and potentially devastating—as laudanum could be. "Why do you wish to know?"

"You can't tell Mama and Geoffrey about it, and you can't tell him I asked you about it."

Good Lord, this family was as secretive as her own.

"Why don't we talk about it first, before deciding how it should be handled? If that means keeping it secret, I will certainly do so. All right?"

Rosy bobbed her head. "Well, the day Papa died, Mama wasn't home. She'd gone out of town to spend the night helping my ill aunt—Mama's sister—and she was expected back before suppertime. She left me and Geoffrey in charge of Papa, who'd been feeling poorly the past week. We thought he had a stomach complaint like he'd had dozens of times before."

Rosy pulled out her handkerchief to dab at her eyes. "When I came in to check on him, he'd already sent his manservant to fetch the doctor, and he asked me to get Geoffrey. So I did. Then he sent me to fetch him some ale. By the time I got back with it, the doctor had come to examine him."

She sighed. "Geoffrey sent me on another errand, but I couldn't stand not knowing what the doctor had to say, so I hid outside the door and just . . . sort of eavesdropped. Papa told the doctor he mistook his bottle of laudanum for his bottle of tincture of rhubarb and took too much. The doctor tried to give him other medicine, but it was no use. Papa had been ill already, and the laudanum was the last straw, I suppose."

Good Lord, Diana had no idea what to make of this. Why had their father been taking laudanum anyway? "Was there an inquest?"

"No. Geoffrey said the doctor ruled it as accidental, so there was no need." Rosy slanted her gaze up at Diana. "You know. On account of the laudanum he took wrongly. The bottle was empty, so the doctor took it and the tincture of rhubarb away with him in case there *was* an inquest later, and he had to testify. But Geoffrey made the doctor promise not to tell Mama about the laudanum."

"Did *you* tell her? Or ask her or Geoffrey about the laudanum?"

"Are you daft? And risk Geoffrey being angry with me? No, thank you. I'd rather eat worms." Rosy's gaze turned troubled. "But lately, thinking of Papa . . . well, I just want to know what laudanum is and why it would make Papa so sick that he died."

Diana only knew that any amount of laudanum could be dangerous. When combined with strong drink, who knew what could happen?

The poor man. No wonder Geoffrey didn't talk much about his father. It must still be painful to know that the man had become dependent on laudanum to get through his days. That was what she assumed had happened anyway. Because what fool mistook laudanum for tincture of rhubarb?

But what was she to tell Rosy?

The truth, of course. The dear girl had endured enough worry as it was. "Laudanum is given for pain mostly, but it can also act as a poison if you take too much of it. No doubt when your father . . . er . . . made his mistake with the tincture of rhubarb, it was, as you said, 'the last straw.'"

"Then why doesn't Geoffrey want Mama to know about it?"

What had he said? *Because* they *don't know it. And I'd prefer to keep it that way. Hence my refusal to tell* you.

But that made no sense. Their father was dead regardless. There was little point in hiding a vice that part of good society already indulged in. Diana had always thought it a dangerous habit—and clearly she'd been right to do so—but no one generally considered it shameful. Or not *too* shameful anyway.

Then again, Geoffrey had strange ideas about such things. Who knew what he'd decided it meant?

Rosy was still eyeing her, patiently waiting for an explanation Diana didn't have. "Honestly, I don't know why your brother wants to keep it from your mother. I'm afraid you'll have to ask him. Anything I could say would be speculation."

"I can understand that, I suppose." With a sigh, Rosy looked down at her hands. "There's something else I need to know. It has nothing to do with Papa."

"All right."

"Did you . . . tell my brother that I danced with Lord Winston last night?"

That *was* quite a shift in subject, but one that made sense, given Rosy's current situation. "No. I saw no point." Diana kept a close eye on Rosy. "How was it? Did you find him as interesting as before?"

Her face lit up. "He's very funny. I like that about him."

"Me too."

Then Rosy caught herself. "But Lord Foxstead is funny, too. He was so kind to me. I just think he's a bit old. He's almost as old as Geoffrey."

Diana bit back a laugh. Foxstead was probably in his late twenties, not old by most people's reckoning. But Diana could see how he might seem so to a woman fresh out of the schoolroom.

Sometimes Geoffrey seemed older than he was. It was the weight of the world he kept placing on his own shoulders. One of these days she might actually get through that tough exterior of his and find out what made him so wary and why he didn't wish to marry right now.

Unless he just didn't wish to marry *her*.

She stiffened. If that were the case, to hell with him. She was a pretty woman with much to commend her. If he couldn't see that, it was his loss. She refused to waste her life waiting for him.

Chapter Sixteen

Geoffrey was at his wit's end. He hadn't seen Diana for more than a few minutes here and there in days. Between his meetings and her race to prepare Grenwood House for an influx of two hundred guests, they hadn't crossed paths very often.

And how they'd left things was beginning to weigh on him. Especially now that Rosy's début ball was here. Or almost here. He, Rosy, and Mother were assembled in the family parlor for inspection by Diana, who hadn't arrived yet. But he was more concerned about Rosy at present. She kept pacing around the parlor, probably nervous about the ball, and for the life of him, he didn't know what to say to her.

He'd seen Mother whispering to her, but it hadn't seemed to change her expression any. Perhaps *he* should say something. "You look beautiful, poppet."

Rosy's gaze flew to him, fraught with worry. "Do I really?"

"Of course. I wouldn't say so if you didn't. Besides, I did my gushing last time I saw your gown, remember?" When she nodded, as if incapable of doing more, he stifled a sigh. "Do I have to gush again? Because I'm not good at that, as you know. I mean, I think the small roses in that band about your head are very pretty. I do like the pink stuff overlaying the white gown and those triangles on your hem and sleeves. And how those triangle things are repeated in larger fashion on the pink stuff so it exposes the white shiny fabric—"

"The white shiny fabric is satin, Son, and the pink stuff is rose-pink crape," Mother said with a roll of her eyes. "Those triangle things are Vandykes. It's Vandyking on her gown."

"Forgive me if I'm not a man of fashion," he grumbled.

"Definitely not a man of fashion," Rosy said under her breath.

"I heard that," Geoffrey said. "And I happen to think it's not a crime to be an ordinary man with no sense of—"

Suddenly Diana bustled into the room with a phalanx of footmen carrying bags of purple flowers and even a couple of bottles of champagne. "I am so sorry to be this late. The larkspur hadn't arrived at the florist's yet, so I promised Verity I would wait for it and bring it on. Where is Verity?"

"She's in the ballroom, waiting for the chalkers to finish up the floor," Mother said.

Diana gestured to the footmen, and they tramped off to the ballroom with the larkspur. "Don't step on the chalking!" she cried after them.

"They should be all right," his mother said. "Fortunately, the chalkers left a wide margin around their art for her to set up the flower arrangements on the sides *and* to allow people to admire the chalk before the dancing begins."

Geoffrey bit his tongue to keep from saying anything. He still did *not* understand the appeal of chalking a floor and then ruining it by dancing on it. But Rosy had wanted it from the moment she'd heard of it, so Rosy was going to get it if he had to chalk the floor himself.

A humorless laugh escaped him. That wouldn't happen in a million years.

Diana looked at him for the first time in days. "Have you seen the chalking yet?"

"I have. It's very . . . whimsical."

She let out a relieved sigh. "Whimsical is good."

"Good for a ball anyway," he said.

His mother laughed. "We wouldn't want an image of your *actual* bridges, Geoffrey. They're very . . . Well, they're not pretty. Let's just put it that way."

"I can't chalk like those fellows, so you will fortunately be spared having to put my utilitarian bridges on the ballroom floor." To be danced away in an hour, at most. "And you lot can keep your pretty bridges. I prefer the ones that actually work to convey carriages and people from one side of a river to the other."

The women looked at one another and burst into laughter. Even Rosy, thank God. Somehow, he'd broken the tension in the room, and that was worth any amount of money spent on chalking. Although he still preferred functional bridges to "whimsical ones" any day.

And he definitely preferred a laughing Diana to an absent one any day, too. Everywhere she'd gone this week—organizing servants, consulting with Eliza about the musicians, helping Rosy pick out jewelry—she'd been kind and helpful and competent.

It was enough to make him wonder if she was right.

Perhaps it was time he trusted his secrets with *someone*. She was clever—she might see a way through the thicket he'd found himself in. He could use another person's perspective. It worked in engineering. Why couldn't it work in everyday life, too?

You just want her in your bed, that's all.

Yes, he did. Very much. But it was more than that. He wanted the right to be in her company whenever he could. Because it was beginning to dawn on him that after this week, he would no longer have that right. And that felt as bad as a crushing blow from an iron wheel.

The fact that the day would come whether he wanted it to or not left him wishing he had more time—a week, a month, a year even. Indeed, the time before him now seemed a yawning void, filled with work and naught else.

"What do you think of how I look, Diana?" Rosy asked, clearly anxious. "I'm worried about my hair. Eliza is so focused on the musicians that I had to rely on my lady's maid. I know Eliza has taught her a great deal, but this style is so simple—"

"It's perfect. Don't let all the ladies with their outrageous hair fashions make you feel as if you have to compete with them. Your coiffure is beautiful in its simplicity." Diana turned to him. "Don't you agree, Geoffrey?"

Every eye fixed on him. Damn. Nothing more frightening than three determined ladies waiting for him to pronounce judgment. "I don't know a thing about simple coiffures *or* outrageous hair fashions. But I know what I like, and I like yours."

Rosy beamed at him, and Mother gave him an approving nod. It made a lump stick in his throat. Their duckling had turned into a swan. He didn't know when or how it had happened, but he was proud of her for being able to transform into a diamond of the first water. Meanwhile, he'd barely managed to become iron of the first water.

And just like that, he remembered why he couldn't marry the likes of Diana. Because he could never be part of her world.

Or could he? She kept saying he was already part of it.

"Well, then," Diana said. "Let's all proceed to the formal drawing room, where the receiving line will begin."

He stepped forward to block her way. "Can you spare a minute to discuss something with me?" At least he could remedy one difficulty that lay between them.

She arched a brow as the other women went on without her. "Before you even mention it, the answer is no. I am not going to attend the ball, and you cannot make me. There are too many things still to be done, and I need to consult with your housekeeper."

"Oh. No, that wasn't it, although if you change your mind about that—"

"I won't. And you still haven't had dance lessons, so it's not as if we could dance together."

"Actually, I have had lessons. What do you think I was doing while you lot were discussing flower arrangements? I'm not very good, but . . ."

Her jaw dropped. "You had dance lessons? You wonderful, sneaky man! I had no idea."

"Does that mean you're willing to change into a ball gown and join me?"

"No, indeed. It means *you* can go out there and do something other than stand on the side glowering at Rosy's every partner." She added in an arch tone, "You might even meet a woman worthy of your trust."

"I already have," he said. "She's standing right in front of me."

For a moment she looked nonplussed. "That's not what you said the last time we were together."

"I know. I was a fool. But then, I'm sure you already realize that."

Her features softened a fraction before she turned suspicious. "How am I to believe you?"

"I'm not sure. Perhaps by considering that most of the time, I've told you the truth."

"Hmm," she said, and crossed her arms.

Rosy darted back in the room. "Diana, we're ready."

"I'm coming," she called out, then turned to him with a frown. "You're telling me this *now*? When there's nothing on earth I can do about it?"

"I just wanted you to know."

"Well, then, thank you. Now, if you'll excuse me . . ."

"Actually, that's not even what I was waiting to tell you. I wished to make you aware that I no longer require Rosy to have five male visitors a day in the ensuing week in order for me to pay you double your fee. I will do it no matter how many visitors she ends up having. Because the things you have given her are beyond price." He meant every word.

Diana stared at him for half a minute at least. "What . . . has brought on this rush of generosity? Are you well?" She touched the back of her hand to his forehead. "Wait, is this your idea of a prank?"

"I'm serious, damn it!"

She laughed. "You must be if you're using bad language."

"Diana . . ."

"It's all right. I'm only teasing. And later we can discuss

this all you please. But right now we really must go to the drawing room."

"Fine." He offered her his arm, and she took it, causing something in him to swell with pride. It was the most peculiar sensation—to be proud of having a certain woman on his arm—a peculiar sensation for him anyway.

"I should probably talk to you later myself," she said.

"About what?"

"Something having to do with Rosy. But it will wait."

"Very well," he said. "Though I confess I would rather be alone with *you* than in a ballroom with a thousand other people."

"A thousand! Where have you stashed this gigantic ballroom?"

"You know what I mean, sweetling," he said softly as they entered the drawing room.

"I do." She gazed up at him. "And I feel the same."

"Good. Just remember that later when everyone is gone."

Mother and Rosy had already spotted them and had come to drag him to the receiving line. They asked Diana questions about what order they were to be in, and they had her go over again their approved responses. And Geoffrey didn't care about any of it.

No matter what else happened, he and Diana would be alone together later. That was all that mattered to him.

A few hours later, Diana was sitting in the family parlor, which had been closed to guests, with her feet on an ottoman. She wished she could remove her shoes, but she didn't dare, because she knew from past experience that the second she did so, someone would come needing her to go take care of some mishap or another. She merely needed a few minutes to catch her breath, find her calm, and remind herself of why she did this sort of work.

Because she could. Because she enjoyed it—most of the time. And because, silly as Geoffrey would probably find it, she felt as if she were helping people, mostly young women who deserved a better existence than they often ended up with.

But tonight it was harder than usual to remember all that. Never had she felt more keenly out of her element than when watching Geoffrey dance with a succession of young women. Oh, he didn't do it out of choice. Before they'd even entered the ballroom, his mother had begged him to dance, probably for the same reason Diana had hoped he would—so he wouldn't glare at Rosy's partners.

He'd grudgingly agreed and had then proved himself to be a decent dancer. Not spectacular, by any means, but good enough to impress his guests, who'd probably heard the rumors about His Grace's unusual profession.

Unfortunately for her, the women he danced with were all gorgeous. She couldn't blame him for that—if one had to do something one found irksome, like dancing, one could at least find an attractive partner to share the task.

Still, it had been hard to watch. Which was ridiculous, really. Jealousy wasn't in her nature. Definitely not.

Except perhaps when it came to him.

Without warning, one of the footmen came running in. "My lady, you have to come. There are some people trying to force their way into the ball. They claim to be relations of His Grace."

Oh, no. That did not sound good.

Tired as she was, she sprang up and joined the footman on his way back to the entrance hall. "Where is His Grace? Does anyone know?"

"One of the other footmen went to find him. But these ladies—if you can call them that—are insistent, and I don't know how long we can hold them back."

When they emerged into the entrance hall, she saw four women and a gentleman arguing in ever-increasing voices with Geoffrey's butler, who was flanked by two of Geoffrey's burliest footmen.

The oldest looking of the women said, in a carrying voice, "I am the duke's paternal aunt. I am certain he will wish to see me and my husband, not to mention my daughters, who are his cousins. He was probably unaware of how to find our direction to send the invitation, but I know he would want us here."

"The hell he would," Diana muttered under her breath.

The footman said, "I beg your pardon?"

"Never mind." She hadn't had to do this very often, but once in a while, her responsibilities included making sure undesirable and uninvited guests were ejected from Elegant Occasions' parties, balls, etcetera.

So she could certainly handle this. Pasting a welcoming but firm smile on her lips, she walked forward to stand beside the butler. "I beg your pardon, madam, but—"

"It is Lady Fieldhaven to you, miss. Now go fetch your master and we can sort this all out."

"The duke is not my master. I am Lady Diana Harper of Elegant Occasions, and I'm in charge of this affair. You may have heard of my father, the Earl of Holtbury?"

The woman had the audacity to sweep her with a long,

contemptuous look. "Hasn't everyone? He and your mother are quite infamous."

"True. But that has nothing to do with this ball in particular. You and I both know that His Grace didn't neglect to invite you because he lacked an address for you. He didn't invite you because you and your family treated him and his family very ill. So I suggest you leave before I order the footmen to remove you."

Lady Fieldhaven drew herself up to her full height, which was still quite a bit shorter than Diana's. "You have the gall to speak to me about my relations! I assure you that His Grace—"

"—wants nothing to do with you," Geoffrey said as he strode into the hall.

For once, Diana was grateful he was so very imposing a figure physically. Because if Diana couldn't cow the woman and her family, Geoffrey certainly could.

He came up beside Diana. "Speaking of someone who has gall, madam, you are a pitiful excuse for an aunt."

"Now see here," Lord Fieldhaven said, "that's my wife you're insulting."

The man should never have spoken, because that merely focused Geoffrey's attention on *him*. "I feel sorry for you, sir, that you married a woman without an ounce of familial affection. Who joined her mother, my late grandmother, in cutting off my father—your wife's own *brother*, for pity's sake—from every person in his family. My own wonderful mother insisted that we should visit when we children were small, but your wife and my grandparents all refused to give us admittance. So it seems perfectly fitting that I deny you the same."

He turned as if to leave, and Lady Fieldhaven said,

"You, sir, may have undeservedly inherited the dukedom, but you are a rude nobody, just as I suspected. And how odd that you should mention your father, given that you murdered him."

Geoffrey froze. Diana couldn't even react. Murdered his father? Ridiculous. Geoffrey wasn't capable of it.

When he turned, rage burned in his face. "Where in God's name did you hear something so vile?"

"I have my sources in Newcastle." She gathered her cloak about her as if to protect herself from Geoffrey's rudeness. "Do you think that simply because I wouldn't expose my daughters to your father's reckless behavior, I didn't know what was going on in your household? I knew. I heard that your father died of an overdose of laudanum. Although no one could prove how he received enough to kill him, reliable sources say *you* were the one to give it to him."

His voice dripped ice. "Aside from the fact that I know nothing about dosing for laudanum and thus wouldn't have dared administer it to him, I loved him. He was my father, for pity's sake. Why would I kill him?"

"To inherit the dukedom, of course."

Diana couldn't stifle her laugh. "His Grace doesn't even want it. Never did."

That threw Lady Fieldhaven off the scent for only a second. "Well . . . of course he wants it. It comes with considerable property."

"And considerable debt," Geoffrey snapped. "You, madam, are a fool if you think I cared one whit about becoming duke. My father never kept track of who would inherit the title, and neither did I. I assumed it would be one of my many distant cousins."

Lord Fieldhaven snorted.

"Are you calling me a liar, sir?" Geoffrey came up so close to the fellow that Lord Fieldhaven could only stare up at the taller, younger man and swallow hard. "If you are not careful," Geoffrey went on, "I will call you out. And I daresay you aren't as good with a pistol or sword as I am."

Lady Fieldhaven pushed herself between the two to poke Geoffrey in the chest. "He'll call *you* out first, sir."

"Quiet now, Ivy," Lord Fieldhaven said and drew his wife to stand at his side.

Geoffrey gave a mirthless laugh. "I would welcome that, Lady Fieldhaven, because it would give me the right to choose the weapons, and I would choose my fists. I daresay I could make quite the dent in your husband's jaw."

"You wouldn't dare, sir." She squared her shoulders. "Because then I would reveal your perfidy from here to Newcastle, and you would be forced to go before a jury of your peers to defend yourself."

For some reason, that gave Geoffrey pause. Which made no sense to Diana. She refused to believe he would ever murder someone, especially not his father. The idea was ludicrous.

Sensing her moment of triumph, his aunt went on. "But I could be persuaded to hold my tongue as long as you made amends by marrying one of my daughters."

Geoffrey's face darkened dangerously. "I am not about to do any such thing, madam." He gazed at the three young women, who were clearly mortified by the entire encounter. "Not that they aren't lovely ladies, I'm sure."

He narrowed his gaze on their mother. "But I would slit my own throat before I would willingly accept you as a mother-in-law. So I suggest you leave now, before I have my footmen escort you and your family to your carriage."

Her eyes went wide. "You leave me no choice but to spread the gossip concerning your father's death far and wide."

Foolish woman. Did she really think Geoffrey the Almighty would give up with one attack? Clearly she didn't know him at all. Which only lent credence to his claims that she and her family had cut off his father because he had married Geoffrey's mother.

"Fine. And you leave *me* no choice but to share with the world your attempt to blackmail me." He leaned close. "How do you intend to get your daughters married when people hear that I rejected them as possible wives? That you had so little faith in their ability to attract husbands that you had to blackmail *me* into marrying one of them? A man you claim killed his own father?"

"You wouldn't! Why . . . why, no one would believe you. You called them 'lovely' yourself."

"And yet I have no desire to marry them."

Lord Fieldhaven took hold of his wife by the arm. "Come, Ivy. You tried and failed. I think we should leave before one or the other of us comes to fisticuffs."

"Excellent idea," Geoffrey drawled. "Leave. It would be so much more civilized than my throwing you out, although much less satisfying."

"We're going, sir," Lord Fieldhaven said, and tugged his wife by the arm out of the door, as the three admittedly pretty daughters followed after.

In Diana's opinion, none of them looked terribly eager to marry the new Duke of Grenwood anyway, but especially not given his response to their mother's blackmail.

Diana wondered if she, too, should rethink the possibility of marrying him, even if he wanted to marry *her*, which was by no means certain. But despite whatever battles might lie ahead for them, she was fairly certain she wanted to be part of them.

As long as it meant she could be with Geoffrey.

Chapter Seventeen

After the Fieldhavens left, Diana turned to find several members of Geoffrey's staff standing there. He looked horrified, as it apparently sank in that the servants had heard everything.

He cleared his throat before addressing them. "I appreciate your help with my relations. I wish I could promise you this won't happen again, but I can't be sure. My father had many distant relatives." Joining his hands behind his back, he said, "I would ask, however, that you not repeat what you heard here tonight. I assure you it was all lies."

"Please, Your Grace, no need to explain," the butler said. He looked back at his fellow servants, who nodded their encouragement. "We don't believe such rumors. We are very proud to be in your service and will exercise the greatest discretion concerning this matter. You need not worry about us." He drew himself up ramrod straight. "We would never betray you. Just tell us what you require."

Geoffrey stood there, clearly dumbfounded by this show of support from a staff who'd only known him a month or two. "Thank you. You humble me, all of you. I appreciate your concern more than you can possibly know."

"And," Diana said, "if you gentlemen will forgive me for interrupting, you can best show your support by . . . er . . . getting back to your duties in the ballroom? At the ball being held for His Grace's sister?"

Everyone, including Geoffrey, looked at her blankly. Then, as if finally realizing most of the footmen were in the entrance hall, everyone hurried away.

All but the butler. He approached Geoffrey with a determined look. "Do you think the Fieldhavens are likely to return this evening?"

"I don't think so. I hope not anyway. So I believe it's safe for you to attend to your other duties."

"Very good, Your Grace."

As the servant marched back to the ballroom, Geoffrey took Diana's arm and said, "Come with me." Then he paused. "Please. If you don't mind."

She fought the laugh bubbling up in her throat. Apparently, Geoffrey the Almighty could actually use good manners when he wanted. "Of course. I'm sure I can be spared for a few minutes."

"It may be more than a few," he murmured as he guided her through rooms where they were unlikely to be seen by anyone.

Next thing she knew, they were entering his study.

"I'm locking the door," he said. "I don't think anyone has seen us enter, but if someone comes looking, I don't want them to be able to walk in on us."

Was he implying what she thought he was? She eyed him

askance. "*Here*? You want to have an intimate encounter here and *now*?"

"Not exactly." A rueful smile crossed his lips. "I wouldn't mind, but that's not why I brought you here. I need to speak to you about my father's death."

"Oh. I see." She sank into the chair in front of the desk. "Believe me, I know there's no chance whatsoever that you killed your father."

He steadied his gaze on her. "You have that much faith in me?"

"Of course. If I hadn't, you and I would never have had our first intimate encounter. I wouldn't even have allowed you to get me alone. I've had plenty of experience fending off untrustworthy clients."

"Sadly, I believe you."

When he fell silent, she said, "You were going to tell me about your father?"

"Yes. You heard the so-called 'evidence' my relations gave. It's only a tiny part of what could be alleged." He sat down behind his desk, unlocked a drawer, and took out a letter. For a moment, he just stared at it, as if debating something. "I'm afraid the only cure for such gossip—this letter—is worse than the disease itself." With a sigh, he reached over the desk to hand it to her. "Read it and you'll understand. What you don't, I'll explain, if you care to ask."

A chill swept over her as she took the document. "Just like that? All this time you could have told me your deep, dark secret, and you choose to do it now, in the middle of a ball. Merely because some distant relations of yours made a fuss?"

"Yes. Because others might also make a 'fuss.' Because the gossip has followed me to London sooner than I expected. Because . . . you seem to actually care about my family and not only as clients. I don't fully grasp why that is, but I'm grateful." His gaze bore into her, haunted, torn . . . vulnerable. "You'll understand when you read the letter."

Should she tell him what Rosy had already revealed?

Perhaps not yet. If she could keep his sister's secret, she would. Because he was clearly already worried about this gossip business. Not on the surface, of course. He always had to be a fearless fellow on the surface. But deep down, he truly was worried. She could tell. How odd that she had come to read his emotions so well.

"Are you going to look at the letter?" he asked impatiently.

"Yes, right away."

As she unfolded it, he said, "Try not to damage it. I may need it one day to save my own skin."

That sounded ominous. She steadied herself and began to read:

Dear Son,

If you are reading this, my plan worked, and I am out of this world and into the next, or very soon will be.

I am hoping to avoid an inquest by making my death appear accidental, so the doctor sees no purpose in calling the coroner to convene an inquest.

If, however, there is an inquest, say nothing of this letter unless they accuse anyone of murdering

me. Let them draw their own conclusions about
the manner of my death. With any luck, they will
deem my death accidental.

Her heart faltered as she realized what she was reading. This wasn't at all what she'd expected. An overdose?
Yes. A case of habitual use gone awry? Possibly. But
this . . . oh, poor Geoffrey. Poor Mrs. Brookhouse and
Rosy!

She glanced over at him. "This is . . . a suicide note?"

"Unfortunately, yes." Geoffrey swallowed convul-
sively. "By the time Father gave it to me, with instructions
not to read it until later, he'd already ingested a bottle or
more of laudanum. He wanted to make sure he was past
the point where anyone, including me, could save his life
by giving him an emetic to empty his stomach."

Geoffrey wouldn't meet her gaze. "He'd also already
sent for the doctor. That enabled him to speak to me in
secrecy and finish his plan, which only involved me because he wanted to put the letter in my hands himself. First,
so it wasn't missed in the confusion following his death.
And so the coroner couldn't use it to declare him a suicide.
And lastly, so no one could use it to blackmail me."

"That's ironic, considering."

"Yes," he said with a faint smile. "Obviously, he didn't
count on his relations being the vile vultures that they are.
Anyway, read on."

So she did.

If there is an inquest, lie to the coroner about
my increasing use of laudanum for pain. Say that
your mother did not know about the laudanum,

Sabrina Jeffries

which is true. I had to tell the apothecary I needed it for my stomach ailment. It was the only way I could ensure I got enough for my purpose. Our apothecary should have a record of multiple visits to purchase the drug, and he can confirm that I asked him not to tell your mother of it.

Speaking of your mother and sister, do not tell them of this letter either. Let them go on to mourn me, assuming it was my stomach ailment that took my life. I will tell the doctor myself of the accident, and ask him not to reveal my use of laudanum unless absolutely necessary. Your mother takes too much blame upon herself as it is—I wouldn't wish to add any.

Now we come to the question that must be uppermost in your own mind. Why am I doing this? Because I am *in pain, though not the sort laudanum could alleviate. I'm of no use to anyone and am only biding my time until death takes me. I've felt this way most of my life, but lately such thoughts prey on me constantly. The only time they leave me is when I see my children carrying on so beautifully, and when I gaze upon your mother's face. We quarrel, it's true, but those quarrels are as nothing when I hold her in my arms. She will be better off by far without me.*

So it makes sense to leave this earth in a blissful sleep, something I rarely had in life. I hope you can understand, and that if you don't, you at least won't blame me too much.

You have been a good son to me, and I hope

you will continue to be so by following my wishes. But don't risk your own life to prevent anyone knowing I took mine. I know you will make the right decision regardless. I leave your mother and sister in your capable hands.

With much affection,
Your father

Only when her cheeks got wet did she realize she was crying. When he offered her a handkerchief, she carefully folded up the letter and handed it back to him before using his handkerchief to wipe her eyes and nose. "Your poor, poor father. How melancholy he must have been to see this as his only escape."

"Now do you understand why I kept the truth about Father's death a secret for so long?"

"I think so." She had trouble speaking for the lump in her throat. "If it ever got out that your father killed himself, you're worried he would be judged guilty of felo-de-se."

"Yes. You may not be aware, but it means 'self-murder.' And you know what happens to those who commit suicide and are so judged in a court of law?"

She stared at him. "Not really. I mean, I know it's a terrible scandal, and anyone so judged is buried with a stake through the heart at a crossroads and some other superstitious nonsense, but—"

"It's far more than that, I'm afraid." He restored the letter to its drawer and locked it again. "If Father were judged as committing a felony—which a felo-de-se is, in legal terms—his property would be forfeit to the crown.

That means the house my mother and sister live in, my grandfather's company, Stockdon and Sons, which was left to Father, and quite possibly the property I inherited with the dukedom. I'm not certain about that last because I'm reluctant to consult an attorney about it and raise questions. But it could be disastrous for my family, not only now but for decades to come."

"Good Lord, that's a stupid law."

"It is," he said dryly. "But it is still prosecuted. And if the only way I could keep from facing a charge of murder was to present this letter, it would save *me* while possibly damning my family. No good would come of it either way."

No wonder he held that letter so close. Diana didn't know whether to feel gratified that he'd finally chosen to reveal this to her . . . or angry it had taken him so long.

That also explained why he had so much contempt for rumormongers. Because such people quite literally could destroy his life and the lives of his mother and sister.

Then a bit of information she'd read somewhere wiggled its way into the front of her brain. "I thought there was another determination a jury could make, which would be less awful. They could deem your father non . . . non . . ."

"Non compos mentis. It means 'of unsound mind.'"

"Yes! I knew I had heard that."

He drummed his fingers on the desk. "Does that letter sound as if it came from a man of unsound mind? He plotted to acquire the laudanum and planned how to make it look accidental. No one would rule him non compos mentis."

Her heart sank. "No. I suppose not."

"Granted, juries are less eager to deem someone guilty of felo-de-se these days, but that doesn't mean they won't."

"I suppose. Although you're a duke now. That ought to work in your favor."

"It depends on the jury." He shrugged. "They may consider me a jumped-up boor who should never have been allowed to become duke in the first place."

His use of "boor" made her wince.

"Sorry," he said, reaching over to cover her hand. "I honestly wasn't thinking of what you called me initially."

Her gaze flew to him. "That's why you're so intent on seeing Rosy marry, isn't it?"

"Part of the reason." When she lifted her eyebrow, he sighed. "Most of the reason, yes. Once she marries, I'll know she's safe from whatever scandal or financial difficulty she might otherwise endure if she stays under my roof, especially if she marries someone protected from the usual laws."

"A peer, you mean."

"Yes. Having endured a scandal yourself because of your parents' actions, I'm sure you understand."

She slid her hand from his. "I do, though my family's scandal didn't result in a loss of so much." She rose and began to pace. "Why are you telling me this now, when you wouldn't before?"

"Because your words about trust affected me. I had already resolved to tell you the truth before my relations arrived, but their lies made it more imperative that I do so." Lifting a somber gaze to her, he added, "And perhaps now you also understand why I can't marry just yet."

She tilted up her chin. "No, I'm afraid you will have to explain that more fully. Especially because I haven't even said I *wish* to marry you."

Judging from the surprise on his face, he hadn't thought she'd make him explain. Or even consider not wedding him. Geoffrey the Almighty always thought things should go according to *his* plan. And while she realized now why he had that belief, it didn't change the fact he was willing to sacrifice her happiness—and his sister's, by choosing the appropriate husband for her—whether they wanted him to or not.

He stood to come around the desk. "I can't marry you yet—because I also don't want *you* to suffer, damn it. I don't know how many more times I can brazen my way out of a conversation like the one I just had with my relations. Plenty of people in Newcastle considered my father high and mighty, solely because his own father was a viscount. Father never belonged, and as a result our family didn't either."

He took her hands in his. "If dislike of my family ever rises to the level of charging me with murder, I couldn't bear . . . I would *refuse* to drag you through that. Or through the scandal of having a father accused and convicted of felo-de-se." He released her hands. "It's better that I get Rosy married as soon as possible to a respectable man—"

"Don't forget—to a *peer*," she snapped. "He must have a title, you said."

"Yes!" He glared at her. "A peer, if she can get one, and you've made me see that she can. So, after enough time has gone by that I'm sure I'm safe, that no one is likely to bring any charge of murder against me, you and I can then consider marriage."

She shook her head. The sheer arrogance of the man never failed to surprise her. "How much time is 'enough,' assuming I would even accept such an offer from you?"

He raked a hand through his hair. "I don't know. It depends on how long these rumors continue."

"I see." She really did understand at last. While she'd given up on pretending she didn't *want* to marry him, she couldn't wed him if he expected their marriage to be on his terms alone. Apparently, he couldn't foresee any future for them where they made decisions together for their mutual happiness.

"You do realize," she said, "this disaster you're protecting us from includes a number of ifs. If Rosy doesn't marry a peer. If you're accused of murder. If you're forced to defend yourself by using your father's letter. If your poor, dead father is brought to trial postmortem. If the jury deems his suicide felo-de-se. If you and your family personally lose your goods and property as a result."

"All of those things could happen," he said defensively.

"They could. But the likelihood that they will happen in that order and with the most damaging result is small, to say the least. So refusing to marry just in case they all do is like refusing to marry until you're sure the Thames won't overflow and flood all of London." She stared up at him. "What if, for example, instead of using your father's letter, you insist that his doctor be called as a witness to confirm your father's tale about confusing his laudanum for his tincture of rhubarb?"

He scowled. "For all I know, the doctor is the one who

started the rumors. Wait, how did you know about Father's 'tale'?"

"Oh!" She probably should have mentioned that sooner. "Rosy told me. She overheard you and your father speaking with the doctor on the day your father died, so last week she asked me what laudanum was."

The blood drained from his face. "What the hell? Has she been going around questioning strangers about Father's death?"

"I don't know, although I rather doubt it." She crossed her arms over her chest. "And I should point out I'm not exactly a stranger to her."

He huffed out a breath. "I didn't mean to imply—"

"No, you never do mean to insult people. But the insult still hurts." Before he could try to apologize and instead make matters worse, she hastily added, "Anyway, as it happens, I believe she asked *me* because she trusted me. But you might wish to talk to her about it yourself if you need answers. And if you want her to stop asking other people. She wanted to know why your father asked you and the doctor not to tell her and your mother about the laudanum."

"Good God," he muttered as he turned to roam his study.

"What *did* you tell your mother and sister when he died?"

"Just what Father asked me to say—that he died of his stomach complaint. He'd had it for a while, and it was getting worse. Of course, I didn't know Rosy had been listening and knew part of the truth."

"You see? That's what happens when you keep your secrets too close. It doesn't just hold your enemies at bay—it holds your friends and family at arm's length as well. And without any guidance, they tend to behave unpredictably."

"Apparently so," he bit out.

"If you keep insisting on fighting your battles alone, you may very well end up hanged for your trouble."

He halted in front of her. "I'm just trying to protect my family, for God's sake."

"But your family might not *want* your protection if it means you either throw your life or your financial future away. They care about you. They might just prefer that you tell them what you need of them, so the three of you can act accordingly."

She tried not to think about the fact that he would prefer *not* to marry her rather than take the chance that the truth coming out might hurt her.

"So what do you mean to do about Rosy?" she asked. "Would you tell her the truth? Or do you merely intend to demand she marry a peer of your choice so she can be saved from a possible disastrous future?"

He arched an eyebrow. "You know I wouldn't do that. The whole point of giving her a spectacular début is to make sure she can choose a man worthy of her, one who will protect her if things get ugly."

"The way my brother-in-law protected my sister when things got ugly with my parents? I thought he was a good man, too, but he may very well have run off to war just to escape the gossip, leaving Eliza to face it all alone. So, what if the saintly husband you wish for Rosy is mortified to find himself married to the daughter of a man who took his own life? Men are unpredictable when it comes to scandal. Eliza's husband certainly proved that, and your scandal is far worse. It could easily scuttle Rosy's marriage before it's begun."

"I think I know how to choose the right sort of husband for my sister." He paused. "Not that I would, mind you. But I know enough to prod her to accept the right sort and refuse the wrong."

"How *dare* you make decisions for your mother and sister? They have a right to hear the truth about your father, to be prepared for what could happen. You've already seen how your servants stand by you. How much more would your mother and sister? Because I am certain—knowing how much they both love you—that they would rather endure scandal and loss of wealth if that was the only way to have you hale and whole with them."

He looked away. "If I tell them, I'll be betraying my father and not doing the one thing he asked of me."

"He had no right to ask!" She clasped his arms. "No one gets to keep making choices for their families from beyond the grave. Even wills can be challenged. But this is final. He chose the darkest path for himself, then left you alone to fight your way out of an impossible situation of his own making." She reached up to kiss Geoffrey's cheek. "The only way to win a rigged game, my darling, is to refuse to play. Then forge your own path. Rely on those who love you, those you love and trust yourself, and then muddle through."

"You don't understand," he ground out.

"I *do* understand. That's the trouble. I understand very well. It's the reason I, too, never let anyone close, never considered marriage. Because too many things could go wrong. I might lack passion or my husband be a philanderer like my father. I might not enjoy being the wife of an engineer or a duke or a man from Newcastle and might find myself trapped in an unhappy marriage like my mother."

She clasped his face with both her hands. "But it seems to me that worrying about every 'if' only leads to being alone and unhappy. Life makes us no promises. You and I *both* know that, which is the very reason we like each other's company and understand each other so well. Surely that's the most important thing to have if one means to marry."

That and true love. But she didn't dare mention love when she still wasn't sure how *she* felt about it, much less how he did.

When he covered her hands, his face reflecting his own uncertainties, she added, "You keep looking for assurances that all will be well if we marry. And Lord knows I'd like the same. But no one gets those. Sometimes we don't even get to choose our situations. Because if we did you surely wouldn't have chosen a father who couldn't bear to live, and I wouldn't have chosen parents who couldn't bear to live with each other." She smiled through her tears. "We would have picked much tidier circumstances, I'm sure."

"We certainly would have."

"You have to give people the chance to show you their support. I know in my heart that your sister and mother would be at your side no matter what. Do you believe me when I say it would be the same for me?"

"It's not a matter of believing. It's a matter of figuring out what's best for my family. And for you, too, if you ever give me the chance to look after you."

"How will you look after me if we don't marry?"

"We *will* marry, just not until I'm sure you won't be marrying a pauper. Unless, of course, you find yourself bearing my child. You have endured enough scandal as it is without that."

"First of all, it would be *our* child. Secondly, you're not making any sense. If I find myself with child, you wish to bring both of us into your difficult situation. But if it's just me, then no?"

He was flustered. "That's not what I meant."

"It sounds as if that's exactly what you meant. The risk of scandal over having an illegitimate child trumps the risk that the scandal of your father's death could take you away from me or impoverish us for life. Well, I have a say in these calculations of yours, and I say you can't make decisions for me. We're not married, and apparently not likely to be for some time, so you have no right to dictate the future of any child I might have if we don't marry."

"Diana, be reasonable. I know you wouldn't jeopardize our child's future out of pride."

"No, I would save my child from growing up with parents in a marriage like that of my own parents. This is about what kind of marriage I intend to have, the only kind of marriage I will tolerate. I reject the kind where you decide things for my own good without consulting me."

"I'm not saying . . . I don't want . . ."

"What about Elegant Occasions? If it flounders, will you dictate that I have no part of it? What if you decide to build a bridge in some dangerous corner of the world? Will you go without me, leaving me to worry about you? And if you take me with you, won't you worry about me being there? If you can't answer any of these things, haven't even considered them, then clearly you're not ready to be married, and I am definitely not ready to be married to someone like my autocratic father, spectacular passion or no."

"Spectacular passion?"

Oh, Lord, she shouldn't have mentioned that.

"Surely 'spectacular passion' makes up for a great deal," he said.

Before she could answer, he lowered his head so he could seize her mouth in a kiss. He wanted to distract her, to end the discussion so he could take care of the matter on his own. But even knowing that, she didn't stop him from kissing her. Because this might be the last time she ever got to. Because his mouth was generous and demanding at the same time. He gave and he took, all in one sweet, passionate kiss.

He pressed her up against the wall, his lips now roaming as her hands did the same. Oh, how she'd missed this, missed having him in her arms. And what would it hurt to be with him again, even if nothing ever came of it?

She didn't get the chance to find out. A knock at the study door put an abrupt end to their kissing, especially when whoever it was tried the door handle and found it locked.

To Diana's horror, it was Eliza who spoke. "Your Grace? Are you in there? You're wanted in the ballroom."

"Damn," he whispered, his eyes showing how reluctant he was to part.

"And we can't find Diana," Eliza added. "Do you know where she is?"

He nodded toward a sort of alcove between the bookshelf and the wall, and Diana slipped into it. Then he strode for the door, opening it forcefully. "No," he lied. "No idea. Have you checked the ladies' retiring room? She said something earlier about repairing her fichu."

Diana stifled a groan as she lay her head against the wall. She wasn't wearing a fichu but a tippet, which Eliza would know. This was what came of not teaching men about fashion.

"Why don't you go on to the ballroom," Eliza said, "and I'll look for Diana in the retiring room?"

"Very well," he said.

Diana waited until she heard both sets of footsteps walking away. Then she crept through his study and out the study door, intent upon figuring out how to reappear in the ballroom without rousing suspicion.

"I knew it," Eliza said from behind her. "I knew you were in there with him."

Diana whirled on her. "Then why did you interrupt us? We were having an important conversation about our future."

"One that includes marriage, I hope."

"I hope so, too. But you interrupted him in the midst of his speech, so now I don't know."

Eliza shot her a pitying look. "If you'd been having that particular discussion, he would have said so to me, and I would have gone away . . . or waited for him to come out and announce the betrothal. But he didn't. He's still a duke, my dear sister. They still marry for reasons that have nothing to do with love."

"The situation is more . . . complicated than you can possibly know. I'm dealing with it. And you have to trust me. I know what I'm doing." Diana drew herself up. "Besides, I'm a grown woman perfectly capable of handling my own affairs."

"Very well. If you insist on having your heart broken, there's naught I can do to stop you." A troubled look crossed Eliza's face. "But I'm not going to help you either. The only thing that gives me hope is the fact that your clothing seems to be intact, and his did, too. No woman can 'repair her fichu' that fast, and Lord knows no man could. So at least he's treating you with *some* respect."

"You have no idea," Diana said. She'd never met a man more intent on saving her from the future than on making love to her. It was flattering and sobering at the same time.

But she hated that they hadn't finished their discussion. Because soon this "project" would end, and afterward, she wouldn't see him again. If her reasonable and sound arguments couldn't change his mind, how on earth could she marry him?

Not that he was asking her to. What if Eliza was right? What if he was more of a typical duke than she'd realized?

No, if that were the case, he would have drummed up some other excuse for not marrying, one where he wouldn't lose his every earthly possession if the truth got out.

She sighed. That merely made it even sadder. He was

being noble and principled, which was all she'd ever wanted in a man. Except she might not ever get to have that man if he decided to martyr himself for the sake of his family.

And *that* would break her heart.

Chapter Eighteen

Geoffrey wanted to be anywhere but here, in the midst of a ball he was supposedly hosting. He wanted time to think about Diana's words and to strategize, in case she really did refuse to marry him. He could see why she had become angry—the situation made him angry every time he thought about it. But surely she could understand that he was handling things the only way he knew how.

Someone announced it was time for the ball supper. Rosy came hurrying up to him with Foxstead trailing behind. "Oh, Geoffrey, it's going splendidly, don't you think? I have danced every dance, and all my partners were so complimentary that I feel like a princess."

"Didn't you just finish the supper dance?" Geoffrey said, giving Foxstead a dire look.

"We did indeed," Foxstead said blandly. The man was tormenting him for fun, damn it.

"Wasn't that sweet of Lord Foxstead?" Rosy put her hand on Foxstead's elbow. "I began to despair that no one would ask me for it, even though all of my other dances filled up very quickly. It looked as if the Duke of Devonshire might dance with me, but he left before supper."

She patted Foxstead's arm. "Then Lord Foxstead came to the rescue."

"That's what friends do, isn't it," Foxstead said, looking serious. "They come to the rescue."

"Yes." Now Geoffrey felt bad for not trusting the man. "That's what friends do."

Rosy frowned. "It would have been mortifying not to dance the supper dance and not to be taken in to supper at my own ball. So I'm very grateful to him."

"As am I," Geoffrey said. "Thank you, Foxstead."

The man nodded before walking off with Rosy. Geoffrey wondered if Diana was right—perhaps he was so busy seeing assassins behind trees that he was missing the friends and supporters and loved ones standing right in front of him.

He sighed. Perhaps. And perhaps this was merely the calm before the storm. Why hadn't anyone else asked Rosy for the supper dance? Had the guests heard of the conflict in the entrance hall with the Fieldhavens? Or was he just seeing trouble where none existed? Again?

Lady Verity approached him. "You really should eat supper," she said absently. "It's a very good one, if I do say so myself." She was scanning the ballroom as if looking for someone. Her eyes narrowed. "There he is. Your Grace, do you see that fellow over there by the pillar?"

"Which pillar?"

She scowled at him. "The only one with a fellow next to it now that everyone is headed to supper. Oh—" She made a frustrated noise. "*There.*" She nodded to the other side of the room. "He's wearing black and has his back to us."

"Every man is wearing black, including me." But just to be agreeable, he scanned the area she was talking about. "The fellow with the chapeau bras under his arm?"

"Yes! Yes." She peered over at the man. "Who is he?"

"I have no bloody idea. Why?"

She didn't even correct his language. He'd grown accustomed to all three of them doing so. He even cursed sometimes just to see if they'd catch it.

"I wonder if he was invited," Lady Verity mused aloud. "Perhaps I could find him on the guest list." She sighed. "Never mind. He's gone now. If he behaves as usual, by the time I go over there, he'll have disappeared into thin air. In any case, I should go to the kitchen to make sure the food is going out as planned."

When she started to walk away, he called out to her. "Lady Verity!"

"Yes?" She halted to stare at him. "What is it?"

"If I were to marry your sister, would you approve?" Damn, he should definitely not have said *that*.

"Which sister?" she asked. When he eyed her askance, she laughed. "It's not my place to approve."

"Then whose place is it? Your father's? Your mother's? Lady Eliza *is* the oldest of you three, so perhaps—"

"Diana's, of course." She shook her head. "Although if you couldn't figure that out, I might have to disapprove on account of your being a dunce." She gazed uncertainly at him. "Have you asked her yet?"

"Sort of."

"What the devil does *that* mean?"

He let out a frustrated breath. "It's hard to explain."

"Well, then, when you figure it out, let me know. I have to go."

As she walked away, his mother came up next to him. "Are you still planning on taking me in to dinner, Son?"

God, he'd forgotten all about that. "Of course."

He offered her his arm, and they headed toward the crowd at the end of the ballroom.

"What were you and Lady Verity discussing?" Mother asked.

"Lady Diana."

Her hand tightened on his arm. "What about her?"

No, he wasn't ready to have *that* conversation with his mother yet. "It doesn't matter." He cast her a bright smile. "So, our girl danced every dance, did she?"

"She did. Too bad you weren't there to see it."

"I had to deal with some relatives of Father's who were trying to force their way in."

His mother stopped short. "Which ones?"

"Lord Fieldhaven and his wife."

"Oh, I hate them. How your father and his sister could be so different is beyond me. They were also mean to you and Rosy when you two were small."

"I remember."

"Your father gave them a piece of his mind for it, too."

"Now *that* I don't remember," Geoffrey said.

"Because he didn't do it in front of you children, of course. He didn't want to upset you any more than they already had." After a quick glance around the ballroom, she leaned into him. "Did the Fieldhavens say anything about you murdering your father?"

Geoffrey blinked. "How did you know?"

"For pity's sake, Son, our house wasn't an island in

Newcastle. I heard the rumors. Why do you think I was so eager to move to Castle Grenwood?"

"I . . . just assumed the memories in Newcastle were too painful for you after Father died."

"That, too, I suppose," she said softly. "But I heard people talking about him having an overdose of laudanum." She raised her eyes heavenward. "Why your father thought he could keep an apothecary and a doctor quiet concerning his laudanum use is anybody's guess. If he'd consulted me, I would have instructed him to send me for his laudanum. I would have said it was for my sister and no one would have thought a thing about it."

Geoffrey's stomach sank. "So Rosy told you, did she?"

"Told me what?" Her jaw dropped. "Wait, how did Rosy know anything?"

He sighed. "Perhaps we should both sit down somewhere private."

"Later. Supper is being served, and I'm hungry." She brightened. "Oh, I know. Let's get our food and then go to your study to eat. And you can tell me all about whatever it is Rosy was supposed to have told me."

He thought about all he should say. All that Diana had said. "Actually, it's not so important that it can't wait until tomorrow. Tonight is Rosy's début. I've already missed a big chunk of it. So you and I are going to enjoy ourselves. As Diana says, our guests have 'danced the chalk out.' I daresay they will dance some more, and I mean to do so as well." He headed for the supper room now that the rest of the guests had pushed through into it. "We're going to eat marzipan and blancmange and cheesecakes—"

"And prawns and truffles and little bitty savory tarts."

"They call those tartlets, Mother. Did you know that?"

She smiled. "I didn't. Thank you for telling me."

"While we eat until we groan, we're not going to be sad about Father. We're going to be happy about Rosy."

Her smile faltered. "I shall try."

"Try hard." And he would, too.

Then, tomorrow, he would begin to talk about his father's secrets to his family. And perhaps then he might learn—from both Mother and Rosy—what they knew and hadn't told him. It was time the secrets among them were unveiled. Because how else could he convince the woman he desired to marry him?

The ride back to Grosvenor Square seemed eternal. Diana was so very tired, and not just from managing Rosy's ball. Talking to Geoffrey was utterly exhausting.

And Verity was on a tear again about the mysterious stranger who kept showing up at affairs they arranged. "At least Grenwood saw him, too, so I know for certain I'm not imagining things."

"Did Grenwood know who he was?" Eliza asked.

"No," Verity said. "But I'm not surprised, are you? We did the guest list almost entirely, except for all the engineer friends he insisted upon inviting."

"You're very quiet, Diana," Eliza said. "Did you think it went well?"

"Oh, it went *very* well, from my perspective," Verity said. "Rosy gained a number of suitors, and Diana gained the only one she wanted."

Diana blinked. "What are you talking about?"

"The Duke of Grenwood asked me if I would approve of his marrying you."

A thrill coursed through her before she quashed it. "What did you tell him?"

"That it wasn't for me to approve. That he should ask *you*."

Diana huffed out a breath. "Well, he hasn't really done that, so don't be building any houses for us just yet."

"*He* said that he'd 'sort of' asked you." Verity cocked her head. "So are you saying he did not?"

"I gather that he muddled that part a bit," Eliza said dryly. "But then, the duke is not known for being good at . . . well . . . dealing with delicate situations."

"That pretty much sums him up," Diana bit out. "The man can be utterly infuriating—taking things for granted and making assumptions. Why, I don't even know if I'd *want* to marry him, even if he asked. Can you imagine what marriage to him would be like?"

"I can." Verity got a dreamy look on her face. "You have to admit it would be lovely waking up to a man with a fine form like his."

"Good Lord," Eliza said. "You've never even woken up to a man at all. How do you know what it would be like?" Eliza turned to Diana. "But she has a point. There are . . . certain compensations to being married to a fellow of his . . . attributes."

Fortunately, it was too dark for her sisters to see Diana's furious blush. She looked out the window. "Oh, thank heavens we're home. I don't think I can bear another moment of you two talking about my . . . possible future husband in such bold terms."

The sleepy footman came to put down the step. When he started to open the door, Eliza said, "Wait for one moment, will you?" and then seized the door handle.

"Eliza!" Diana chided. "The poor man is about to fall over. And I no doubt will fall on top of him. Let us out."

"Just answer one question for me," Eliza said, "and you may leave the carriage."

Diana dragged in a heavy breath. "What?"

"Are you in love with the duke?"

Glancing from Eliza to Verity, Diana contemplated fobbing them off with some mealymouthed answer. But they would just keep badgering her until they got to the truth. "Of course I'm in love with him."

Oh, Lord, she *was*. And she'd never even meant to be so. How could she have lost her determination to hold firm so easily? When had things changed from *How can I slide past Geoffrey to get this thing done?* to *How can I get him to slide inside me again?*

She groaned. "Who wouldn't be in love with the man?"

"I wouldn't," Verity said, "although I must admit that his body—"

"Yes, yes, you were rather vocal about that already," Diana said irritably, then looked at Eliza. "Now, are you going to open the damned door or not?" Before she started crying. Before she could think about how hard it was to be in love with a man who probably only loved her for her body and her breeding capability, because he clearly didn't respect her opinion at all.

Eliza let go of the handle, then turned to Verity. "She's already cursing like him."

"Perhaps that's why he likes her so much," Verity said. "Or perhaps it's her rather large bos—"

"Enough!" Diana said as she opened the door. "I am not

going to sit here while you start cataloging *my* attributes. I'm going to bed."

"She gets so fussy after a ball," Eliza said. "Have you noticed that?"

"I haven't," Verity said. "But I'm noticing it now."

Diana didn't grace them with a reply. Instead, she made for the steps as quickly as possible. Unlike her, the two of them were always energized after any ball they organized that turned out well. Afterward, they loved to dissect the entire evening and figure out whether it had been a success.

But with the sun peeking above the horizon, she had no desire to do anything but go to bed. Not only was she too tired for any sensible conversation, she'd been unavailable for at least half the ball—either with Geoffrey or watching him deal with the Fieldhavens. So she couldn't exactly chime in on certain aspects of the evening.

As soon as they'd entered and divested themselves of bonnets and shawls, she said, "Good night to you both. I'll see you in the morning."

Thankfully, they let her go. They didn't always.

Once she was undressed and in bed, she lay there a while replaying everything he'd said and everything she'd said, and she got angry at him all over again. So she finally stopped thinking of *that*.

Instead, she worried she'd never get to be with him alone again. Elegant Occasions hadn't contracted with him for anything beyond Rosy's ball. Granted, he would have to pay them for what they'd done so far, but that wouldn't necessarily be something he must do in person. He could send his man of affairs over.

Wait, did he have a man of affairs? She'd never seen one if he did.

She had to stop thinking of all those things—they were making her daft. Instead, perhaps she would think of Geoffrey and his kisses and how amazing it had felt to have him inside her. As she did so, she began to touch herself. Unfortunately, it was unsatisfying compared to doing the real thing with him.

A pox on the man! He'd both convinced her she wasn't too cold for passion . . . and made it impossible for her to be passionate with *him*.

If she ever had the chance to be with him intimately again, she would enjoy that part first and then get into an argument. Or perhaps skip the argument. Because if they couldn't find a way to compromise, they would never find a way to make a marriage work. And she began to think that marriage to Geoffrey was precisely what she wanted.

Now if only she could figure out a solution to the issue of his late father's situation. Clearly the gossip in Newcastle was a problem. But how much of a problem was it? Was it as bad as the Fieldhavens said? Given that Lady Fieldhaven had a vested interest in presenting it that way, Diana doubted it. She fell asleep contemplating the suicide of Geoffrey's father.

Well into the afternoon, she woke up to discover her courses had come. She burst into tears. Now she couldn't even hope for a child with which to force Geoffrey into marrying her. Not that she wanted him that way. But now she would have to wait on him, and she didn't want that either, because she might be waiting for *years*.

So if she ever disentangled her heart from Geoffrey, who now held it hostage, she was *not* going to fall in love ever again.

Being in love was utter misery if you couldn't be with the one you loved.

Chapter Nineteen

Geoffrey had considered going over to Grosvenor Square a hundred times in the past four days. But he'd been busy reassessing his situation. Thanks to Diana, he'd started thinking of possibilities beyond the horrible box he'd built for himself, the one that cut him off from every person he cared about.

Between the ongoing social events Rosy was attending now that she had so many invitations and the daily visits from suitors whom he felt honor-bound to scowl at, he hadn't had much of a chance to pay Diana a visit. Especially because he'd been working up the courage to tell his mother and sister what had really happened to Father. And why he hadn't told them before.

Indeed, now that they were past the time for callers and his sister and mother miraculously had no social affairs for the evening, they sat in his study, with the door closed and locked, and he still scarcely knew how or where to begin.

The letter. That had worked for Diana. He would let his father tell his own story. That was what Geoffrey should have done in the first place with Mother and Rosy.

He truly believed he'd done the right thing by waiting to tell Diana until he was surer of her. But not to tell his mother and his sister? That was unforgivable.

Now he realized it was a betrayal of the deepest kind. It may have been his father's wish, but Diana was right when she'd said, *No one gets to keep making choices for their families from beyond the grave.*

Diana was right about a lot of things.

With a sigh, he took the letter from his desk. "I should have done this a long time ago. You both had the right to know. I had hoped to keep from causing you pain, but I think I may have just mucked things up even more." He dragged in a heavy breath, then handed over the letter. "This is what Father wrote and gave to me right before he died. He already knew he was dying because he ensured it himself by drinking two bottles of laudanum along with his usual brandies."

His mother's eyes went wide and she seized the letter as if it were the key to a vault of jewels. As they both began to read, Rosy started to weep. But his mother just became angrier with every word.

When she was finished, she tossed the letter down on the desk without even waiting for Rosy to be done. "If he weren't already dead, I'd kill him myself. How dare he? Now he will never get to see Rosy marry well or his grandchildren grow up or . . . or his son become the greatest duke in all of England!"

"I'm not sure he would have seen that last one, anyway, Mother, but I take your meaning. And I share your outrage."

Rosy lifted her head from reading. "That's why he had me run all those errands on that day?"

"I'm afraid so, poppet," Geoffrey said. The expression of betrayal on her face cut him to the bone.

"Why did he tell you and not me?" Rosy asked plaintively.

"Because he knew I would protect the two of you from the consequences of his actions if anyone else should happen to find out. He wanted it to remain a secret."

His mother snorted. "The truth is your father didn't want to be declared non compos mentis. He was always worried people would think him mad."

Geoffrey stared at her, stunned. When Diana had told him about Rosy's question concerning laudanum, he'd begun to figure out that there were pieces of the story he was missing, but his mother's pieces were particularly sobering.

She rose to go stare out the window at the garden. "I suppose he had no trouble at all with being declared a suicide and losing all his family's money and property to the Crown."

"He was trying to avoid that, Mother," Geoffrey said. "That's why he wrote the letter only to me in the first place."

"What's non compos mentis?" Rosy asked.

For the next hour he had to explain what it meant. It took much longer to lay out the laws for his sister than for Diana. Rosy simply couldn't imagine why someone choosing to kill himself could translate into a choice either to allow the Crown to take all the worldly goods of his family or to be publicly declared insane.

Seen through her eyes, it did seem unfair. Putting aside the religious strictures against it, it hardly seemed right to punish people posthumously for committing suicide by punishing their families financially. It wasn't as if it would have any effect on the dead person's behavior.

And once his explanations to Rosy did sink in, she had a moment of panic. "Oh, no! I told Diana about Papa and the laudanum!"

"How did *you* know?" their mother asked. "About the laudanum, I mean. From the gossip?"

"Not . . . exactly," Rosy said sheepishly.

Questions and answers like those meant it took a while to explain Father's complicated plot to kill himself while protecting their finances. Then, of course, Geoffrey had to reassure Rosy that she'd chosen the right person to ask about the laudanum.

"But you didn't tell anyone else, did you?" Geoffrey asked sternly.

"Who would I tell? My suitors? I know better than that. And my only two female friends are in Newcastle."

Their mother sat down again to put her arm around his sister's shoulders. "Haven't you made new friends here?"

"I suppose." Rosy brightened. "The ladies at Elegant Occasions have assured me that they consider me a friend. So that's three right there."

"We can return to Newcastle anytime you like, you know," Mother said, sparing a severe look for Geoffrey.

"No." Rosy mused a moment. "I like all the things to do in London. And once I marry . . ."

"What happened to your promise to keep house for me wherever I went?" he teased.

"You'll have Diana for that," she said simply.

His mother stared at her. "Is there something you know that I don't?"

"I just think . . . they would make a grand couple," Rosy said. "Don't you?"

"I certainly do." Mother looked over at him. "So you should take care of that as soon as possible, Son."

He sighed. "I'm working on it."

"You are not," his mother said. "You're sitting here with us."

"I see," he said with a faint smile. "You're trying to push me out the door now."

"If that's what it takes," Mother said.

"And I know it hasn't been a whole week," Rosy added, "but since I've had thirty visits in four days, I should think you still have every reason to go there and pay them double their fee."

"How do you figure that?" he asked. "Not that I mean not to pay it—I already told Lady Diana that I would, because I was so impressed by their efforts. But technically four days is not a week."

"The number of visitors averages out to five a day."

He lifted a brow. "Five times seven is thirty-five."

"You said a week. I assumed you meant six days because no one pays visits on Sunday."

When she shot him a triumphant smile, Geoffrey couldn't help it—he had to laugh. "You are going to lead some poor fellow a merry dance, poppet. Now, I have to go."

"To see Diana?" she asked hopefully.

"That will have to wait until tomorrow, I'm afraid. I have to meet with some of my investors at the Old Goat Tavern. The meeting has been scheduled for weeks."

In the meantime, he had some thinking to do about

how to manage a shifting world where more people knew of his father's issues than he'd realized. Not to mention he needed to consider everything Diana had said. He began to think she had a point. There might be a middle solution to his problem.

Or they might have to just wait it out. And if she was willing to wait it out with him, as his wife . . . "But to-morrow," he said to Rosy and Mother, "I will put on my best clothes and march right over there."

After which he hoped he could coax Diana somewhere they could be together for a while. Four days of not seeing her or touching her was too many days by any calculation.

Diana sat at breakfast, alone as usual, but this time because Eliza was at a client's house looking over the woman's pianoforte and harp while Verity consulted with the woman's cook. Clothes were not the issue in this case. Lady Sinclair had exquisite taste in that respect and always had.

Diana had expected Geoffrey to take a day or two to think through all that they'd said to each other. But *four* days? It made her despair.

Norris walked in. "His Grace, the Duke of Grenwood, to see Lady Diana. Shall I send him away, my lady?"

She rose, her heart thundering in her chest. "You mean he didn't follow right on your heels as usual?"

"No, my lady. He was very specific that I should an-nounce him and wait to see if you were at home to him."

Who said a boorish duke couldn't learn from his mis-takes? The very fact that he was following a few societal rules for a change was taking her breath away. At least he was here at last. "Please show him up." When Norris lifted a brow, as if to question her lack of chaperone, she said firmly, "*Now*, Norris."

"Yes, my lady."

That gave her just enough time to make sure her gown was straight, her hair in place, and her cheeks pinched sufficiently enough to pinken them. Thankfully, her courses were over. She'd always been blessed with courses that lasted only a few days. Then he was there before her, and she lost the power of speech.

He looked magnificent in a brown coat and light blue trousers, with a cravat that couldn't have been any more starched or masterfully tied. If they did ever marry, she would make sure he never got rid of his valet. The man was well worth his salary.

But she was getting ahead of herself. "You look well."

"You look beautiful," he said in a tone of such seriousness that she knew he was here for more reason than just to pay them or some such. "Then again, you always do."

The way he was looking at her made her nervous. "Have you had breakfast? You're welcome to join me with mine."

"I could eat something, I daresay."

She laughed. "I do believe you could always eat something. Indeed, I would assume you were ill if you couldn't."

"You know me well. Better than I expected, actually."

They took seats at the table, and Diana sent Norris for more food, mostly just to gain a few moments alone with Geoffrey. She had to tell him one thing privately.

"I thought you should know," she murmured, "I am definitely not with child."

"How do you know?"

"Because I had my monthly visitor, if you know what that means."

"Ah. But you do want children," he said, taking her by surprise. "I mean, if we marry. You want them, don't you?"

Her heart in her throat, she nodded. "Children would be lovely."

"Yes. I agree."

When he lapsed into silence, she asked, "Has anything changed with regard to your . . . willingness to marry?"

"So much has changed." With a glance at the door Norris would come through, he scooted his chair a bit closer so he could take her hand. "I've discovered that my family was more aware of Father's machinations than I realized. But that's not why I'm here. I wanted to tell you that—" He straightened and said in a more formal tone, "I am here to pay you the doubled fee I promised."

Thrown a bit off guard by that, she frowned. Then she realized Norris had reentered the room. "Are you? But we're only up to the fourth day, by my calculation."

"Ah, but Rosy has had thirty young men pay her visits. And now she insists that because thirty visits divided by six days is five visits a day, the terms have been met."

"That's very kind of her," Diana said, already trying to figure out what lengthy errand to send Norris on so they could have privacy.

"You're not going to question the six days?" he asked.

"No. That's perfectly clear. No one pays visits on Sunday. I always assumed we would not count Sunday."

He laughed. "You and my sister are clearly of one mind. Perhaps you should marry *Rosy*."

She was about to say she'd rather marry Rosy's brother when Norris approached her with an envelope. "I was told to put the note in your hand myself, my lady." He bent to whisper, "It's from Lady Rosabel, and I was told to make sure you were alone when I gave it to you."

Diana's attention immediately shifted to the envelope. "Did she say why?"

"*He*, the servant, said only that you would understand when you read it."

She unsealed it at once, but as she read, her heart sank.

Dear Diana,

I have a favor to ask. By the time you receive this, your cousin and I will be on our way to Gretna Green. So if my brother or mother come looking for me, will you please instruct Norris to say I am out shopping with you? It will gain us enough time to get away. Your cousin says you will understand and help us, but I ask that you do it for me as a friend. If you do, I promise I won't tell Geoffrey the part you played.

Gratefully,
Rosy

She dropped the envelope into her lap. "Oh, Rosy. You foolish little girl."

"What is it?" Geoffrey asked.

She handed it over to him. "Your sister has eloped with my second cousin."

"What? Who's your second cousin?"

"Lord Winston Chalmers."

And that probably spelled the end to any future romance between them.

Chapter Twenty

Geoffrey read the letter, growing angrier with his sister as he went along. Clearly she was taking advantage of her friendship with Diana to impose on her. His sister had even gone so far as to bring *him* into it with a not-so-subtle bribe to keep Diana quiet!

It wasn't fair of Rosy in the least. And he knew beyond a shadow of a doubt that Diana had nothing to do with the elopement. He'd seen the shock and horror on her face as she was reading. No one could pretend that well, even his mindful-of-words Diana.

He shot up. "I have to go. I must at least *try* to catch them before they reach Scotland."

She rose, too. "Geoffrey, I want you to know that I—"

"It doesn't matter."

She looked stricken. "Please, hear me out—"

Suddenly realizing how that must have sounded, he seized her hands and kissed both in turn. "It doesn't matter because I know you had nothing to do with it, the same way I know that I love you."

"You do? Truly?" she asked in a tremulous voice.

"I do, truly and until death do us part. Nor is that going

to change simply because my sister is a fool and your cousin is apparently one also. But I still have to go."

"Then I'm going with you." She turned to Norris. "Please have Cook pack up whatever is left from breakfast. Tell her to use that picnic basket and include plenty of coffee. Then have her send it out to his lordship's carriage. We'll need to eat on the way. Oh, and if you could explain to my sisters where I've gone and why—"

"But . . . but, my lady, you can't go with . . . with *him*. It's improper and will quite possibly ruin you! If you insist on going, I can send for Mrs. Pierce to accompany you."

Before Geoffrey could even protest, she said, "That would take too long. Besides, by the time the gossip has gotten around, we will already be engaged to be wed." Then she paused, as if realizing he hadn't actually proposed marriage to her yet. "Is that correct, Your Grace?"

"That is absolutely correct," he said, unable to stop a silly grin from crossing his lips.

She gave Norris a hand motion that apparently meant *Do as I say*, because the butler gave no more protest and hurried off in the direction of the kitchen.

"Norris is right, you know," Geoffrey said. "If you come with me, the gossip will be merciless."

"Actually, if I come with you, we might save Rosy from that merciless gossip. Assuming we catch up to them before nightfall, we can always claim we went on a day trip as couples. It wouldn't quite be acceptable, but he's my cousin and she's your sister, so in a way, we're both chaperoning our relations. Whereas, if you just ride after them alone in your carriage, you lose that as an argument."

"You really want to go, don't you?" he asked.

She nodded.

"Why?"

"So I can help with Rosy and . . . well . . ."

"Keep me from murdering your cousin?"

"Precisely."

He shook his head with a rueful smile. "And I don't suppose my promise *not* to kill him will suffice, under the circumstances?"

"You might just maim him. Or worse, call him out, and then you could *both* end up killing each other." She frowned. "And I refuse to go to your funeral if you do something that foolish."

He chuckled. "Very well. How soon can you be ready?"

"In the time it takes for me to fetch my bag and put on my gloves and bonnet."

That took him by surprise. "Well, then. Let's go."

A short while later, they were in his carriage, along with the picnic basket and Diana's mysterious bag, which she seemed to carry everywhere. While she'd been getting ready, he had run after the servant who'd brought the note and threatened him with dismissal if the lad didn't tell him everything he knew.

By the time he got back, Diana was in the carriage. He told his coachman where to go and climbed inside.

As they were racing through town on their way north, he closed the curtains so no one could see Diana with him. "Does your cousin have an equipage of his own?"

She tensed. "A phaeton. But it needs work, so I don't know if he would have taken that."

"He didn't take a phaeton. From what my servant

described, he's in a post chaise, probably rented. I just wanted to make sure it wasn't his. So, assuming he rented it, he has to be taking the usual roads to Gretna Green." He drummed his fingers on his knee. "My damned sister told the servant that she wanted that note left for you because she was planning to meet you at a shop, and her 'friend' was taking her there."

"Oh, no. I'm so sorry."

"Why? Did you plan the elopement?"

"No, indeed!"

"Then you have nothing to apologize for," Geoffrey said. "If anything, you showing me that note and not taking part in Rosy's deception will enable us to find her in time. If you had done as she asked—which you could have, because I had no clue that the note came from her— we wouldn't now be on the road with some idea of how and where to find them."

"I know, but I still need to explain about Winston."

"You don't have to. Honestly, you don't."

"I want to." She set her bag on the seat next to her. "When your sister first told me about Winston, I cautioned her exactly as I told you."

"I know. She confirmed it."

"What you don't know is that I wrote a note to Winston, asking him not to tell you of our personal connection. I was afraid you would change your mind about hiring us if you knew he was our cousin."

"I might have. Or I might have seen it as a way to keep watch over the enemy."

She winced. "Regardless, it was very wrong of me."

"It doesn't matter." He smiled at her. "Now, are you finished reciting your sins?"

"I—I believe I am."

"Good. Because I'm ready to give you absolution." Reaching across the carriage, he hauled her over and onto his lap.

"What on earth are you doing?" she cried, but he noticed she didn't try to get off.

"Didn't you wonder why I brought the cumbersome carriage to Grosvenor Square in the first place, instead of coming over in my curricle, for example?"

"I confess I hadn't even considered it."

"I did it so that in case everything went according to plan and you agreed to marry me, I could take you for a drive in the park and do *this*." He gave her a long, deep kiss, relishing every minute of her swift capitulation. "And this." He removed her fichu, then kissed his way down between her breasts. "And this." He reached one hand up beneath her skirts to caress her bare thighs through the long slit running along the inner sides of her drawers.

But before he went any higher, it occurred to him he should probably check something first. "Are you still on your courses?" He knew some women preferred not to make love then.

"No, I'm not." She parted her legs. "And if you had tried this in the park, I would most definitely have been ruined. But I suppose we're far enough away from Grosvenor Square that no one will recognize the carriage at once, and if they do, they'll assume you merely wanted privacy to sleep or something. There's really not much to the northwest of Hyde Park."

He moved his hand higher. "Excellent. Although that

only means Lord Winston probably has a good lead on us."

"Wait. How do you know about women's courses?"

He froze. "Um . . . Rosy told me?"

"Rosy blushed whenever she mentioned her own breasts, which she always called her 'bosom.' So there's no way she told you." When he opened his mouth, she added, "And before you suggest that your mother told you, be aware that men's mothers *definitely* do not talk of their courses to their sons."

"Right." He sighed. "Actually, I learned of it from a merry widow I kept company with in my salad days."

She stopped his hand before it could go any higher. "You're not still—"

"Oh, no. It ended when she found out I was fourteen."

"Fourteen! Good Lord, you started young." When he tried to move his hand, she tightened her grip. "How many of these dalliances did you have while you were sowing your wild oats?"

"A few."

She arched a brow. "Perhaps I should sow my own wild oats to catch up."

"You wouldn't do that," he said softly.

"What makes you so sure?"

Her hand still gripped his, so he had a fairly good suspicion this was a test. But the answer was the same either way. "Because my oat-sowing was finished long before I met you. I would never have a dalliance now. I love you. And people who love each other don't have affairs with other people, especially once they've vowed in a church to cling only to each other."

That must have been the right answer, because she

released his hand. As he moved it up to stimulate her where he knew women liked it most, she murmured, "Your oat-sowing does explain why you're . . . so good at this."

"Are we going to talk?" he whispered in her ear as his cock thickened. "Or swive? Because in less than an hour we'll be changing horses, and I don't think you want to be doing this then."

"No more talking," she said and kissed him boldly.

He fondled her, loving how it excited her. And once he could feel her warm wetness coating his fingers, he shifted her onto the seat next to him just long enough to unfasten his trousers and drawers and slip them down to his knees.

"All right, sweetling," he said, "time for you to straddle me."

"What?" she asked, her face filling with confusion.

"This will be easier if you ride me. You don't even have to remove any clothes. Here, I'll show you. You put this leg on this side and the other leg—"

"Oh. *Straddle*. I see now."

She straddled him at the middle of his thighs, and his cock got bigger and bolder. He loved that she was such a quick study when it came to bedsport. She drove him wild with her enthusiasm.

"Now," he said, "if you'll just place your knees on the seat and rise up . . . Not too high! Don't want you bumping your pretty head." Or his other head, for that matter. "Good, good. Now come down on my . . . on my . . ." He refused to call it a "pencil" ever again.

"The fallen females call it a 'cock.'"

His would begin to crow if she kept talking that way. "I think those fallen females of yours aren't very reformed."

"Why? What do *you* call it?"

"A cock." He went a little insane when she adjusted him so she could come down on him. "And you must . . . never say that word . . . in polite company unless you're talking about . . . chickens."

"Ooh, a naughty word. So, let's see . . . I come down on your *cock* . . ."

Just having the tip of it inside her was driving him to distraction. "Farther down, my love. More." He threw back his head. "Oh, God, more. Yes. Exactly like that."

"What now?"

"You move . . . up and down. As we did before, but in reverse."

Her face brightened. "Oh, I see!" And she began to move, hesitantly at first, and then more enthusiastically as his measured thrusts gave her the rhythm of it. "Geoffrey . . . that is . . ."

"Incredible? Because that's how it feels . . . to me." His blood pumped through him, a potion giving him energy, making him feel fierce, reminding him he was *alive,* as heat surged in him.

And it was all due to her . . . his goddess Diana making him feel this rush of excitement. She rode him like an Amazon queen of old, who needed no crop but her luscious body to get him racing.

"Your cock is so . . . *hard* . . ." she whispered.

"As it should be."

She grabbed his hands and pressed them to her breasts, making his cock even harder. He caressed her full breasts through her gown and shift as best he could, glad that she wasn't wearing the type of corset that covered her nipples.

"Next time we do this, sweetling . . . you'll be naked so . . . I can see you . . . in all your glory."

"Oh, yes," she choked out, throwing back her head as her eyes slid closed. "I would like . . . I want . . . I need *you* . . . my love."

He could feel her muscles tighten around his cock, spurring him to find his release with her. This time, as he poured his seed into her, he prayed that it *did* take root. Because he wanted nothing more than to have a child with her, one life brought into the world to replace the one who chose to leave it too soon.

Clutching her to him, he kissed her bold chin and firm jaw, which showed her strength . . . and the rapidly beating pulse at her throat, which showed her vulnerability. A sudden flood of peace washed over him as she nuzzled his hair and his temples, her breathing still quick, but the pulsing of her muscles down below slowing.

She drew back from him with a contented smile. "Now, aren't you glad you brought me along?"

"Gladder than you can possibly know. I wish I could remove your gown and take down your hair. I still haven't seen you that way."

"You know you can't." When she smoothed back his hair, he smelled her strawberry scent, but mixed with something else. Jasmine? He couldn't be sure.

"You always smell so good," he said.

"So do you." She sighed. "I brought my sponge in my bag. But I forgot to use it again."

He chuckled. "Why do you think so many women have so many children when some of them know how to prevent it?" He tilted his pelvis up against her. "Because we randy fellows are so good at this that we make you forget." Then he sobered. "I love you, my sweet goddess Diana."

"I love you, too, Your Grace." When he frowned, she released a peal of laughter. "I love you, Geoffrey Brookhouse, whether you're a duke or an engineer of bridges or an ironmaster. Although some day you'll have to tell me what an ironmaster is."

In that moment, he realized she hadn't said she loved him until now. Well, he might have taken her love for granted in the past hour, but he would never take it for granted again.

Past hour? Damn. The hour was up.

The carriage was already slowing as it approached the inn where they would change horses. "Better get back into your seat, Diana. It may take you a few moments to straighten your clothes."

"Oh," she said dreamily. Then her eyes went wide as she, too, could feel the slowing. "Oh! Damn." Throwing herself onto the seat across from him, she started putting her clothes into some semblance of order.

He laughed as he wiped himself with a handkerchief and restored his clothing to its former state. "I see I'm having a very bad influence on you."

She tucked in her fichu with a saucy smile. "No more than I'm having on you."

Only with difficulty did he resist the urge to sweep her back onto his lap. "I need to get out when we stop," he said. "We have to make sure we're on the same road as they are."

She nodded and patted her hair. "Do I look all right?"

"Yes. You look like a woman who has been well-pleasured by a stalwart fellow."

"Geoffrey!"

"I'm joking, I swear! You look fine. Why?"

"I want to go to the necessary while we're stopped, that's why."

"Just don't take too long. We don't know how far ahead of us they might be."

Chapter Twenty-One

Diana returned to the carriage feeling a bit more presentable. She had sprinkled strawberry water on the pertinent places and dabbed on some of the precious Floris Jasmine scent she'd bought the week before. She only hoped that if . . . *when* they caught up to Winston and Rosy, nothing of her and Geoffrey's behavior showed. It would be hard to lecture the pair if she and Geoffrey smelled of sex.

She wasn't terribly surprised to find Geoffrey still talking with the ostler as she approached.

"Here she is, sir." Geoffrey pressed a coin into the man's palm. "Thank you for your help."

Once they were back in the carriage and on their way, she asked, "Any news?"

"We're not as far behind them as I feared, perhaps even as little as an hour apart."

She let out a breath. "What a relief. Surely we can catch up to them if that's the case."

"I should hope so. And they are indeed in a rented post chaise, so it's good to have that confirmed, too."

"Who did you tell the ostler that *we* were?"

"Husband and wife, of course. But Mr. and Mrs. Brookhouse because he'd remember a duke. It isn't much of a lie—we'll be marrying as soon as it can be arranged. I'm assuming your sisters will take on the task of planning our wedding?"

"I beg your pardon? All *three* of us will plan our wedding. And I might even let you put in a suggestion or two."

"The only thing I want a say in is the food. I've sampled a number of Lady Verity's dishes, and I am prepared to list them all in descending order of preference."

"Let me guess. Marzipan anything is at the top."

"Exactly."

The conversation stalled as she tried to think of a way to ask him her most burning question.

"Out with it, my love," he said.

"So now you read my mind, too?"

"Sometimes."

She decided to just march right ahead with it. "What made you change your mind and decide to pursue marriage to me, despite all the gossip still swirling in Newcastle and the deplorable behavior of your distant relations?"

"Hmm. Well, first of all, four whole days spent not seeing you."

"Oh, spare me that nonsense. You avoided me for three weeks after our first kiss."

"Ah, but I hadn't yet been 'inside' you, as you may remember saying."

She felt heat rise in her cheeks. "True. Although we also barely saw each other after that."

He held up a finger. "But not on purpose. And I lived for those glimpses of you. They were one reason I got up the courage to tell you the truth." He crossed his arms over his chest. "After which, you gave me a lecture and chided me about not telling my sister and mother."

Her heart began to pound. "Oh, no. Is *that* why Rosy ran off with Winston? Did you tell her?"

"I told Mother and Rosy, yes. And I don't regret it. Thanks to that—thanks to *you*—I learned things I didn't know. Like Rosy knowing more than I realized. And the fact that Mother had already heard gossip in town about the laudanum. Granted, she'd thought he'd had an accidental overdose of laudanum, but she did say my father was a fool for thinking an apothecary and a doctor would keep laudanum use a secret. At least she knows now that there was nothing she could have done. He'd been planning it for a while, apparently."

"And Rosy? How was she?"

"Upset. Angry that he entrusted me with his secret and not her, too."

"That's to be expected. I think she gets tired of you getting all the attention and her getting none."

"So she did this to get attention?"

"I don't think so. I think she did it because she's in love with him." Reluctantly, she told him about her encounter with her second cousin at Almack's. She waited for his reaction.

"So you think he might also be in love with her?"

Surprised he hadn't condemned her for not telling him about the conversation, she said, "I do. Or at least infatuated enough with her to want to treat her well. He's not a bad man, you know. He just sowed his wild oats a bit longer than you did."

"To be fair, he didn't start at fourteen, I would imagine." He looked as if he was at least considering the idea of

Lord Winston with his sister. "And you're sure he's not a fortune hunter."

"Well, a fortune would certainly allow them to live more comfortably. Last week, I saw his grandmother while I was shopping with Eliza. We chatted a bit, so I asked what his marriage prospects were. Once I assured her I wasn't asking for myself, she said they were good. He has a healthy allowance from his father, although he's unlikely to inherit the title. But I already told you that, and I can't promise that his brother, the heir to the title, will continue his allowance. It vastly depends on how their father's will is written."

"Did she say how much the allowance is?"

"I personally think it's not enough to live on in London." She told him the amount, and Geoffrey agreed. "But when paired with her dowry, they should do well. How much *is* her fortune, anyway?" When he told her the amount, she gaped at him. "You mean, all this time you've been worried about fortune hunters and her fortune is that little?"

"W-e-e-ll, I thought it was large when Father set it up. But yesterday, I received the bills for the gowns." He winced. "Between that and your fees, I realized that a large dowry by Newcastle standards was a fairly small one by London standards, especially London nobility standards."

She gave a rueful laugh. "No wonder neither Rosy nor your mother ever told us how much it was."

"They couldn't. I never told *them*." When she frowned at that, he added hastily, "I was worried they would tell people indiscriminately, and we'd have fortune hunters beating down our doors. How was I supposed to know it was practically a pittance compared to the expenses of living in London?"

"Speaking of that, if they try to live in London on that little money, they would always be in debt, I fear, especially if they tried to live the lives they'd been living heretofore."

"Do you think he'll be faithful?"

"How can anyone predict that? I assumed my mother would be the faithful one in my parents' marriage, but I was wrong. If you can find a way to determine that ahead of time, let me know. Elegant Occasions would make a fortune selling that secret."

His brow was knit in a frown. "Actually, I might have a way to make it less likely that he'll cheat. But we're getting ahead of ourselves. We haven't caught up to them yet."

"Yes, and once we do, we won't be able to discuss anything concerning your father. So I need to know what you mean to do about *that*. Because if you still intend to wait a while to marry—"

"No. Actually, Mother said something that got me thinking—that Father dreaded the possibility of being considered non compos mentis and feared having people think him insane. That's why he went to such great lengths to make it appear to be an accidental overdose. He wanted to die, but also wanted not to be considered a suicide."

"And it might also be why he preferred to frame his death as a possible felo-de-se by leaving you that letter." She took a deep breath and reminded herself that he needed to hear this. "Perhaps—and I'm just saying it's a possibility—your father might have been manipulating you for his own purposes."

"Do you think so?" he said dryly. "Yes, that has occurred to me. After years of watching me side with my maternal grandfather, Father might have felt abandoned. This was his way to keep himself ever in my mind even after his death."

"Exactly. In your mind and trying fruitlessly to find a way out of the box he'd put you in. Forgive me, but he sounds like something of an—"

"Arse. Yes, I realize he does. But honestly, he spent most of his life trying to fight his way out of melancholy. That's why he drank, which only seemed to make it worse. Not that you could tell *him* that."

The bitterness in his voice was laced with something else. And she recognized it, having been through something similar when her own family was shattered. "You haven't yet really mourned him, have you?"

He sat there, clearly stunned by the observation.

Her heart hurt for him. "You've been so busy trying to meet his impossible requirements that you haven't taken time to mourn him."

"It's just . . ." He scrubbed one hand over his face. "I don't want to be like him. I don't want to . . . lose my will to live."

"I'm not saying you should throw yourself into the river over it. I'm merely saying you should make your peace with the fact that he's gone. And with who he was."

"A melancholy man deep in his cups, you mean?"

"And a man who cared about your mother in his own peculiar way." She folded her hands in her lap. "By the way, melancholy is one of those things they consider when looking at whether someone is non compos mentis. If you have evidence—other than the letter—that proves his spirits were often depressed, you could use that to help have him declared non compos mentis. If it comes to that, that is."

"I still say it's better that it not come to that."

She sighed. "True, but if it does, at least you will only suffer the awful gossip and the scandal of it. As far as gossip goes, people will talk. I know that better than anyone. You just have to take your life in your own hands and find a way around them. Rosy once told me you were considered quite the eligible bachelor in Newcastle. And you're a success in your field, who has to be one of the more exalted graduates of Newcastle-upon-Tyne Academy. I suspect you'll find more people to champion you than think you guilty of murder. I say you just brazen out the gossip."

"Like you and your sisters did."

"Yes. Like we did." She reached over to seize his hands. "Honestly, there's no real evidence to imply that you killed him, is there?"

"No. I did dispose of the other empty laudanum bottle in the Tyne. But if it ever did turn up in the river, no one would connect it to me."

"Perhaps it's also time you consult a solicitor or even a discreet investigator, who can find out if anyone is even taking seriously the rumors of your murdering your father. Or perhaps ask a friend in Newcastle. Surely you have some there."

He smiled. "A few. I would hope none of them would believe me capable of murder."

"And you did say that the dukedom came to you long after he died."

"Yes, but that doesn't prove anything. They'll say that anyone paying attention to the title would know Father was next in line." He squeezed her hands. "That's what I get for not paying attention, I suppose. But don't worry about it."

"I won't. Because you and I are going to face whatever happens together. That's the most important thing."

"You're right."

The carriage abruptly halted.

She looked out the window. "We're not at an inn. What's wrong?"

He climbed out of the carriage, then came back all smiles. "We've found them."

"I'm not coming home with you, Geoffrey, and that's final!" Rosy cried.

Why she'd had to choose *now* to assert her independence was anyone's guess, but much as Geoffrey wanted to take her over his shoulder and treat her like the child she was behaving as, he knew that wouldn't work. For one thing, Winston looked fiercer even than Geoffrey felt at present.

Perhaps it was time to compromise. "Well, you're not going on to Gretna Green either," he said. "Because if I leave you with a broken-down post chaise, what are you going to do about it? The post boy over there doesn't seem to be having any luck with repairs."

"We'll walk to the next inn on the route," Winston said, taking Rosy's hand.

"I can assure you, sir, that my sister cannot walk five miles in that gown. And if you carry on toward Gretna Green, I won't give her a penny of her dowry. Which will no doubt make your *father* cut you off." Before Rosy started to protest, he held up his hand. "But I do have a proposal that you might both find amenable. A perfectly fair one that will allow the two of you to be married the proper way, in a church with both families present."

"Let's at least get back into our more comfortable carriage to discuss it," Diana said. "We've got a picnic basket with plenty of food and drink."

Winston looked at Rosy. "What do you think, love?"

"I suppose we should hear them out. Papa's family cut him off, and it hurt him deeply." Rosy edged closer to Winston and glared at Geoffrey. "But no sneaky business, like trying to rush us back to London in your carriage before we can get out."

"That would be impossible," Geoffrey said. "We'd have to turn the carriage around, and given how slow that process is, you could leap out quite easily."

Even Rosy had to concede the soundness of his logic.

Once they were all situated in the carriage and foraging in a picnic basket for food, Geoffrey presented his idea. "I will approve your marriage *if* Winston first spends a year working for me."

"Working at what?" Winston asked.

"Whatever you wish. Stockdon and Sons has projects all over the country. Or, if you prefer, you can work at my estate, learning to be the estate manager."

To Geoffrey's surprise, Winston seemed intrigued. "I've some ideas about crop rotation I'd like to try out. My father won't even consider them."

"I will. I've never had an estate. So, if anything, you could show *me* how to run one."

"It's Castle Grenwood in Yorkshire, isn't it?" Winston asked.

"That's the one. I have a project in Manchester I wish to finish first. That's why I said a year. Because that's what's left on the project, and I was thinking you could help me finish it. But if you'd rather play lord of the manor, I'm fine with that.."

"Then we could see each other," Rosy said, squeezing Winston's hand.

"No, Rosy," Geoffrey said. "That's my one condition. I will help Winston try whatever sort of post I can offer. But I will only do it if the two of you stay apart for a year."

"A year!" she said.

"That's the offer," Geoffrey said.

Rosy looked at Diana. "You understand why a year is too long, don't you? He's your cousin!"

"You weren't supposed to say that," Winston said under his breath. "We agreed."

"Diana already told me," Geoffrey said. "We have no secrets from each other."

"The year will be up before you know it," Diana added. "But your brother wants to make sure your fiancé can afford a wife on his income. And Geoffrey wants to give Winston an alternate position to fall back on if the two of you need it."

"So I'm just meant to stay at home with Mama for a year?" Rosy asked.

"Actually," Diana said, "I'll be marrying your brother, so I was hoping you could help me plan the wedding. It will give you ideas for your own wedding in a year."

How clever of his wife-to-be. It would force Rosy to see how much everything cost in London and to weigh that against what little the couple might have if they went against their two families.

"Who knows?" Diana said. "I may just hand my position over to you. You've learned a great deal about fashion in the past couple of months. With my tutoring, in a year you will be quite the expert."

Geoffrey bumped Rosy's knee with his. "I'm trying to treat you better than the Brookhouses treated Father and Mother. I don't want to cut you off, poppet. But I also want to make sure that you—that both of you—realize what you're getting in to."

"Well . . . what do you think?" Rosy asked Winston.

Winston squeezed her hand. "I think it's a fair offer. Except for one thing." He looked at Geoffrey, who braced himself for anything. "We should be allowed to spend one day a month together—well-chaperoned, of course."

Geoffrey had to struggle to hide his relief. "Provided that it doesn't interfere with your work," Geoffrey said, "that's fine."

Winston drew a deep breath and smiled. "I suppose I should go get our bags from the post chaise."

As he climbed out, Rosy said, "I'll help!" and joined him.

Geoffrey started to climb out, too, but Diana stopped him. "They're not going anywhere—they can't. And you can't blame them for wanting to consult in private for a few moments."

"So, what do you think, my love? Will they be all right?"

"Only time will tell, as they say." She cupped his cheek.

"But if they truly love each other, they will find a way to make it work, don't you think?"

"I *think* I am marrying a very clever wife. Time to go home, sweetling."

Then he kissed her, and his heart felt as if it might burst out of his chest. Because with Diana, he knew he'd always be home.

Epilogue

April 1812

Diana, Duchess of Grenwood, stood with her sisters and husband on Grenwood House's terrace at the very edge of the garden as the vows were spoken. Lady Rosabel Brookhouse, now Lady Winston Chalmers, turned to her brand-new husband for the kiss.

"Now that's a kiss," Eliza murmured. "There's a man who knows what he's about."

Geoffrey snorted. "He ought to. He's done enough of it through the years."

"Do I detect a note of envy?" Verity asked.

"You do not," Geoffrey said, sounding offended.

"Well, I can't judge your kissing," Eliza said. "Diana won't let me."

"Trust me," Diana said. "He's beyond compare." She added in a stage whisper, "He makes me say that. He's really dreadful."

"Hey!" Geoffrey said, drawing the attention of everyone seated. Not that it mattered, because Rosy and Winston were already down the aisle and headed inside to enjoy the wedding breakfast.

Diana laughed. "Surely you know I'm teasing you."

"All the same, just see if I give you any more kisses," he said, tipping up his chin in an exaggerated show of snobbishness.

Placing her hand on her rounded belly, she said, "Perhaps that's for the best, considering."

Her sisters laughed. The rest of the guests—a fairly small gathering, in keeping with the wishes of both Rosy and Winston—headed indoors to find their seats at the breakfast.

But the three sisters lingered. "That was the perfect wedding!" Verity said. "You outdid yourself with the design for that gorgeous gown, Diana."

"Honestly, I barely had a hand in it."

"The piping along the sleeves makes it perfect," Eliza said.

"That was Rosy's idea," Diana said. "That and the ruffles on her hem."

"I've never seen a woman with such a love of ruffles," Verity said. "She would put ruffles on her shoes if she had room for them."

Diana shook her head. "I only wish I had her tiny feet. Right now, I feel both bloated and fat-footed."

"You look radiant," Geoffrey said. "But then, you always do."

Verity rolled her eyes. "Perhaps we should move inside for the next stage of judging."

"What are you judging?" Geoffrey asked.

"The wedding, of course," Eliza said. "My part will have to wait for later, when there's dancing."

"But why are you judging a wedding that you all had a hand in planning?" Geoffrey persisted as they entered the dining room.

Verity whirled on Diana. "You haven't asked him yet?"

"I've been trying to find the right moment."

"Asked me what?" Geoffrey said.

"To judge Rosy's handling of the wedding," Diana said. "Or rather, each part of the wedding. It was her idea. She has learned a great deal in the past eleven months, but she wanted a test to be sure she could do everything to a certain level of competency. So we agreed to teach her each area, and then we're each judging her handling of the various parts. But we wanted a layman's judge for each of the parts as well. We asked your mother, but she pointed out that she was too biased to judge."

"And I'm not too biased?" Geoffrey asked.

"You are the most critical brother I know," Diana said. "But don't worry. You're not alone. Norris agreed to judge the music and your valet is doing the fashion."

"So what part am I doing?"

"The food," Verity said.

"Ah, that I can do. May I just ask one question: Where's the marzipan, so I may sample it?"

"There isn't any," Verity said. "Lord Winston doesn't like it, and Rosy's not all that keen on it herself."

"I see. Then that's ten points off right there, for not considering their guests' needs and wants."

Diana eyed him askance. "Or rather, one particular guest's needs and wants."

Geoffrey drew himself up. "I'm the brother and the groomsman. I ought to get a say in whether there's marzipan."

"I told you he would make a terrible judge," Diana said. "But give him a waterwheel and a mill, and he'll give you a grade in a heartbeat."

"Is that a category?" Geoffrey asked. "Because I will judge that all day long. I could judge the placement of the terrace right now, if you wish."

"None of us wish that," Eliza said.

"Not ever," Diana added.

He shrugged. "Suit yourself."

"Oh, look, Rosy is throwing the bouquet," Verity said and dragged Eliza off to try their luck.

"Do you mind if we sit down?" Diana asked. "His Lordship-to-be is kicking."

Geoffrey hurried to her side, and she grabbed his hand to put it against the spot. He laughed when his child kicked again. "You realize it could be a girl."

"That would be wonderful," she said. "The baby could inherit the business."

"We could horrify all of society again."

For Geoffrey, that was probably more appealing. He loved horrifying society, which they did regularly. He started to lead her to their seats at the breakfast, and she whispered, "Would it be too awful if I sat in the drawing room for a few minutes, in that comfy chair by the fire?"

"Not for me, it wouldn't."

The two of them crept out and went straight to the drawing room. She released a blissful sigh as she lowered herself into the chair. "I won't stay long."

"I'm staying with you."

"But the food—"

"Will wait," he said firmly.

She eyed him closely. "How do you feel about Rosy marrying Winston?"

"She's happy, which is all I ever wanted. And to be honest, so far he's shown himself to be willing to work. If anything, he's more interested in the estate work than I am."

She laughed. "Admit it: You and my cousin work well together. You plan the engineering aspects of updating Castle Grenwood and the mine, and he takes care of the tenants and all of that."

"All right. I confess he's been quite an asset."

"But I daresay you miss living in Newcastle," she said.

He sat down on the sofa. "Rarely. So far, visiting has been enough. It took a while for the gossip to die down, but once people saw I acted no differently than before, and I was still hiring and paying people to work at Stockdon and Sons, they realized I wasn't some high-and-mighty duke who couldn't wait to be rid of my humble beginnings."

It had certainly helped that Geoffrey had hired a solicitor whom he'd been told by friends would be discreet. When Geoffrey laid out the situation with his father, the attorney had assured Geoffrey enough time had already passed without an inquest that it was unlikely anyone would try to prosecute either Geoffrey for murder or his father for self-murder. Whatever evidence there was would be gone.

The solicitor had also laughed at the idea that Geoffrey's relations could pressure the authorities in Newcastle to investigate. The same distrust of his father's aristocratic legacy that had worried Geoffrey would be amplified against them. They'd never lived there. They would be seen as interlopers trying to stir up trouble in the town.

And if, by some small chance, anyone did attempt a prosecution, the attorney said he could easily prove Geoffrey hadn't murdered his father without resorting to revealing the suicide note. He'd also recommended that Geoffrey burn it. Geoffrey had done so.

"We should go to Newcastle together after the baby is born," Diana said.

"They would love that at Stockdon and Sons—seeing the next generation of Brookhouses." He gazed into her eyes. "I hope you realize you saved my life."

"Hardly," she said.

"I mean it." He reached across to seize her hand and kiss it. "Who knows how long I would have gone on with that hanging over my head? You opened up a window in the box my late father put me in."

"Ah, but you climbed through it. That was the truly brave thing."

"If you say so." He knelt beside her chair. "Have I said today that I love you more than life? That you are the sun in my universe, the moon in my night sky?"

"Not today, and never so poetically," she said, fighting tears. "In answer, I will only say this: I love you, too. You taught me that passion only works with one's own true love. And I'm so glad that you're mine."

Watch for Eliza's story . . .

An Earl for Eliza

The second in

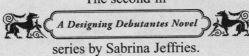
A Designing Debutantes Novel

series by Sabrina Jeffries.

Coming in the spring of 2023!

Connect with Us

Visit us online at
KensingtonBooks.com
to read more from your favorite authors, see books
by series, view reading group guides, and more.

Join us on social media

for sneak peeks, chances to win books and prize packs,
and to share your thoughts with other readers.

facebook.com/kensingtonpublishing
twitter.com/kensingtonbooks

Tell us what you think!

To share your thoughts, submit a review,
or sign up for our eNewsletters, please visit:
KensingtonBooks.com/TellUs.